THE MAXWELL STREET BLUES

A *PAUL WHELAN* MYSTERY

MICHAEL RALEIGH

DIVERSIONBOOKS

Also by Michael Raleigh

Paul Whelan Mysteries
Death in Uptown
A Body in Belmont Harbor
Killer on Argyle Street
The Riverview Murders

Diversion Books
A Division of Diversion Publishing Corp.
443 Park Avenue South, Suite 1008
New York, New York 10016
www.DiversionBooks.com

This is a work of fiction. Names, characters, places and incidents either are the product of the author's imagination or are used fictitiously. Any resemblance to actual persons, living or dead, events or locales is entirely coincidental.

For more information, email info@diversionbooks.com

First Diversion Books edition February 2015.
Print ISBN: 978-1-62681-765-4
eBook ISBN: 978-1-62681-621-3

Prologue

It was late in the day when the fire started. The sun seemed to have been yanked from the sky, and the sprawling Maxwell Street flea market was shutting down. People still stood in the doorways of some of the smaller shops on Halsted, and a few waited in a bunched-up line for Polish or hot dogs from Jim's, but most of the vendors and pickers along Maxwell and Liberty and Peoria had already gone home. Over near the viaducts, along Fourteenth Street and Fourteenth Place, the Mexicans were still selling produce and tamales and *tortas*. The record store at Halsted and Maxwell had finally shut off its speakers, but the strains of a mariachi recording could still be heard from farther south.

The last vendors were all packing it in for the day when someone noticed the flames. A fire here on a windy day was nothing memorable, usually just a diversion, but this one was special. A pile of papers in one of the big dumpsters had caught fire, and the wind had carried burning ash out and deposited it in half a dozen places along Fourteenth. It started small fires on the top of a canvas tent and in a pile of trash sitting out in one of the vacant lots on Peoria. One big slab of burning cardboard landed square on the top of a big white Lincoln whose owner was in the process of negotiating a new set of hubcaps. But the real fire came from a pile of old magazines on Liberty and spread quickly to a stack of card board boxes and then to a little pyramid of old tires. The tires made the difference.

A column of dense black smoke coiled and curled and scratched at the darkening sky; the air was acrid with it. The wind tugged at it and it changed shape and direction, and in a few minutes it had everyone's attention.

The vendor paused in his work for a moment and looked around. Everyone else was running toward the fire, but in twenty years of selling on Maxwell he'd seen a lot of fires. He began to work faster. In the distance the sirens of the fire trucks could be heard, for the third time that day.

He watched the fire as he packed up. His stall was a piece of plywood set atop a pair of small sawhorses. Across it stretched a square of carpeting and, spread on this, a pair of hubcaps, an old table lamp, a handful of Bic lighters, boxes of finishing nails and masonry nails and wood screws, a woman's purse—real leather, still in good shape—a ceramic knick knack, a doll, a toy pistol, two boxes of doorknobs, a cheap set of screwdrivers, and a box of Christmas lights in their original box. On this chilly autumn day he'd sold a man's wallet for three dollars and four packages of C-cell batteries for a dollar apiece. Seven bucks for the day. He'd had worse, a lot worse; other people hadn't sold a thing.

He wrapped some of his wares in an old piece of canvas, covered that in plastic, and put the package in a cardboard box.

The temperature had dropped ten degrees in little more than an hour. The wind made tumbleweed of newspapers and hot dog wrappers, and the street dust and the smoke were beginning to bother his eyes.

He looked down the street to the fire and saw it was spreading. People were beginning to move back, and he thought he could see new flames growing from the top of a wooden shack.

A car moved by, skirting pedestrians like a halfback in trouble. He gave the passengers a quick look and they stared back idly, incurious about an old black man packing up his junk.

He worked quickly, packing and wrapping with practiced movements, and in a few minutes his spot on the curb was empty. He was getting ready to load his boxes onto the truck when he heard a footstep scrape against the sidewalk behind him.

Someone was standing a few feet away, looking at him. The newcomer wore a shabby gray cloth coat with the collar pulled high and a stocking cap covered with lint. The vendor was about to inform the newcomer that he had closed up for the day but then he stopped. There was something familiar about this one.

The figure in the gray coat stared at him for a moment, then seemed to mutter something. From inside the coat a gun appeared, and just as recognition dawned on the vendor the gun fired twice.

ONE

DAY 1, FRIDAY

The things in Sam Carlos's window were dead things. Whelan could tell that much because they didn't move. The various signs made claims Whelan couldn't verify, that these were Hispanic delicacies, bargains at Sam's prices. Whelan studied the dried-out pieces of meat and the deep-fried things that curled up as though from embarrassment and decided that any Latino person who bought his delicacies from an Armenian deserved what he got.

Sam's door was open, and smells issued forth that matched the looks of the dead things in the window. Inside the store, the Man Who Would Be Mexican shouted angry Armenian insults into the phone, presumably at his supplier, a Greek from the Haymarket down on West Randolph.

He paused for a moment, looked at the earpiece, shouted, "You sell shit!" and slammed the phone down.

Sam Carlos looked up at Whelan and grinned. "Hey, detective man, how you doing?" Then he laughed. "I got problems with those Greeks."

"Yeah, I got that impression."

Sam Carlos pointed a tobacco-brown finger at Whelan. "You can't trust the Greeks," he said.

Whelan jerked a thumb in the direction of Broadway. "Spiros over at the Wilson Donut Shop, he says you can't trust Armenians."

Sam tried to look insulted, but a customer entered the store so he just laughed. Whelan waved to the grocer. As he turned toward his office building, he noticed a woman examining the produce displayed in boxes outside the store.

She was a tiny black woman, wizened and wrinkled like one of Sam's ancient grapes, and she held a small brown oval in her hand. Like the woman, the brown thing was dried and wrinkled. It had a light covering of fuzz, and she held it up close to her face to get a better look at it. As Whelan watched, she shook it, turned it over to examine it from a better angle, then rubbed her gnarled fingers over the furlike covering. Finally she wrinkled her nose and held it up to Whelan.

"What is that? Sir, do you know what this is?"

Whelan pretended to be puzzled, then nodded. "I think it's a kiwi fruit."

The woman looked at it. "Got fur on it."

There was just the faintest trace of horror in her voice. Whelan knew this lady had seen food grow a layer of fur before, and no one had had the nerve to tell her it was supposed to be there.

"A kiwi fruit?" she repeated.

"Yeah. An old one. They're supposed to be sort of a brownish-green." He looked at the crude lettering on the sign. "And they don't cost a dollar anywhere but here."

The woman gave him a quick look, showed beautiful teeth in a grin that made her twenty years younger, and then laughed as she tossed the evil-looking kiwi fruit back into Sam's basket. She peered into Sam's store, where the shopkeeper could now be seen repackaging peaches so the bruised ones were on the bottom.

"You never have to make a decision fast here, ma'am. You change your mind, you can come back next week and buy that same kiwi fruit, and it'll still be a dollar." She laughed and Whelan nodded toward Sam Carlos. "Watch him."

He gave her a little salute and walked on. There was a new feature to the door of his office building. Someone had kicked in one of the glass panes in the doorframe and it now sported a thin plywood plank. He stepped back and studied it. Somehow it went with the rest of the building, with the rest of Uptown. The brisk wind had trapped pieces of old newspaper and fast-food wrappers in the little doorway, and the local kids had covered part of the wall with their peculiar stylized graffiti. He looked up at the front of his building and could see streaks and smudges on the windows. The next time this building was washed would be the first time.

He went inside and trotted up to the second floor.

He was now the sole tenant of the second floor, with hopes of moving down soon to One, where the restrooms were. He hit the light switch and two bulbs came to life, one at each end of the hall, and he unlocked the frosted glass door that said PAUL WHELAN INVESTIGATIVE SERVICES.

Yesterday's mail sat in a pile on the floor. The mail now came so late in the afternoon that he frequently didn't get to it till the next day. He tossed the khaki vest he was wearing over the back of the guest chair, sat down at his desk, opened a Styrofoam cup of coffee, and started going through yesterday's mail.

The door made a loud springy noise and Whelan looked up. His door didn't open often, so any visitor was a novelty to him, still worth at least his curiosity. A man's head pushed in through the half-opened door.

"Mr. Whelan?"

Paul Whelan dropped the letter he'd been about to open and nodded. "Yes. Come on in," he said, but he had misgivings; the man looked like a door-to-door evangelist.

No. He wasn't carrying religious reading material. More likely a salesman. He was black, light-skinned, late twenties or early thirties, with a vague hardness in his face that put Whelan in mind of the young Malcolm X. He wore glasses and a dark blue suit over a white shirt starched enough to stand by itself. The rest of the ensemble was there—the dark narrow tie, the matching pocket square, the smooth black shoes—and the man was carrying a large black briefcase. Men dressed exactly like this boarded trains in squadrons at every station in Chicago each morning.

He closed the door behind him and remained standing

just inside the doorway, eyeing the office as though he'd made a mistake.

"Changing your mind?" Whelan asked. The man looked confused for a moment. Then he seemed to realize he'd been staring and collected himself. He crossed the room, holding out his hand.

Whelan got up and held out his. He saw the man's eyes take in the loose-fitting blue shirt and the jeans.

"Paul Whelan," he said.

"David Hill," the man said. "We spoke one afternoon last week." He smiled and attempted to break all the small bones in Whelan's hand.

"Have a seat," Whelan said, mildly surprised. Hill was one of those people possessed of a deep, resonant voice, and Whelan had expected a much older man. Older and perhaps even white, for on the phone, David Hill had sounded like a white television announcer.

The visitor looked at the guest chair and caught himself in the act of wiping off the seat.

Whelan smiled and looked down at the small stack of paper on his desk. It had hardly been worth the effort, nothing in it to make a colleague jealous: an advertising flyer from one of a thousand companies selling car phones, a postcard from a new pizza place on Clark, and a letter from a man in Milwaukee making inquiries about Whelan's fees. The letter was badly written, brief, and evasive; in eight lines, the writer mentioned Whelan's reputation for finding young runaways and twice stated that he was writing only for information purposes. The real ones were easy to identify: the writers were embarrassed at their problems, uncomfortable at the notion of hiring a private investigator, strapped for cash, and miserable. This was the real thing. He put it aside to answer later. He'd get a little more information about the case and try to suggest that payment was a flexible thing.

There was also an item in the mail that amused him: a note from the manager of the decrepit Lawrence Avenue building informing the tenants that the building would be fumigated against the horde of crawling things that had long since taken up residence in its walls and corners. Like all previous missives from the building management, the letter bore the unmistakable signs of someone struggling mightily with English and losing. It said, *This building will be exterminated on Thursday, October 24. All tenants must vacate this building because of poison.*

He tossed the letter, shaking his head. The critters in this building were by now inured to any form of pesticide ever used; the only thing that would kill them was likely to kill all the people in the building as well.

He looked at David Hill.

The man sat at the very edge of the chair, clutching his briefcase in one hand. There was something in the unblinking intensity of his face that suggested he was about to spring.

"As I said on the phone, Mr. Hill, I would have been perfectly happy to come to your office. There wasn't any need for you to come up here."

Hill pursed his lips. "It was no trouble. I had business just up the street from here. The bank."

Whelan nodded but gave an inward shudder: lawyers and banks, a heavy combination. Sounded like trouble for somebody.

Hill cleared his throat. "I was told you have a certain expertise in your field."

Whelan blinked. Whatever became of English? "It's a pretty big field, and I wouldn't want to claim expertise or even success in most of it. What were you looking for? From our conversation I got the impression that you wanted me for some routine investigative work."

Hill made a little wave with his free hand. "I understand that you've had no small success in finding people." He spoke with the diction of a drama coach and modulated his tones like a stage actor. This was a man in love with his voice.

Whelan nodded. "Yeah. I find people. Mostly young people, but not always. You have someone you want to find?"

Hill frowned slightly. "*I* don't."

"A client?"

"Yes." Hill looked down at his perfect shoes for a moment,

and when he looked up, he wore his first smile of the meeting. "And this is not a young person we're interested in locating. My client is attempting to find a family member. She…we believe he is in the Chicago area. He's from here originally."

"And you're from…the East Coast?" Whelan asked.

Hill raised his eyebrows and smiled. "I'm from New York. How did you know that?"

You talk like Marv Albert, Whelan thought, but said, "Just a hunch."

"I guess I'm not aware of it."

"Nobody's aware of his accent. It's why they're so hard to lose. How long have you been in town?"

"A little under six months." Hill frowned and gave his head a shake. "But I'm not here to talk about my residency."

"Sorry. What can you tell me about the person your client is looking for?"

"The information I have is irritatingly sketchy. My client has been living in another part of the country and, as I indicated, wishes to find a relative believed to be in the Chicago area."

"These people lost track of one another sometime in the past?" A nod from Hill. "And is there a particular reason why this person wants to find the relative?"

"Why do you want to know that?" He frowned again and stared for a moment before speaking. "The detectives I've worked with have usually been willing to negotiate their fees and go about their business without—"

"Without asking questions, right? But the detectives you've worked with haven't been me. I like to know who I'm looking for and why, and what will happen when I find them."

"There's no money involved, no money whatever. These people…" The young attorney seemed to feel some disapproval of the client and his—no, *her* family. Hill had said "she."

"All right, it's not a matter of a family estate."

"My client wishes to locate this individual for personal reasons, nothing more. The relative is believed to be here. The client is unfamiliar with Chicago. As I am myself."

"What can you tell me?"

"The man I am trying to locate is named Samuel Burwell. He is originally from Georgia, came north with his mother in the nineteen thirties. From what I've been told, he appears to have left town in the fifties, got into some sort of personal trouble, and returned sometime around 'sixty or 'sixty-one."

"How old would he be?"

"Fifty-eight or fifty-nine."

"And does the client have evidence that this man is still alive?"

"Well, there's no evidence to the contrary. My client received a letter from him years ago. It was from Chicago, and he gave his address. The client attempted to contact him but the letter came back. He'd moved on. I gather he was something of a drifter."

"And then what?"

"Then nothing. Now, after several years, the client wishes to establish whether or not this man is still alive."

"You have the last address?"

"Yes, and other addresses the client remembered."

"Do you know the neighborhoods?"

"West Side neighborhoods, Mr. Whelan. I have a rough idea of the geography but little more. Why? Are you assuming I would have a better chance at finding a man in these neighborhoods than a white man would?"

"Not at all. There are parts of the West Side that are dangerous for anybody, and parts that are dangerous for nobody. But I don't worry about that. I walk and talk like a cop and people generally assume that I'm still one. I was just wondering if you made any attempts to find him yourself."

"I have no time to traipse around town, Mr. Whelan. I made several phone inquiries, but..." Hill didn't bother to finish the sentence.

Phone inquiries indeed. Whelan suddenly had a mental picture of David Hill knocking on doors in the inner city and trying to sound "down home."

"And the West Side is a little different from what you're used to, I suppose."

The lawyer's jaw muscles went tight. "Have you ever heard

of Harlem, Mr. Whelan?" More consonants seemed to appear in Hill's speech when he was angry; his pronunciation grew even more precise.

Harlem. Yeah, Harlem, Whelan thought. A place you've only read about in the papers, Mr. Hill. He realized his attitude was showing. Don't let the client think you're a smartass, Whelan.

"I just meant it's hard to scope out a new city. So what do we have to go on? A couple of addresses and what else?"

"The names of a few people he knew here. People he knew in the past, at any rate. I don't know what else."

"No family here; wife, children?"

"Not as far as I know."

"A description? Better yet, a picture, a recent picture?" He made no attempt to hide the hope in his voice.

Hill reached into his breast pocket and pulled out a couple of snapshots. One was small and square and blurry, and age had yellowed both the paper and the image. It showed a tall man in his twenties standing near what appeared to be a riverbank, with the faintest hint of mountains in the distance. The second snapshot was a little better, a photo of the same man, now in his late forties, dressed in a baggy suit and looking ruefully at the camera, as though unhappy to be caught in its lens. It was a clear picture. He flipped it over and saw it had been dated by the developer. August 1975: nine years old.

"This is everything?"

"It is what I have from the client." There was dismissal in Hill's voice. He looked around at the office and made a little sniffing sound.

"Just out of curiosity, can you tell me who referred you to me?"

"A colleague," Hill said, pursing his lips. He pushed his glasses back up on his nose with a knuckle.

Suddenly you're a man of few words, Whelan thought.

"Well, there are only three lawyers I know of who'd recommend me for anything, and one is out of town and another one is in the hospital, so I'll guess it's G. Kenneth Laflin."

"That's correct. It was Mr. Laflin."

"Well, if you're accustomed to doing business with Ken Laflin you might not like doing business with me. I tend toward the informal."

Hill's eyes went to Whelan's corduroy shirt. "I see that," he said crisply.

"It's clean," Whelan said.

"I meant no offense." He looked at Whelan without expression, but his right hand slipped into the side pocket of his suit coat. A cigarette case came halfway out and then, as Hill became aware of it, disappeared back into the pocket.

Whelan fished his cigarettes out of the pocket of his vest and brought out a pair of ashtrays from the desk drawer.

"I could use a smoke, Mr. Hill. I hope you don't mind."

Hill brightened. "Of course not. I think I'll join you."

The cigarette case made its second appearance. It was flat, square, and magnificent: tortoiseshell and, from the peculiar color of the brass frame, an antique.

They went through the steps of the smokers' ceremony: pulled out their smokes, tapped the filtered ends against box and case, lit up, filled Whelan's office with little gray-blue clouds, and avoided each other's eyes like a pair of rug traders about to do business.

Whelan found himself studying the lawyer surreptitiously. He noted Hill's face, his haircut, the manicured hand holding the cigarette, the shoes polished to brilliance, the suit without a wrinkle, and the word that kept coming to him was "perfect." It was just as well that Hill wasn't going to do his own legwork. The folks in the projects weren't gonna give up a whole lot to a guy who came in talking New York through his nose and looking like an ad from *GQ*.

A thought struck him. "Mr. Hill, do you belong…are you by any chance a new partner of Ken Laflin's?"

Utter silence in the room. They looked at each other, and Whelan was conscious of the street noises on Lawrence, an argument in front of the pool hall, the noisy, gaseous-sounding brakes of a bus.

Hill's eyes widened and a smile transformed him, sent color

spreading through his face. He shook his head and laughed. "Mr. Whelan, do I look stupid to you?"

Whelan laughed too. "No, it was just a scary thought, that's all."

"Be a whole lot scarier if it were true. Mr. Laflin is..." He waved a hand in the air.

"A piece of work. Yeah, he is. I've always thought his law degree is the one thing keeping him out of the joint."

"He may get there anyhow, Mr. Whelan. They put lawyers inside now, you know."

"In what capacity do you come into contact with him?"

"We—uh, collaborate occasionally. You see, Mr. Laflin doesn't like to deal directly with the brothers, if you know what I mean. I'm a middleman."

"You mean he needs somebody to translate Laflin-ese into English when he deals with street folk."

"Exactly."

Hill puffed on his cigarette and Whelan waited for a moment, then said, "So what's your gut feeling about this man?"

"No idea. He might be out there, he might be dead. I just need to tell the client something firm. If Mr. Burwell is still alive, I hope you'll find him."

"And if I don't?"

Hill shrugged. "I report that to the client." He cleared his throat. "And now to the matter of the fee."

"If you've done business with Ken Laflin, my fees won't scare you off."

Hill looked at him with amusement. "Does the man pay you, Mr. Whelan? Does he actually write you checks?"

"Yes, but our financial arrangements are what you might call Byzantine. He never, ever pays without a reminder, never pays on time, and never gives me the whole thing in one shot. I swear he lives to jerk me around over my bills and receipts."

Hill nodded and looked around and pushed his glasses back up on his nose again and cleared his throat.

"What do you charge, Mr. Whelan?"

"Two and a half a day, plus expenses."

Hill raised his eyebrows but said nothing.

Go on, Whelan thought. I've been waiting all my life to hear a lawyer tell somebody else he makes too much money.

Hill considered his words. "If this should stretch on without resolution, Mr. Whelan, we will have to curtail our efforts. My client is willing to spend only so much." He reached inside his suit coat and came out with a long slender checkbook similar in color to the cigarette case, except that it was alligator. Turtles and alligators had given their lives so that Mr. Hill could look nice.

A pen appeared in Hill's hand from nowhere, a companion to the cigarette case. He wrote out a check and signed it with a flourish, looked at it, waved it in the air the way Whelan had seen people do in old movies, and handed it over.

"There's your retainer, sir. Will that do it?"

"You bet." Five hundred would do it indeed. Nicely.

"Now, what else do you require?"

The party was over; Hill had crept back into his shell. Once more he was a lawyer from the East Coast.

"The addresses you have. Names of the people you mentioned, from the old days. I suppose it would be too much to expect some of the old letters themselves." Hill gave one brisk shake of the head. "Any names he used."

Hill tilted his head slightly to one side. "Interesting. Why do you assume he used more than one?"

"You mentioned he'd been in some kind of trouble and left town. A man who starts over after legal trouble generally uses a new name."

"I never said he was in legal trouble."

"No, and I'm not assuming he was in any. Just that if he found reason to roam from place to place he might also have found reason to change or alter his name." Whelan shrugged. "I know people who change their names just to get the utilities turned back on. Money trouble is enough reason for a man to change his name. And God knows there are enough people having money trouble at any given time in this country. It's the one thing that never changes."

Hill shook his head slightly and reached into his jacket

pocket again. When his hand reappeared, it held a tiny notebook in the same alligator cover as the checkbook.

"I'll have to take your word about that, Mr. Whelan. It would never occur to me to change my name. Have you ever considered changing yours?" He looked at Whelan with a cold half smile.

"Yeah, when I was sixteen, I wanted to join the Ringling Brothers Circus. Thought about changing my name to Barney Bates. I wanted to be a juggler. My mom wouldn't let me take food with me, so I had to give it up."

The lawyer said nothing and began writing with the tortoiseshell pen in the little notebook. As he wrote, he recited.

"Actually, this man did use another name. He has gone by the name Samuel Terry." He tore a sheet from his notebook and leaned forward to lay it on the desk. "I've listed the addresses I have for him."

Whelan picked it up and glanced at it. There were two addresses, a pair of first names—*Oscar* and *Henry*—and the words *Maxwell Street.*

"Who are these two men?"

Hill shrugged. "People he knew at some time or other."

"No last names?"

"I'd have given them to you."

"And Maxwell Street? Why Maxwell Street?"

"Apparently this man operated a booth of some kind on Maxwell Street."

Whelan looked away. A "booth" on Maxwell Street? More likely a card table on three legs or a blanket laid along the curb.

"Do you know Maxwell Street?"

"I've been down there." He shook his head. "I stopped by one afternoon. Someone had told me it was an interesting place, with an open-air flea market. Perhaps it was once, but now it just seems to be a lot of shops selling things at discount. A lot of hats, cheap watches, gold chains, cassettes. A funky place. I saw no flea market. And it smelled. Onions and garbage."

"It always smells. You get used to it. And Maxwell Street, Mr. Hill, is like a back-alley Brigadoon. It only comes to life on

Sundays. That's when you see the real thing. It's not what it once was, not as big and not nearly as good, but it's different."

Hill nodded and looked past him.

"And you can't tell me anything more about this man? No idea why he left town or where he went?"

"I believe there may have been some trouble with creditors. And my client thinks the man spent at least some time in Mexico."

"Might help if I could have a few words with your client."

"That is not going to happen, Mr. Whelan. My client has already given me everything possible about Mr. Burwell. And I don't see what there is to be gained by going through—"

Whelan held up one hand. "Easy there, barrister. I don't tell you how to practice law, and you can keep your opinions about finding people to yourself. This is what I do. You find a man by learning about his life, by looking for names and places that had some meaning for him. You put together a mental grid about where he's gone and who he's known, and sooner or later you find him, if he's still there. If this man is still around, I'll find him."

"You have a high opinion of your skills, Mr. Whelan."

"Somebody has to."

"Have you ever failed?" Hill looked amused.

"Sure. I once spent some time looking for a man who didn't exist, because somebody wanted to keep me occupied. And a couple of times I've found who I was looking for and was sorry, because they were dead and I had to tell their people."

Hill made a little right cross in the air and shot his cuff back to look at his watch. It looked to be a fine watch. "Is there anything else?"

Whelan held up the photos. "No. Guess not. These are dog-shit pictures, by the way. Might as well give me his baby photos."

"They're what we have."

"You said late fifties. Tall? He looks a little taller than average in this picture."

"About six-one. I'm told he has a scar over the right eye. Scar tissue like a boxer's, was the way it was described to me. And going bald near the top of his head."

Whelan studied Hill for a moment, and then the lawyer ground out his cigarette in the ashtray.

"Well, Mr. Whelan, I have appointments."

"How about a number where I can reach you?"

"I prefer to contact you. Do you have an answering service?"

"Oh, do I ever. Yeah, twenty-four hours. But I need a phone number. It's something I ask for from every client."

"All right." Hill frowned, took out a little leather case, and drew out a business card.

Whelan looked at it. "Near North Side."

"New Town, they call it."

"Realtors in Chicago have a name for everything.

"I must be going." He stood up and then seemed to be taken by a sudden thought. "Excuse me," he said, and walked past Whelan to the window. "Damn!" he said. "*Hey!* Get off that car!" He looked at Whelan. "There are a bunch of kids on my car!"

"Local custom, Mr. Hill," Whelan said, but Hill was already at the door.

The door slammed.

He went to the window that looked out on Lawrence. In a moment David Hill appeared, striding purposefully across the street against the traffic. There was a gleaming dark-blue Buick Park Avenue in front of the pool hall with half a dozen of the neighborhood kids sitting or leaning on it. Hill yelled something at them and made imperious gestures. The boys slid off his car in movements rich with lethargy and nonchalance and didn't look back at him. David Hill looked at the glorious navy finish on his car and leaned over to stare at one spot. He fingered it, shook his head, walked over to the door, and opened it. Just as he was getting in, he looked quickly up at Whelan's office.

Whelan nodded. Hill turned away and gave him a curt wave as he slid in behind the steering column.

"Nice meeting you too," Whelan said.

Two

DAY 1, FRIDAY

The first address on David Hill's paper was 1036 South Racine. It was an entrance at the very beginning of the Jane Addams Homes, a housing project that formed part of what they were now calling the ABLA Homes Complex. As projects went it was neither forbidding nor particularly big, a low-rise complex of red brick three stories high that stretched to the west and the north for several blocks. Beyond it to the west rose the real thing, one of the infamous high-rise projects. A few hundred yards away was the tight little cluster of Italian homes and businesses called Taylor Street, unchanged and unchanging for generations. The families in this project were black. They could do their business in the Italian neighborhood, they could wander in for a pizza or an Italian ice or a bag of garbanzos or a beef at Little Al's, but the welcome mat was withdrawn after that.

Whelan's father had once told him that Chicago was like the Middle Ages: a bunch of little fortified towns continually at war with one another, but occasionally sending each other restaurants. There was a Greek town and a Polish town and a Chinese town and several Irish towns and a couple of Italian towns and a whole lot of black towns, and the geography was murder on the tourists.

He parked in front and noticed with amusement that the car two spaces ahead of him was a dead ringer for his own car, the redoubtable Jet: a badly rusted brown Oldsmobile whose insides were a mass of wounds and transplants, a car near death.

From a window on the second floor, a black woman

watched him get out of the car. She was gray-haired and fleshy and stared in straight-faced curiosity as he locked his car and walked toward her entrance.

The entrance faced a little courtyard with a rectangular lawn gone to rust brown and a pair of trees of heaven at each end. The entrance on the opposite side had a small bench, and two old black men sat beside each other, talking quietly and sharing what looked like a bag of peanuts. One watched Whelan. The other man looked straight ahead and nodded to his friend's conversation, and Whelan would have bet the rent that he was blind.

He pushed open the heavy green door and found himself in a small hallway that wore a coat of graffiti. Some of it was gang graffiti, some simply the semiliterate ravings of boys obsessed with the need to write about the local girls. There were phone numbers and sexual boasts and badly spelled profanity.

And there were smells that took him back many years, to a housing project on the North Side along the Chicago River, the Lathrop Homes, that was a mirror image of this one. His grandmother had lived there and as a boy he'd spent his share of time with her, for his family had lived just down the street on Clybourn.

He remembered these smells: pork chops or chicken frying in a cast-iron skillet, cleaning compound, disinfectant and roach killer, and over it all the pervasive odor of incinerated garbage, as though the air were made of smoke.

He studied the names on the mailboxes for a moment and then rang the first-floor bells and went on up. There was no answer at any of the three doors at the first landing.

At the second-floor landing he paused in front of the garbage chute and looked at the doors on either side. He knocked on the one on his right.

From within he heard the shuffling sound of someone coming to the door, someone not in a hurry.

"Yeah?" Who's that?"

"Hello? Ma'am?"

"Yes?" The door opened two inches, just the length of the

narrow chain that held it.

Whelan held up his wallet and showed his license. "My name is Paul Whelan. I'm a private investigator. I need some information about a former tenant."

The woman looked him up and down.

Come on, lady, he thought. You made me for a cop as soon as I got out of the car.

The door closed, the chain came off with a metallic snap, and the door swung open. The heavy woman he'd seen in the window now stood in the doorway and threatened to fill the hallway. She still looked uneasy, but she had thirty pounds on him, maybe more.

"Hi," he said.

She nodded. "I'm Mrs. Greenlee. What you need?"

"I'm trying to find a man named Sam Burwell. He used to live in one of these apartments."

She looked him in the eye.

"You sure you not the po-lice?"

"Used to be. People shot at me, so I got a new line of work."

She laughed quietly, but her whole body rumbled with it.

"That man don't live here no more."

"Did you know him when he did?"

"Just a little while. He lef' 'bout a month after I got my place."

"What about the other tenants, would any of them know him?"

"He in trouble, that man?"

"None that I'm aware of."

She thought for a moment. "No, don't nobody here know 'im. They all moved in after I did. But you could try Mr. Ellis."

"Where would I find him?"

"He live across the way. Maybe he's on the bench right now. He likes to sit there with Mr. Crawford."

"Is one of them blind?"

She nodded. "That's Mr. Ellis."

"All right. Thanks for your help."

"You're welcome, sir."

She nodded and said good-bye, and the door and chain were returned to their places.

Whelan went back outside and walked around the little rectangle of grass. The old man who had watched him enter looked up now and paused in his conversation. The blind man stiffened a bit, took on an air of anticipation.

"Hello," Whelan said.

The sighted man nodded and said "Hello." The blind one said "Morning."

"Mrs. Greenlee across the way there told me you might be able to help me. My name's Whelan. I'm a private investigator. I've been hired by an attorney who is attempting to find a man for one of his relatives. The man in question lived around here for a time, probably back in the seventies, maybe earlier. His name is Sam Burwell."

The blind man nodded almost imperceptibly. He was thin, almost emaciated, with high cheekbones and a narrow nose that gave him an ascetic look, and the hair that showed from under his Sox cap was white. The other man looked down. Neither said anything.

"You know him? Mr. Ellis?"

The blind man straightened slightly. "Yes, sir?"

Whelan smiled to himself: too polite. You call him by his name, he answers, even when he wants to ignore you.

"You're Mr. Ellis, so that might make this gentleman Mr. Crawford."

The blind man smiled. "It might."

The other man laughed. "That's me. I'm Crawford." He looked Whelan in the eye. He was shorter than Ellis, and heavier, almost pudgy, and it took no time at all to see that he was clever and alert and he hadn't yet made up his mind whether he was going to tell Whelan anything.

"Why can't this lawyer go lookin' for him his own self?" Crawford squinted up at Whelan and inclined his head slightly.

"He's not exactly what you'd call streetwise. He's also from New York. They're different."

"That explains something," Mr. Ellis offered, but Mr.

Crawford made a little shrug as though he wasn't convinced that it explained anything.

Whelan watched Crawford chew on that for a moment, then asked, "Can you tell me anything about this man?"

Crawford pursed his lips.

Mr. Ellis nodded. "We know 'im. He moved in over there where Mrs. Greenlee lives after his wife passed, but that was a long time ago. He moved back out to the West Side, over there by Douglas Park."

Crawford looked at Ellis. "That was a long time ago."

Ellis nodded. "He was from around there. Let's see. Last I heard, I think he was up north. Up by Foster Avenue. My daughter lived up there once."

"No, he didn't live up that far," Crawford said. "He live on Wilson, one of them streets."

"My neighborhood," Whelan said.

Crawford looked at him. "S'pose to be pretty rough."

"It can be. I like it, though. We've got about forty-nine kinds of people up there."

"Sound like forty-nine kinds of trouble to me."

"We've got that too. You wouldn't have an address for Sam Burwell, would you? Either on the West Side or up by me?"

"The thirty-two hundred block of Douglas Boulevard, that's what I recall," Mr. Ellis said. "But I know you won't find him there. He's long gone from there."

"Okay, what about an address for his place up on the North Side?"

Ellis smiled. "No, young fella, I don't have that."

"What was his wife's name?"

Ellis shook his head. "Erma. Name was Erma."

"Anything else you can tell me about him?"

"Sam used to tend bar at a place over on Roosevelt. Rundown kinda place. This was a long time ago, you understand."

"I was told he used to sell a few things down on Maxwell Street. And he had a partner named Oscar."

Mr. Ellis gave a little start and snorted. "Oscar? Oscar." The old man smiled to himself.

Whelan studied the rigid pose of Mr. Ellis. "What did I say that was funny?"

"Who told you the man's name was Oscar?"

"The lawyer. Why?"

"That's how they are, lawyers. This man's name is Oscar, young man, but can't no one *call* him Oscar. People call him O.C."

"Is he still alive?"

"Oh, yes. O.C. is still alive."

"Got a last name?"

Mr. Ellis hesitated, and Whelan saw Crawford give the blind man a sidelong glance, as though hoping he wouldn't answer.

"Brown," Mr. Ellis said at last. "The man's name is Brown."

Whelan glanced at Crawford, who gave him a quick look, then looked down at his shoes.

"Any way I can get a hold of him?"

"O.C. been gone from here a long time," Crawford said. "He lef' before Sam did." Ellis nodded agreement.

"And where could I find him now?"

Mr. Ellis shook his head and Mr. Crawford looked straight ahead and the interview was just about over.

"Okay, let me tell you what I think. I think you know where I can find this man, but you don't want to tell me because you think I'm a cop." When neither man responded, Whelan dug out his wallet and let Crawford see the license.

Crawford glanced at it and shrugged.

"It's legitimate. I'm what I said. I'm not a cop—"

"Look like one," Crawford said, looking straight ahead.

"I was a cop a long time, but I work for myself now. I'm not working with the police, and as far I know there's no reason the police would be looking for this man. You can check me out, or check my story out, and I can come back."

Crawford met his eyes this time. "So you got a license, so what? Could be somebody hired a detective to give this man trouble."

Mr. Ellis made a little nod and cleared his throat. "And you aren't the first one."

"What? What do you mean?"

"You're not the first one to come looking for Sam Burwell. But I suppose you know that."

"No. Who was looking for him?" He looked at Crawford. "Did you see him?"

Crawford made a little shrug and indicated Ellis with a nod. "Naw. I wasn't here. Luther talked to him."

"Who was this man, Mr. Ellis?"

"Somebody saying he was an old friend of Sam's. A white man."

"How do you know he was white?"

"I heard the man talk. There's some voices that are just white, some that are black. This man was white. Sounded like Fibber McGee."

"Did he give you a name?"

"Yeah. Said his name was Charlie something. I don't recall the last name. Said he knew Sam in the old days." Mr. Ellis shook his head.

"Did he say why he was trying to find Sam?"

"Just said he wanted to look him up. Didn't sound like it to me."

"Why?"

"He asked his questions very fast. He was an impatient man, and I could hear things in his voice. He was angry, I'd bet good money on that."

"And you told him less than you're telling me."

"You're a smart young man," Ellis said quietly.

"I spend a lot of my time around smart old men. It's catching."

Ellis laughed and Crawford tried on a half smile.

"Was this recently?"

"About a year ago, this was."

"Well, thank you for your time. Now I'm going to go find O.C. Brown."

"How you going to do that, young man?"

"I'm good at what I do. I'll find him. And when I do, I'll tell him you wouldn't give me the time of day."

Ellis chuckled.

"Here's my card." Whelan handed it to Crawford, who gave it a dubious look. "Give me a call if you hear anything. I'll see you around."

Walking away, Whelan took a quick look over his shoulder at the two old men. Crawford appeared to be staring at Whelan's business card and Ellis looked straight ahead. Old men on benches.

He suddenly remembered a moment from his boyhood. They were leaving his grandparents' house in the projects and walked past a trio of old men on a bench in front of a building very much like these. His father had said simply, "Old men on benches," and his mother had said, "I think it's so sad."

"Sad?" He could remember the surprise in his father's voice. "What's so sad about it? I hope I live long enough to be an old man on a bench."

It was less than a mile from the projects to the little bottleneck along Halsted where Maxwell Street really began, but Whelan ignored the temptation to drive by. It was only Friday, and the open-air flea market and junk emporium that was the true face of Maxwell Street wouldn't appear until early Sunday morning.

Maybe it wasn't time to cruise Maxwell, but it was time for a late lunch, it was *always* time for a late lunch, and the Almighty had sent him to an address three blocks from Little Al's. Had to be an omen.

At Al's he had a beef groaning under its heavy load of hot *giardiniera* and an order of fries. They made their own *giardiniera,* a mix of chopped peppers and celery and olives and half a dozen spices, including anise, and though Al's was famous throughout the city for its beef, Whelan was certain they could serve him an old running shoe with these peppers and he'd like it.

He spent the afternoon on the phone, calling Ma Bell, People's Gas, Com Ed, Public Aid, Social Security, Unemployment Compensation, the Veterans Administration and the two area VA hospitals. The VA Lakeside Hospital had a record of treating Samuel Burwell for emphysema in 1979.

The address they had on file wasn't the same as the one Hill had given him but was in the same block.

He ran the same kind of check on O.C. Brown and struck out. There was no shortage of Browns in Chicago—you could have created an army division with them—but there was no O.C. The Chicago phone book told him there were a couple of Browns within blocks of the address he had for Sam Burwell, an O. Brown and an Oscar Brown, and he wrote them both down.

Driving time.

He called his answering service and heard the husky, reassuring tones of Shelley, like Lauren Bacall with a smoker's cough.

"Well, hi, hon. Thought maybe you went on vacation without telling anybody."

"Hello, Shel. No, no vacations here. How's your life?"

"Oh, things are looking up. I got a new fella on the line. Who knows?"

"What happened to your—uh, main squeeze."

"Ray? He's history. He broke the rules. Broke the two big ones, baby. He went in my purse, and then he got drunk and took a swing at me. I showed him the way out. He's on the street where he belongs. You'll probably run into him on one of your cases. You talk to all those folks."

Ray. He never heard her use names until it was over. For several years it had been simply "My old man."

"So who's the new guy?"

"The milkman!" She burst into joyous laughter, a deep throaty rumble that soon took off, gained altitude, and became a high cackle. He found himself laughing along with her.

"The milkman, huh?"

"That's right. My old milkman was this pretty little black guy, and he quit and they replaced him with a tall, skinny guy. Walks like Gary Cooper and wears a—you know, a sun helmet? Like Ramar of the Jungle. He's adorable. And he likes big girls, baby. Thinks he died and went to heaven."

"Well, he did."

She laughed again, a delighted laugh.

Whelan had never seen Shelley, but he had a vivid mental

image of her: a heavily made-up woman in her forties, with dyed red hair and a shape somewhere between Mae West and Kate Smith. She was tough, smart, and streetwise and liked martinis and a good laugh. She was also lonely and never without a man for more than a short period of time. He had long since made up his mind to drop in and surprise her some day, just to meet her in the flesh, but he put it off. Something told him it would embarrass her.

"Shel, I'm going to be out of the office for a while. Probably the rest of the day."

"Goin' out to play hooky?"

"Gotta go digging up information in strange neighborhoods."

"Well, that's what you do best. Where you going?"

"West Side."

"Oh. 'The West Side is the Best Side,' " Shelley sang into the phone. "Careful, baby. I'm from the West Side. It was never the best place to go wandering around, and now—"

"I know. Talk to you later. You working the weekend?"

"Sorry, baby. Abraham's working the weekend."

"Goddam."

She laughed. "Him and a new girl. Cracks gum into the phone. Just like in the old movies."

"Oh, excellent. That'll help business." He sighed into the phone. A gum-snapper and Abraham Chacko, a little Indian immigrant whose eternal struggles with English made each conversation a foray into the unknown.

He walked back from the office to his house and went inside to check the mail. Nothing interesting.

He got into his car, pumped and turned the key, and listened to the Jet cough a few times before it started.

You'd better start, he told the car. We're going to a place where there are lots of cars like you.

He drove Halsted to Madison, hung a right, and took the Grand Tour.

West Madison Street. Willard Motley Country: "Knock on any door on Chicago's West Madison Street and you'll find a

Nick Romano," the book began.

You wouldn't like it now, Willard, Whelan thought. Your neighborhood's gone.

Entire blocks had gone up in flames during the riots in '68. There were still buildings standing along the miles of bare concrete that had once been Skid Row, but not many: a few shelters and soup kitchens and the occasional greasy spoon. There were still homeless men and women and derelicts here as well, but now just a remnant. For several miles west, vacant lots took up the places of the old buildings, the small businesses and cheap grills and Skid Row taverns.

As a child, Whelan's grandfather had brought him here on the bus. Grandpa knew an old Irish tavern keeper who ran a small saloon. He would drag the boy down here for company on the long bus ride, always on the pretext of getting little Paul a haircut at the Moler Barber College, where inept men destined never to become barbers would hack away at the boy's head till his left and right profiles no longer matched.

Whelan drove past the empty lot where the "college" had been and shuddered. Grandpa thought it was a bargain, a haircut for a quarter, but Grandpa had forgotten the anguish that a bad haircut could cause among a young boy's social circle, and Whelan's mother had given the old man hell for allowing these atrocities to be performed on her son's head.

The barber college was long gone, and there was hardly anything else left. Rumor had it that there were plans in high places to build things here on Skid Row—a new stadium, shopping centers.

How about a few houses? he thought. A few houses wouldn't hurt.

Just past Ashland a great gray shape appeared, the huge concrete cube of the grand old lady of Chicago sports, the Chicago Stadium. It didn't look so forbidding in the full glare of the sun, but Whelan had seen the Stadium at dusk on a cold day, and it looked like the ruin of some misguided civilization.

• • •

David Hill's second address for Sam Burwell was a vacant lot on West Ogden. At the moment there was a car in the lot, a car without wheels or doors. Along the sides of the lot, prairie grasses grew four feet high.

The third address still had a building on it. It was a gray sandstone three-flat down the block from a modern-looking Catholic church. School was just letting out, and a group of black children walked by in the blue-and-white uniform of a Catholic school. There were eight of them, three girls and five boys, and they were all chattering away at once. The boys were doing their best to uphold masculine tradition by bedeviling the girls, and the young women were striving mightily to ignore the boys, and none of them paid Whelan any mind.

He parked in front of the graystone. The front yard showed signs of someone attempting to grow grass. A pair of young men on the next porch paused in conversation to stare at him, made him for a cop, and quietly resumed talking; he could feel their eyes following him as he went up the front stairs.

The first-floor windows were covered tightly with thick old-fashioned curtains with ruffled edges. He went up the stairs and looked at the names on the doorbells: McKee on the first floor, Willis on the second. He rang the lower bell first.

A curtain moved in a first-floor window and a moment later the front door swung open. A fleshy dark-skinned woman in a blue T-shirt filled it and said, "Yes?"

He looked back at the name on the bell. "Mrs. McKee?" A slight nod but nothing more.

Great. I just proved I can read.

"Are you the landlord?"

"If I was the landlord, the sidewalk would be fixed. Be new back stairs and some glass in that window up there." She pointed up behind her to a third-floor window covered with plywood.

The woman studied him with dark, penetrating eyes. She was almost six feet tall and he was betting she hadn't lost an argument in twenty years. The T-shirt said WE ARE THE ENEMY.

"My name is Whelan. I'm a private investigator, and I'm attempting to locate a man who I believe lived here sometime in the seventies." He handed her a card.

Her eyebrows went up and she seemed to read the card several times.

"The man's name is Samuel Burwell. He's a tall thin man in his late fifties. He's also gone by the name Sam Terry. I'm trying to find him for a relative."

She hesitated and then looked him in the eye. "Well, Mr. Whelan, I can honestly say I never met anyone by either of these names. I only been here for two years. We moved here in 1983." She was silent for a moment, then handed him back his card. "I'm sorry I can't be any more help. Maybe you could ask the other folk around here."

She stood there holding out his card. A faint but familiar stubbornness came into her face, and Whelan understood what had just happened.

"Ma'am, it's never easy to give out information to strangers about your neighbors, especially to people from outside the neighborhood. But you keep the card. If you think of something you can tell me without making yourself feel uncomfortable, call me. I've got an answering service, so you can leave a message any time of day."

"All right," she said tonelessly, but he knew he'd probably had his last conversation with her.

"Mind if I talk to the people upstairs?"

"That's your business."

"Thanks for your time."

She nodded and closed the door quickly. Whelan moved up the stairs, thinking of what little she'd told him: she'd "never met anyone by either of these names." Okay, what did that mean? Maybe that she knew nothing whatsoever about the man, but more likely that she had met Sam Burwell under some other name, or that she had never actually met him but knew who he was. He knew that look: the look of someone about to use semantics to get out of a tight spot, the look of somebody who thinks she's been wonderfully clever.

He knocked on the door to the second floor.

A young woman's voice said something, and he heard

footsteps approaching the door.

"Who is it?"

"Mrs. Willis? My name is Paul Whelan. I'm a private investigator looking for a missing man. His name is Sam Burwell, and I was told he used to live here."

Nothing. The door remained closed.

"I could slip my business card under the door, ma'am."

The door opened and Whelan found himself eye to eye with a tall, slender woman in her early twenties. She was wearing a nurse's uniform. She gave him a quick scan, didn't like what she saw, and held out her hand. "Let me see the card, please."

She looked at the card he offered, turned it over, and handed it back to him. "I'm on my way to work."

"I just need some information, and I don't need to take up a lot of your time. Do you know a man named Samuel Burwell or Sam Terry? I was told he lived in this building for a while." He showed her the picture.

The young woman took a quick glance at it. "I don't know him." She gave him a challenging look.

"Have you lived here long?"

"Four years." A look of irritation crossed her face. She stared at him, and when he said nothing she shook her head. "Mister, I don't know nobody like that. And I got to get to work."

"Thanks for your time," he said. The door closed before he finished the sentence.

A few feet from his car, a dog was sniffing at what appeared to be a dead pigeon. It was a scrawny dog, filthy and bony, with matted fur that showed signs of mange. It was also at least part German shepherd and it did not like him.

The dog growled and then barked sharply, moving several steps toward him. He backed away.

"Easy. I like dogs."

The dog advanced, barking louder, and Whelan walked a little faster. The dog yelped and growled at his departing back, exulting in its first piece of good luck in weeks.

In Asia they'd eat you, dog.

• • •

He drove on up Douglas Boulevard and skirted Douglas Park, driving slowly and allowing himself a few seconds to look at the old place. In another time Douglas Park had been one of the city's showpieces, one of a small handful of parks with their own lagoons. In the seventies, the city had pulled off one of its few original notions, creating a beach area near the Douglas Park Lagoon and giving the residents of the neighborhood a tiny lake of their own, complete with sand and lifeguards. Swimming season was over and the lifeguards long gone, but there were still people strolling through the park as though hoping to conjure up a little more summer before returning to reality.

Reality was a neighborhood with 40 percent unemployment, where rents for unsubsidized housing kept pace with those in the upscale neighborhoods on the North Side, paid to an absentee landlord who might or might not ever get around to putting a nickel for repairs into his buildings and who probably had never heard of the city building code. Subsidized apartments went for 30 percent of the resident's income, which didn't sound like much if he was pulling down minimum wage but added up to pretty amazing rent if he went out and found himself a decent paying job.

Almost everywhere in the neighborhood were vacant lots and decaying buildings, and from almost any angle he could see the dark monolithic structure that had housed Sears, Roebuck and Company before its sudden departure from the West Side. He wondered what the shock waves had been like the day Sears announced it was shutting down and taking its jobs and money somewhere else.

O. Brown proved to be a harried woman in her forties who was babysitting a number of small children. One of them took the opportunity to bolt for the street while she was talking with Whelan.

The other address, on South Troy, offered an education, as did South Troy itself. The house was a trim red-brick two-flat on a narrow street of well-kept buildings, lawns and gardens crowded with a dozen kinds of flowers, an island of color and growing things in the midst of depression. There wasn't the faintest hint of flaking paint or crumbling masonry on the street. It was tidy and gaudy at the same time, cleaner than any street in his own neighborhood, a showpiece. It wasn't the first well-maintained black street Whelan had seen, but all the others had been in far more affluent neighborhoods.

The name on the first-floor bell was BROWN. He rang it, then the one above it, and got nothing. Then he went downstairs to the basement—to what enterprising realtors would call a garden apartment—and rang a bell marked WELLS. The bell made a high tinny sound. A moment later, a short black man in his sixties answered the door.

He nodded to Whelan and Whelan took a shot.

"I'm looking for O.C."

The old man gave him a long look. He started at Whelan's shoes, lingered for a moment at his vest, and then came to a stop around eye level. There was a slight cast of amusement in his eyes that said, So what?

Whelan produced his card. "That's me on the card."

The old man held the card out at arm's length. "Private investigator? I don't think I ever—"

"That's what everybody says. And I'm not really looking for O.C., I want to talk to him about a friend of his. That's who I'm looking for. A man by the name of Sam."

The man looked at him. "Sam who? They lots of Sams."

"Sam Burwell."

The old man nodded. "I know him. But I'm not in the habit of talking 'bout folk to strangers, y'understand."

"Yes, I do. It's an idea most people have. It's why I get paid for what I do. Okay, tell you what. I'll tell you why I'm here, and you decide whether to tell me anything."

"All right."

"I've been hired by a lawyer to find Sam Burwell on behalf of a family member. The lawyer told me about O.C., and although you haven't told me anything, I know *you* know O.C. Brown."

"You do, huh?" The old man looked amused.

"Yes."

"Sam Burwell…I haven't seen Sam in a long time. Long time. Couldn't tell you anything 'bout him."

"But you can tell me where to find O.C. If not, I'll talk to the landlord."

Mr. Wells smiled for the first time.

Whelan thought a moment and then nodded. "Let me guess: O.C. is the landlord."

Mr. Wells nodded. "O.C.'s at work. You can talk to him there. I'm gonna call him and let him know you comin'. He don't want to talk to you, he won't."

"Fair enough. Where's work?"

"The Blue Note."

"Sounds like a tavern."

"That's right. Over on Kedzie. O.C. work the bar during the day."

"Thanks, Mr. Wells."

The old man looked at Whelan's vest again.

"You don't like my vest?"

"Got a lot of pockets. You fish?"

"Once in a while. I haven't fished in a long time, though."

"All those pockets, look like it be nice for fishin'."

"Good for a lot of things. You can never have too many pockets."

The old man nodded, and Whelan gave him a little wave.

THREE

DAY 1, FRIDAY

The Blue Note was a tiny red-brick cube in the middle of a residential stretch of Kedzie. The wide windows of the old days had been covered up by block glass so that only a pair of small slits allowed a glimpse of the inside, and a gaudy electric beer sign had been jammed into each of them.

Never look in the window when you can actually go in, Whelan said to himself, and pulled open the door and let the smell hit him. All taverns smelled alike, all of them, whether Mexican places on Ashland or black lounges on the far South Side or Irish gin mills in Canaryville or Indian bars in Uptown; they all smelled the same because they were the same. They served the same functions, offered the same things to very similar people. And in the middle of the afternoon they were all dark, quiet places, and this one on the West Side was no different.

There was no music on and the back door was open to let in some air. The Blue Note was having a slow afternoon: four men sat at the bar, three of them together and in the middle of an animated conversation, and one by himself at the far end. They were all in their fifties or sixties, all of them smoking, as was the fifth man in the tavern, the bartender. He was of an age with the others, but a little more alert, and he looked up before they did at the sound of the door opening.

The man had seen trouble enter taverns before, perhaps even the serious kind that lurks in the back of every bartender's imagination. Whelan nodded and the bartender moved his head forward almost imperceptibly. The other men didn't stop talking but gave him a sidelong glance—curious but not enough to stare. The bartender watched him without moving.

Whelan took a seat, two stools away from the nearest patron. The bartender moved over to him and tossed a coaster on the bar.

"Afternoon," Whelan said.

The bartender nodded. "What'll it be, sir?"

"That coffee?"

The bartender looked at the half pot on the burner behind him and smiled.

"Useta be. Don' know what it is now."

"I'm feeling brave. How about a cup? Black."

"All right, sir."

The bartender's eyes lingered on Whelan for a moment. He was very dark and the gray hadn't taken over his hair completely yet, but the skin around his eyes and mouth was heavily lined. He turned and grabbed the coffeepot and a white ceramic mug. The lip of the mug was chipped. He poured coffee and set the cup down on the coaster.

Whelan put a five on the bar. The barman said, "Fifty cent," took his money, and put it into the register without ringing anything up and came back with Whelan's change. Whelan smiled.

"Somethin' wrong?" the bartender asked.

"Nope. I'm just trying to remember the last time I saw anybody ring anything up in a tavern."

"We ring it up, Mr. Reagan gonna get it."

"I think he's got mine already. You O.C. Brown?"

One of the old men at the bar stiffened slightly, and Whelan looked at them in the bar mirror. He had everybody's attention now.

"Who's asking, sir?"

Whelan stuck a thumb and finger in a vest pocket and came up with a business card. "Not an IRS man, anyway."

"I see that. Private investigator." He held the card up and looked at his cronies. "This man a private investigator."

Whelan heard a general murmur from the audience and

then, a little more clearly, one voice saying, "Ask him who he investigating, O.C."

O.C. Brown looked at the card again and then at Whelan. "I think the man is investigating O.C. Brown." He smiled, but there was a slight look of tension in his eyes.

Whelan took a sip of coffee and felt scar tissue form on the inside of his mouth. "Good God."

"Told you it was old."

"You didn't tell me it was dangerous. No, I'm not investigating you. I'm trying to find Sam Burwell."

"Ain't seen him." The answer was more a memorized response than a statement, and Whelan grinned.

"A good bartender says that half a million times in the course of a career. How many times have you said that about Sam?"

The bartender fought a little smile and shrugged. "What you want Sam for?"

"I don't. He's got relatives looking for him. Relatives and a lawyer."

The old man pursed his lips and shook his head. "Relatives, huh? Relatives looking for him."

Whelan laughed and took another sip of the fearsome coffee. "I love talking to bartenders. That's how you talk to salesmen, isn't it?"

O.C. looked past him and gave the faintest shake of his head. "I never heard about any relatives that might be looking for him."

"I'm working for an attorney. You might actually feel more comfortable talking to him."

O.C. Brown frowned slightly. "Yeah? Why's that?"

"Because he's black. He doesn't look like a white cop."

"Where's this man's office at?"

"North Side."

"He try lookin' himself?"

"I believe he gave it a shot, but he's not a homeboy. This is your New York variety of lawyer. Here." He dropped Hill's card on the bar. "You can call him if you want."

"I don't need to talk to no lawyer. I'm not afraid to talk to you. Ain't seen Sam. Not in a while."

"But you are a friend of his."

"Yeah. Don't see him much now."

"Does he still set up on Maxwell Street?"

Brown stared at him. "Far as I know. I don't go down there no more myself. I'm too old to stand out there all day for a couple dollars."

"You used to sell things down there?"

"Yes, sir. Just one more way to get by. Tryin' to make a dollar. Sam, he didn't have much to sell, last I heard." O.C. looked out the little window. "Some folk down there just be selling junk, just trying to get by. It's not what it used to be, Maxwell Street."

"I remember."

"Gonna be gone soon, all of it." O.C. looked at him for a moment. "What if you can't find Sam?"

"I still get paid for my time. And maybe this lawyer hires another private detective and you get to do this dance all over again. The lawyer would be throwing away good money, though."

"Oh, yeah? Why is that?" O.C. Brown looked amused.

"Because I'm good at this."

"Lookin' for folks."

"Yeah. But I think if I can't find Sam, it's because Sam isn't here anymore. That's what I think."

He took another sip of his coffee and set it down without looking. It missed the coaster, and a little bit sloshed onto the bar. The old man quickly produced a bar rag and wiped the spill, then put the cup on the coaster.

"So this is your bar."

"Who said that?"

"It's the way you sit there, for one. The way you move behind the bar, like you enjoy it. And the way you pounce on a little spill."

O.C. Brown smiled at him. "Little spill, big spill, they all stain the wood. Can't get wood like this no more. Can't build a back bar like that no more, either." He indicated the beautifully carved and varnished bar behind him, a long dark piece of maple with a diamond-shaped mirror in the center.

"And I saw your house. I stopped by there first."

The other man studied him for a while. Suspicion mixed with pride, and pride won a unanimous decision.

"You been by the house, huh?"

"Yes. It's a fine-looking building, and bartenders don't usually own houses like that. Not here, not anywhere."

A satisfied look came into O.C. Brown's eyes and he seemed to relax.

Whelan looked at his money on the bar. "Why don't you buy these gentlemen another cocktail."

O.C. nodded. "Hey, you all got a sponsor here."

Whelan waited till they all had a drink, saluted them with his cup, took one last sip of its dark, possibly toxic contents, and set it down. O.C. Brown was studying him.

"This lawyer—what if you find Sam and he don't want anything to do with this lawyer?"

"Not my problem. Not my job, either. I'm supposed to find him, that's all." He nodded to Brown. "See you around."

O.C. held up Whelan's card. "I see Sam, I'll give him this, hear?"

"Fair enough," Whelan said, and left.

He headed home and drove past Douglas Park. The park was already beginning to fill up with children. A group of kids clung to a pair of park benches and watched two boys break-dancing to a small boom box. Deeper into the park, a number of football games had gotten started, including one that appeared to be tackle: little boys grabbing other little boys and yanking them down onto the soft grass and piling on. Baseball season had ended less than two weeks earlier. For Whelan, it had ended in shock and ignominy, as the heartbreaking Cubs had managed to turn their best season in forty years into a disaster and found yet another way to teach their dewy-eyed fans to expect the worst. A pair of ground-ball outs by San Diego hitters in the final game of the playoffs had been parlayed by the Cub infield into base hits, and another team had gone on to the World Series instead of the boys from Wrigley. Whelan still replayed the final game of that mordant playoff series in his mind every day.

But for these children, the death of each season's hopes simply meant a change of sports: the Cubs and Sox had each gone into the toilet in their own way and it was now another season: in most places, football season. And to city kids, basketball season. But then it was always basketball season in the city.

You wouldn't know from watching these little boys running their circular pass patterns that they spent a good deal of their time hoping they wouldn't be shot from a passing car for looking like somebody in a rival gang.

Something made him glance in the rearview mirror and he saw the car, a white car that looked to be a Ford Escort, and realized he had seen it once already today. He felt a little jump in his heart, a tight little rush of exhilaration and fear. To test his theory he made a sudden right, and when he was in midblock he looked up to see the Ford turn onto the street behind him.

My very own tail. Just like old times.

He'd been followed many times before, by professionals and semipros and unpolished talent just up from the minors. This one had a lot to learn; he was too close and it was broad daylight. Whelan drove to the corner and hung a left, then proceeded north on Ogden Avenue. The Ford crept out into the traffic a couple of car lengths back and stayed there. Whelan slowed down a little and tried to get a glimpse of the driver. He saw a black man in a baseball cap, wearing sunglasses and slouched back in his seat, doing what they called the gangster lean. The face was backlit; that was as much as he was going to see unless he got closer. A couple of blocks later the tail turned off and was gone.

Whelan turned at the next opportunity and doubled back, hoping to catch up with the Ford. He drove two blocks to the south, turned west, came back north, even cut into an alley, where a group of teenagers interrupted what appeared to be a business transaction and melted into the gangways. When he came back to traffic, his visitor was gone.

Whelan drove east in time to catch the rush-hour spill from the hospitals clustered along Roosevelt. From time to time he checked the mirror, but the tail never reappeared.

At seven o'clock that night he was in his car again, trying to figure out something to do. He hit the buttons on the radio till he got a jazz station and drove through his neighborhood listening to the quiet guitar of Kenny Burrell. He resisted the temptation to drive down to Rush Street and pop in on a certain fortyish waitress named Pat.

At this point, that would be a disaster. For a brief time the previous summer, Whelan had found himself in that rarest of experiences, a sudden serious relationship. A few weeks of infatuation, a calming-down period during which they realized they genuinely liked one another, another short period of romantic intensity, and then each had begun to pull back. Pat was very much like Whelan, a person single so long that involvement was a painful, often alien experience.

Whelan found himself asking whether he'd grown too set in his ways for a serious commitment. After many bouts of late-night brooding, he had decided he wanted to try, and at exactly that point, life had grown a bit more complicated for both of them: Pat's ex-husband had come back into her life.

"What does he want?" Whelan had asked.

"I don't know. But I don't know what you want either."

"This guy walked out on you. He 'booked,' as they say. He couldn't handle his liquor or his money or having a kid, and he just split. Now that the child is grown and his life hasn't exactly turned out the way he expected, he wants to come back."

Pat's gray eyes watched him for a moment. "Maybe. Maybe he's never found anything better and now he knows what he let go of. I know he's quit drinking. He's in a program."

"I'm sure he never found anything better, Pat. But only an asshole would have left."

She smiled. "Two weeks ago, you weren't sure you wanted to sign on, sailor."

"I'm not anybody's husband. I wouldn't walk out."

"You sure of that?" She raised her eyebrows. She was smiling, but the eyes told him she'd never trust another man, not completely.

"Yeah. I am. So…what are you going to do?"

"I'm going to see him. I've got to see what happens."

He was about to say something and then stopped himself. He remembered what a divorced friend, a woman, had once told him: that there would always be, in some women, the need to try once more to have that first marriage work out.

"So you're going to give this guy one more shot, huh, Pat? Like he deserves one."

She looked at him for a long time and then nodded slowly.

"Well…"

"Sorry, Paul."

"I'll call you anyway."

"I hope so. Give me some time, though."

"Deal."

So there would be no crime in driving by the hamburger place where she still worked, this woman who deserved better, a better job, a better husband, a better life, but if she saw him he'd be embarrassed, and he was humiliated enough about the new dynamics of their relationship.

He drove instead to the House of Zeus, to feed his sense of the bizarre. He hung a left at the corner of Wilson and Broadway and waited patiently while an elderly black man pushed a shopping cart laden with his worldly possessions across Broadway. Whelan could see aluminum cans and a bundle of clothes and what appeared to be the side-view mirror of a truck. The old man labored against his shopping cart—pilfered from the local Jewel—and paused for just a moment to tip his baseball cap to Whelan.

Whelan drove up Broadway past the point where the El cast its skeletal shadow on the street and pulled up in front of the restaurant.

There was trouble in the House of Zeus.

In the front booth a chunky woman was wrestling with

her preteen son, who had her purse. She grabbed his cheek and pinched till he let go.

A few feet away, a drunk slept at a corner table. He was face down in the little red basket that held his food.

At the counter, the entrepreneurs of the House of Zeus were arguing quality control with a dissatisfied customer.

Comfortable as old shoes, Whelan said to himself, and parked himself in a booth a few feet away. He took a quick reassuring look around at the garish murals on the walls. Like any self-respecting Greek restaurant in Chicago, the House of Zeus boasted huge murals intended to give a little of the flavor of Greece. Usually the wall paintings showed peasant villages or happy Greek fishermen pulling in their nets, or even the occasional tourist view of a ruined temple or amphitheater.

Here at the House of Zeus the artwork ran to the more sensational: the walls here showed Greek warriors dying in battle, most of them at the hands of Persians and Medes. It was gory, gaudy, oversize, and not quite what Whelan wanted to aid digestion. But then, if you wanted a more mainstream dining experience, you didn't go to the only Greek restaurant in town run by a pair of Persians. Especially these Persians, who had cut their teeth running the town's oddest fast-food place and then gone to California to participate in the Good Life. A "misunderstanding" with the Los Angeles Board of Health had sent them back here, where they most certainly belonged. There was no one like them. There was no restaurant like the House of Zeus. Or any other restaurant they ran.

Whelan leaned his chin against his hand and watched the floor show.

The customer was a young black man in his twenties and there was apparently a problem with his gyros, which he held up to his nose and then quickly thrust away from him.

"Damn! Smell that."

Rashid showed his enormous teeth in a nervous grin, and Gus, his fat, brooding cousin, looked sullen and shrugged. His attitude was plain: after all, it wasn't his sandwich.

"This shit is old, man."

Rashid shook his head. "No, this guy is fresh. He's fresh." He pointed to the huge cone-shaped gyros turning slowly on a spit a few feet away.

"See? It's a big one. Not old. When they're old, they get real little."

"Man, I don't care. This is old. I can tell when meat is bad, and this shit done gone bad on you."

He thrust the sandwich farther. Gus took a chance and sniffed, then recoiled in obvious horror.

"You see that?" the customer asked Rashid.

Rashid shot his cousin a murderous look and then leaned forward. He sniffed, and shrugged, then smiled and attempted to create an air of Middle Eastern wisdom. He shook his head.

"It's what he's supposed to smell like."

"No, man."

"Yes. This one is lamb. All lamb smells like shit."

"Lamb?"

"You don' know gyros, this is lamb?"

"I don't know what it is, but the shit is *old*."

"Well, this comes all the way from Greece. Takes a long time."

Whelan listened closely, awaiting a final argument from Rashid.

"Comes on boat, boat is slow," Rashid said, smiling.

The customer slammed the sandwich down on the counter. "Gimme my money back, man."

Rashid sighed and turned to his cousin. "Give this man his money back."

"You give it to him," Gus said. "I didn't make it."

Rashid put his hands on his hips and shook his head at the truculence of Americans, the treason of his cousin. With a visible effort he turned and opened the cash register. With a pained look on his face, he pulled out a couple of singles and then some change. He reminded Whelan of a man pulling an arrow from his own body. He handed the money to the customer.

"Two seventy-five? Cost me four bucks, man. With tax and the orange pop."

"Awright, okay, tax, I give him to you, but you pay for pop."

"Pop probably poison too. I'm probably gon' die on the street goin' home. And I took a little bite out of that sucker." He indicated the offending sandwich with a little thrust of his chin. Rashid handed him some more change, and the man took the money and left.

Rashid watched him leave and then looked over to Whelan's booth. He showed his wondrously huge teeth in a grin.

"Hello, Detective. How is tricks?"

"Hello, Rashid. Little problem, huh?"

"Ah, no big deal." He shrugged and winked and looked at his cousin.

Gus glared.

"Okay, so we got a problem with refrigeration. One cooler, he went out of commission. Maybe some of the food, it's not so good now."

"It's spoiled." Gus pointed at Rashid with a large fork. "He fucked it up. I told him call the people to fix, but no, he wants to fix it himself. He is genius now at electricity. Hah!"

"Electronics. I am engineer in Iran."

"You were clerk in Iran."

"You were street sweeper in Iran." Rashid grinned at him.

"So what? You want to make trouble with me?"

"Ah, you crazy."

"Maybe so," Gus said, walking away.

"And your father was in jail in Iran."

Gus turned slowly. Whelan thought he might have to referee this one. "My father was political prisoner of the Shah," Gus growled.

"My father too."

"Hah! My father spits on your father."

"Is there anything that's not spoiled?" Whelan asked.

Gus looked at Rashid for a moment and mumbled something in Farsi.

"The souvlaki, he's okay."

Gus said something else, and Rashid nodded again.

"And the Persian food, we put him in little refrigerator, and this one he's still okay. Shalimar kabob, maybe."

"Fine. I'll have the shalimar kabob and a root beer."

Rashid put his hands on his hips. "You heard the detective. Get the food."

His burly cousin stared at him for a long moment, then looked at Whelan. "Someday, this one, he's dead man. They will find this one in river. He will have cement underwear." Gus nodded.

"Overshoes," Whelan corrected. "Cement overshoes."

Gus smiled slightly. "Yes, cement overshoes." He went back into the kitchen.

Whelan looked at Rashid. "I see you finished the murals."

"Yes. What do you think?"

"A little bloody for a restaurant. We generally don't go in for a lot of battle scenes at mealtimes, but it's colorful." He stared for a moment at a vivid re-creation of a Persian warrior about to behead a Greek warrior.

"And I'm not sure your—uh, motif will go over well with the Greeks."

Rashid showed a thousand teeth. "The Greeks are barbarians." He shrugged. "Who cares what they think? They are a backward people. All culture in world came from Persia."

"The Chinese will give you an argument."

"From Persia, their culture comes. All is from Persia. All culture in whole world is from Persia."

"You sure?"

"Yes, for sure."

"This will come as a blow to the French."

He looked around. The woman in the front booth was still struggling with her twelve-year-old. She pointed a finger in his face and said something. He apparently gave her an unsatisfactory response because she smacked him in the head with her purse. Like any healthy child, he laughed. He was still laughing when they left a few minutes later, and he had his hand in Ma's purse.

Dorothy was right: there's no place like home, Whelan thought, looking around.

"Add some onion rings to that order, Rashid."

"You bet. The onion rings, they are still good."

I doubt it, Whelan thought, but it's worth the risk. He looked at the sleeping drunk a few feet away.

"This guy had the gyros, huh?"

Rashid looked at the drunk. "Yes, but he didn't finish."

"If he hasn't moved by closing time, you'd better get a lawyer."

Rashid paused in the act of chopping lettuce. He stared owl-eyed at Whelan and after a moment let out a nervous laugh.

"Ha-ha. Very funny joke. Get lawyer." He laughed again, but Whelan thought Rashid's complexion was just a bit lighter now. The Iranian stood with the big knife in his hand and stared off into space, presumably remembering his unfortunate experience with the Los Angeles Board of Health and various legal representatives of the Golden State.

A few minutes later Whelan's food came, in a recycled A & W red plastic basket: steaming shalimar kabob in a Persian pita, the whole mess covered with a spicy green curry whose components were better left to the imagination. It came with cole slaw and a mound of bad fries that made his golden onion rings an unnecessary excess, but there were times when the human body cried out for deep-fried food in large amounts and this was one of them.

The drunk was still sleeping when Whelan left, but he had at least changed position, and Rashid looked relieved.

A more normal clientele was beginning to arrive, and half the tables were filled. At the door, he waved.

"Good night, Detective!" Rashid called out. Half the people in the place turned to look at Whelan, and Rashid grinned delightedly.

He thought about stopping for a beer at the Green Mill and then decided it wasn't what he wanted. People had begun to discover the old saloon and it was now a night spot, with live music and poetry readings. The Bucket of Suds was too far, and no other place appealed to him at the moment. In the end, he decided to go home and have a couple bottles of dark beer and watch television.

The night was looking up: *Boom Town* was on Channel 9: Clark Gable, the great Spencer Tracy, Claudette Colbert, Hedy Lamarr. Tough guys and redheaded women and brawls in the mud, and one of the great drinking scenes in movie history.

The call came about midnight.

There was a pause when he answered. He could hear the noisy brakes of a bus in the near background, cars going by. Pay phone.

"Hello?"

He thought he could hear breathing.

"You don't want to talk, I'll catch you later."

"Whelan?" It was a young man's voice, a young black man, and he pronounced the name *Wee-lin.*

"That's right. Who's this?"

"You come to the West Side again, you gonna get hurt."

"I'm terrified."

"You *gonna* be terrified, you come back."

"Who're you, Joe Louis?"

"Sam Burwell don't need nobody botherin' him."

"I'm not bothering him. I'm working for a member of his family."

"His family, huh?"

"That's right."

The caller made a little snorting sound, and then said, "Sheeeit. I don't know who you working for, man, but it ain't his family."

"No, huh?"

"No, mister, Sam's family know where he at. You ain't workin' for his family."

"Want to tell me who you are, so I know whether to believe you?"

"You *best* believe me, or your white ass is kicked. You hear?" He hung up before Whelan could say anything.

Whelan put the phone down and sat back in front of the TV. He wondered what Mr. David Hill, Barrister, would make of this caller's information, then decided there was plenty of time to talk to Hill. He had left his business card all over the West Side and it had already earned him a tail and now attention of a more personal kind. He decided he could afford to take Saturday off.

Sunday, he'd be working. On Sunday morning, he'd get up early and wander down to Maxwell Street and see what kind of attention he could attract there.

FOUR

DAY 3, SUNDAY

Sunday morning broke hot and sunny. Whelan took a quick shower and then went out for a quick cup of coffee. There was nothing like a Sunday-morning stroll through Uptown to make one appreciate how hard people lived here and what could happen on a warm Saturday night. There was broken taillight glass in the street at several intersections, a demolished car parked halfway up the sidewalk at Wilson and Magnolia, blood on the sidewalk in front of the Wooden Nickel.

Uptown was conscious but groggy. The wounded were gathering on Wilson Avenue in front of the taverns, outside the hot-dog stand that boasted MAXWELL STREET STYLE POLISH SAUSAGE, in front of the Day Labor Office, and in the doorway of the Wilson Club Hotel, which had taken "Men's" out of its name in deference to the liberated spirit of the times.

A short gray-haired man stood in the shadow beneath the El tracks with his hands in his pockets. Whelan had questioned the man in a case a couple of years back. The man nodded and Whelan stopped for a moment, gave him a cigarette, made small talk, and then went on. He got a *Sun-Times* from the happy little Pakistani who ran the green newsstand on the corner of Wilson and Broadway and then had a quick cup of coffee in the Subway Donut Shop.

A half hour later he was in his wheezing brown Oldsmobile cruising south on Halsted. There were a dozen more convenient ways to get to Maxwell Street, but this was the route that let you know you were driving through Chicago. This way you went past the hard dun-colored beehives that made up the Cabrini-Green projects, you went across the North Branch of the Chicago River, past the tracks at Hubbard Street where kids in a summer program had covered the viaduct walls with almost a mile of incredible murals. It took you past railroad yards and the place where Greyhound buses slept, past the produce warehouses at Haymarket Square where trucks unloaded crates of strawberries and melons, through a sleeping Greektown where the smells of Saturday night's meals still hung over the street, and past the University of Illinois—Chicago campus, a maze of nearly identical buildings apparently designed to confuse the unwary freshman.

Then Halsted crossed Roosevelt Road and the world of order was replaced by the crowded, noisy, smelly welter of shops and street peddlers and strolling salesmen collectively known as Maxwell Street. The glitter of the Loop and Michigan Avenue was just a mile to the east, but on a hot dusty day on Maxwell Street you might as well be in Calcutta.

He could smell the onions before he was fifty feet past the intersection, and after an initial moment of nausea he decided he was hungry.

Nine o'clock in the morning and I have a craving for a Polish.

Midway through the first block the traffic stopped cold, and he found himself sitting in front of a crowded-looking shop that sold stereo equipment. A stern young Korean stood in the window with his arms folded across his chest.

"Check it out, man."

A "salesman" had materialized at Whelan's window. He held out a thick gold chain. He appeared to have four or five more on a piece of cardboard.

"No, thanks," Whelan said.

"Come on, man." He held the chain up against Whelan's shoulder. "Yeah, look good on you."

"No, it would look good on Elvis. On Wayne Newton. James Brown, maybe. Not me."

The young man gave Whelan a sly grin and said, "How

'bout a watch?"

Whelan smiled and waved him away. The man moved to the car behind Whelan's and his place was immediately taken by a black teenager with a plastic bag.

"Everything in this bag, ten dollars."

"What's in it?"

This caught the young man off guard. He put his face into the bag for several seconds, looked up at Whelan, and said, "Tube socks."

"Ten bucks for a bag of tube socks, huh? You might want to rethink your price structure." The kid gave him a half smile, and then the traffic began to move and he never got to hear the next sales pitch.

In the street, on the sidewalks, in the doorways, and from the backs of trucks, people were selling things. Things in bags, things held in the seller's hand, things in boxes. At the corner of Halsted and Maxwell, people lined the windows of a little wooden shack that sold hot wings, rib tips, and hot sausage links.

"I'm coming," Whelan said.

Directly across the street in Jim's, half a dozen men in white paper hats scraped grilled onions into piles and handed out hot dogs and reddish-brown Polish sausage. Everywhere else in Chicago people were having scrambled eggs and hash browns. Here on Maxwell Street it was the middle of the day. Some of these people, he knew, had been on the street since five; others hadn't quite finished with Saturday night yet.

He had to brake as a couple of young white guys in Bears jackets staggered in front of his car. They gnawed at hot dogs as they walked, shoving massive bites into their mouths. One of them gave Whelan a loopy smile and fell against the front of the car.

Young drunks on Sunday morning, he thought. My favorite.

Another half block and he was past the shops and into the real Maxwell Street. The entire area took its name from the great open-air flea market that had once lined both sides of Maxwell Street for blocks, packed with immigrants trying to turn that first buck in the new country. Maxwell itself was little more than an alley now, a narrow dusty street of vacant lots and crumbling sidewalks. But along these curbs and back lots for the length of Maxwell and Liberty, and up and down both sides of Peoria and Thirteenth Street, and all the way to the viaducts and railroad tracks to the south, people were selling things.

The landscape was marked by huge mounds of discarded tires, by abandoned buses that now served as temporary quarters for the sellers, and by shacks and lean-tos. There were sleepy-looking sellers and vendors who made eye contact from half a block away, and bored kids working long hours for an uncle or a cousin. This was where stray dogs came to live out their fantasies, where old car parts got a second chance at life, and where your hubcaps came when someone lifted them.

He drove up and down the narrow streets once and then parked in a muddy lot just behind the old Maxwell Street precinct house.

When he stepped out of the Jet he put his foot in a hole filled with gray water.

I hope this isn't an omen, he thought.

He looked down at his feet: he now had one gray running shoe and one white one. People would try to sell him shoes here.

He began by making his way over to Fourteenth Street, where the Mexicans came on weekends to buy and sell produce and odds and ends. There were hundreds of sellers and, on a warm day like this one, thousands of buyers. He walked through the crowd at a leisurely pace and took in the noises, the babble of Spanish and English, the smells of citrus fruits, onions, tomatoes, fresh or dried peppers—every variety of peppers that grew on God's hot spicy planet—plus chorizo, hot sauce, eggs, and tapes of mariachi bands and operatic tenors. A person could buy mangoes here, and guavas, and avocados, and even cactus, needles and all.

And there were cooking smells here as well, as though all of creation had come down to Maxwell Street looking for Paul Whelan. There was a little man stirring strips of beef and onions on a portable grill and slapping the mixture onto tortillas, a stand where a dollar got you three homemade tamales awash in an angry red salsa, a little fat man selling *tortas* and ice cold cans of mango and guava juice from the back of his vending truck. You could buy long sugary *churros* for dessert and coffee or Mexican hot chocolate to wash them down.

People were hawking other things as well, hammers and cheap toys, T-shirts and aluminum foil, but there were no black people selling here. He left the world of cheap oranges and homemade tortillas and walked east a block, to Peoria.

The sellers here came in all colors; there were Arabs and Asiatics, whites and homegrown blacks, and they all wanted to sell him something.

A Korean tried to talk him into new shoes: "These shoes, just like Nikes. Twenty dollars."

"Three-vay light bulbs. Vun dollah." A heavyset white man with a Slavic accent held up one fat finger. He pointed to a package of double-A batteries. "Vun dollah." He pointed to a large bottle of laundry detergent. "Vun dollah."

Whelan pointed to a tiny portable television. "One dollar?"

The man laughed. "You crazy? Hundred dollah."

A few feet away, a Greek-looking man and woman sat on folding chairs behind a card table on which they had displayed two dozen ax handles. They stared impassively at passersby. The ax handles were brand new but paled in comparison to the prize item of this little patch of Maxwell Street: a pair of matching toilets, untouched, pristine, canary yellow. If you were looking for a good buy on a matched set of bright yellow commodes, this was your spot.

Whelan stopped for a moment and looked at them. He felt it was the least he could do.

At the corner of Thirteenth Place and Peoria a battle was in progress. A chubby white man in vile-looking coveralls had attracted a small crowd for his performance, a loud, profane, sweating struggle with a hubcap that refused to fit onto a customer's car. The man's head seemed to wobble slightly as he worked at the hubcap, and Whelan guessed that in addition to all his other offenses against society he was drunk.

Judging by the tiny flag hanging from his rearview mirror,

the customer was Mexican. His car was a rolling wonder of chrome and decals and decorations, and he was short one hubcap. The grimy white man had hubcaps to sell him, thousands and thousands of hubcaps, all visible to the passerby in shining steel piles behind a plywood shack. Particularly noteworthy hubcaps had been displayed on the walls of the shack, like choice heads in a hunting lodge.

The Mexican watched the efforts of the white man and shook his head with a worried look. This was bad business. He looked at his car and shook his head again.

"It's not gonna fit."

The dirty man looked up from the hubcap. "It'll fit. I'll make it fit." He whacked the hubcap with a beefy fist, slammed it sidelong with his forearm, stood, and kicked it.

"Come on, you sonofabitch!" He kicked it again, filling the morning air with sounds a blacksmith might make. His face grew red beneath its layer of grease and dirt, and finally he let it all go and began cursing the hubcap as he kicked away at it, pausing only to change feet. He called the hubcap all the things he'd ever called people and more, inventing new combinations and unlikely marriages of noun and verb till he had the onlookers laughing and himself on the brink of exhaustion. He backed off a step, wound up, and fetched the offending hubcap a great dropkick dead center. The car rocked, the hubcap made grinding noises and flew off into the air, and the man in the coveralls landed on his back in the dirt.

The Mexican leapt at this opportunity to save his beloved car and slid in behind the steering column before the white man was even halfway on his feet.

He laid rubber going east, and the chubby white man just watched. He got himself righted again, made a pantomime of brushing himself off, and muttered something to himself. Then he picked up the reluctant hubcap. He squinted at it, spat on an apparent imperfection, rubbed it with his filthy sleeve, and said, "Shit. I coulda got this fucker on."

Then he bent his grimy form and came up throwing, flinging the hubcap into the air like a cut-rate discus. The hubcap gained altitude, amazing the onlookers with its stability and grace in flight. Whelan could make out each tight rotation as it flew over Maxwell Street in search of less troubled climes, a high-tech Frisbee seeking happiness. The hubcap's owner seemed awed by what he'd accomplished. He stood with his hands on his hips and stared openmouthed at the missile he'd given life to.

"No shit," he said.

Then, as they all watched silently, the hubcap came down, hard and fast like a Cub pitcher's hanging curve landing in the bleachers. It came to earth somewhere in the vicinity of Halsted and O'Brien with a sound unique to city life, the inimitable street music of a windshield giving up the ghost.

"Whoops!" somebody said.

The grimy man walked away. "Not my fault," he mumbled.

I love this place, Whelan thought.

The audience broke up and Whelan walked on, only to be stopped a few feet away by a dog. It was not much of a dog, a skeleton wearing a rug. He was a skinny, runty thing with one bent ear and holes in his coat, and at the moment he had what remained of his dentures sunk into a teddy bear that he gnawed and shook and growled at. He swung the bear up into the air and then slammed it down on the pavement, and his growl changed pitch when he saw Whelan. He looked up at Whelan with his little dark eyes and made unfriendly noises.

"Easy there, tiger. Easy."

"Dog ain't interested in you. He just want to beat on that bear."

Whelan took his eyes off the dog for a moment. The speaker was a black man in his sixties. He was sitting a few feet away behind a makeshift table, a plywood sheet laid across two sawhorses. He had a silver beard and amused eyes and wore a dark raincoat and a little leather cap tipped jauntily over one eye.

"Your dog?"

"No, sir. My bear."

The dog lit into the teddy bear one more time, and stuffing appeared from one corner of the head.

"I don't think you're gonna sell that one."

A smile was working its way out into the light. The man shook his head. "That one ain't for sale. I bring it for the dog. Sonofabitch gimme some peace then." The man chuckled. "He's always here, waitin' on me."

"He likes you."

"Oughta like me." The man looked at his wares, then up at Whelan. "See anything you need, sir? It's all good, no junk here. Give you a nice deal."

At his little curbside store the man had displayed an impressive collection of flathead and Phillips screws, carriage bolts, nuts, screwdrivers and pliers, boxes of nails in three sizes, tacks, and staples. There were rolls of packing tape and a big silver block of duct tape. He also had boxes of trash bags, bags of salted peanuts, fresh eggs, a boxed set of crescent wrenches, and a neat little wooden box of drill bits.

The most interesting piece in this shop, however, sat behind the black man: a section of chain-link fence with the gate still attached. It had been painted forest green but the rain and salt and snow had eaten holes in the color, and the gate part still wore a sign that said BEWARE OF DOG.

"Nice." Whelan nodded at the gate.

"Gonna buy it? Naw, didn't think so."

Whelan felt the man watching him, and when his glance lit on the drill bits the man spoke.

"That's a nice set. German."

Whelan picked it up: *$10* was written in faint pencil on the side of the box.

"I can do better," the seller said.

"How much better?"

"Nine dollars."

"Eight," Whelan said.

"Eight-fifty."

"Deal." Whelan smiled.

The old man smiled. "Give you that gate for eight-fifty, too."

"No, thanks. Don't need any gates."

"Sell you that dog for five bucks," the old man said, and laughed.

"You here every week?" Whelan counted out eight singles and some change.

The man nodded, took the money without looking at it. "Every week. Rain or shine, every week. Christmas come on a Sunday, I'll be here. Every year for thirty years."

"You know all the folks around here?"

The man shook his head. "Know 'em to see 'em, but we don't all speak. We don't all talk English, for one. They all right, though."

"It's a good place."

"Yes, sir, it is. Sometimes folk come down, expectin' something different. They don't like what they find here, but it's a good place. Interesting. Nothing like it was, though."

"I remember, a little bit. I used to come down here with my mother and my grandmother on Sundays. My father thought a lot of it was junk." Whelan smiled.

"Well, a lot of it was. Still is. But you got to go through junk to find something special. And that's half the fun." He squinted up at Whelan. "You know what Waterford is, my man?"

"Irish crystal. It's beautiful, and it costs a lot."

"That's right. I found a Waterford crystal pitcher in an alley on the South Side. In a box of junk. Old lady, maybe it was an old man, I don't know, but somebody old passed and folk come along and dumped out all their possessions. It was a nasty-looking old house on a real poor street and the people didn't have much. Old things, and they were in bad shape. And in this one box with a whole lot of busted-up plates and glasses, I found this pitcher. I knew what it was, too. Took it home and cleaned it up, and then I took it down to an antiques man on Archer. He offered me a hundred dollars for it, so I knew what I had. *He* offers me a hundred, it's gotta be worth three, four."

"You sell it?"

The old man chuckled and gave him a wry look. "I ever get to where I don't know where I'm gonna get my next meal, then maybe I'll sell it. And maybe not." The old man grinned at him and took out a cigarette from a flattened pack in his shirt pocket.

Whelan lit the smoke for him. "My name's Paul.

What's yours?"

"Jesse."

"Do you know Sam Burwell, Jesse?"

The man nodded, looking down the street. "I know Sam."

"Seen him lately?"

"No, sir." The old man looked down at his hands.

"Where does he set up?"

Jesse thought for a moment, studying Whelan. Eventually he decided there was no harm in this information. "Up there on Liberty. He like to be up there near all the food places. Sam don't have much to sell, so he needs to be where there's more, you know, traffic. Up by that tire place."

He pointed off toward the corner. Whelan could see a corrugated iron wall around what appeared to be a mountain of old tires. In the center was a bus, painted blue, its windows covered with curtains.

"That one with the blue bus inside?"

The old man looked at the bus and it seemed to loosen him up. He chuckled. "Yeah. When Sam is here, he set up right around the corner from that place. But I don't think he been doing himself any good. Think Sam's got trouble. He's a sick man. That's why I haven't seen 'im." He seemed to think for a moment. "I don't think Sam's been here in a couple weeks. Last time I saw him, it was a Sunday. I had myself a drink after I packed up my goods, and I come by here on my way home, and Sam was gone, but he didn't even pick up all his stuff. The tarp he uses was still there, and a pack of C-cell batteries. I got 'em right here." He reached under his makeshift table and brought out the batteries. "Keepin' 'em for 'im, but I haven't seen the man." He shook his head. "A shame. Young man like that. He's twenty years younger than I am, you know."

"You're holding it well."

Jesse nodded once and then squinted up at Whelan. "What you want with Sam, sir?"

Whelan thought about telling him a quick story but one look at the candid brown eyes told him that would be foolish. "A family member is trying to get in touch with him."

This seemed to amuse the old man. "Everybody got a family member lookin' for him."

"That's a fact. See you around." He picked up the drill bits and waved.

Jesse smiled and nodded and said, "All right, young man."

A few feet from the corner, Whelan encountered a pair of white women in their fifties. They had set up a pair of card tables in front of a rusted Chevy van and were selling candy and gumballs and squirt guns and old comics and outdated baseball and football cards. Except for a row of watches at the far end of one table, it was the traveling version of the local candy store.

Both the women were blond, looked like sisters. The younger of the two had been watching him as he approached, and he got the impression she didn't like his looks.

"Morning," he said, and the women both nodded but said nothing. Whelan looked casually at the items on their tables and asked how much the mixed nuts were.

"Fifty cents for the small bag," the younger one said. She had long honey-blond hair shot with gray and large pale-blue eyes. "Dollar for the large one."

He handed her a dollar and she pushed a bag of nuts toward him.

"Thanks. I was looking for somebody who sells down here sometimes. A black fellow named Sam. He's kinda tall, about fifty-five, sixty. Has a scar over one eye. I was told he sets up around here."

"That colored man with the green pickup truck?" the older woman said cautiously. She shot a quick glance at her companion.

"Have you seen him lately?"

"No. I don't think so." The younger one moved in front of her. "We don't know none of these people. We just come down here to sell our merchandise, that's all."

"Okay. I just thought you might know him."

"We're not here every week," the younger one said, and then she turned away to open a cardboard box with a single-edged razor. "Ask them up by the place on the corner," she said, without looking at him. The conversation was finished.

At the next table, a potbellied white man took a puff off an unfiltered cigarette and nodded. His table held an array of pocket knives, fishing knives, kitchen cutlery, and several odd-looking pieces that appeared to be some sort of commando knife.

"I can do better on prices," the man said.

"They're not bad prices. I'm looking for somebody, though, a guy who sells down here, a black guy named Sam Burwell. Supposed to set up around here usually. Do you…"

The man was shaking his head before Whelan could finish. "I don't know him. I just started selling here a couple months ago." He looked past Whelan as he spoke, at a young Latino man who was eyeing the pocket knives. "I can do better on prices," he recited, and Whelan walked on.

At the place on the corner they wanted to sell him tires.

"See anything you like here, sir, you let me know. I got tires to fit anything. I got semi tires and jeep tires."

The speaker was a bald black man in his forties, with a hard round stomach threatening to burst free from his T-shirt.

"Got new tires, no retreads. Any kinda tire you like."

"No, thanks. Next time I need tires I'm gonna buy a car with them. What I need is some information."

"Yeah? What about?" The man put his hands in his hip pockets and feigned interest.

"Sam Burwell."

The man shook his head.

"I was told he sets up right around here. Sells things."

A shoulder shrug. "Everybody here sell things, man."

"A man in his fifties. Tall, a scar on his cheek."

The man shook his head again but had to look up the street to hide the fact that he was lying.

"Doesn't ring any bells, huh?"

"Naw."

"Anybody else around here I can ask?"

The man's eyes strayed to the blue bus. "Maybe."

Whelan held out his hand, palm down. The man reached out and met it and closed his fist tightly around the ten. He peeked at a corner of the bill.

"You can ask the old man. He know all the pickers. He know everybody. Name's Nate." A boy of about twelve appeared at the man's side.

"In the bus?"

"Yeah."

"Is he in there now?"

The man grinned and looked down at the boy. "The man want to know is Nate on the bus now." The boy smiled and the man looked at Whelan. "Mister, Nate live on the bus. He always there."

He stepped aside to allow Whelan to enter the land of bald tires.

Whelan made his way through ten-foot walls of tires to the bus. The door was open, and he hopped up onto the first step and knocked on the side panel.

"Yeah?" The voice was deep and hoarse. "Who's that?"

"Nate? My name is Whelan. They told me you might be able to give me a little help."

"Yeah?" There was doubt in the voice, and the speaker didn't invite him in. He went in anyway, up the stairs and past the driver's seat. It was hot and airless inside, and the windows appeared to be painted shut. Much of the bus was dark, but the back was illuminated by a Coleman lantern. An old black man sat on the back seat. Half a dozen of the side seats had been removed to allow for a card table and a cot and an easy chair. The old man watched him approach and said nothing.

Nate was eating a cold pork chop sandwich. The meat hung out over the white bread on all four sides: hell of a pork chop. He was dark and very old, bald on top, and after peering at Whelan through a squint he reached for a pair of thick glasses and looked him over again.

"What you want?"

"The man outside said you might be able to help me find Sam Burwell."

"Ain't seen him."

"The man out there said you might be able to help me."

"He was wrong."

"When was the last time you saw him?"

The old man stared at him, and Whelan saw that one lens was missing from the glasses. Nate licked his lips and looked down.

"I ain't seen him in a long time. He ain't been down here."

"How long?"

"Long time. Couple years."

"Not what I heard."

"Don't care what you heard." Nate looked away, and Whelan realized the old man was nervous.

"Was somebody else down here looking for Sam Burwell?"

"Wasn't nobody down here looking for him," Nate muttered.

"A white man, maybe." Whelan pushed.

Nate looked down at his pork chop and then glared at Whelan. "Only you."

Whelan stared at him for a moment, then dropped a card on the table.

"If you hear from Sam, or if you remember anything, give me a call. I'll pay you for any information you give me."

Nate looked down and said nothing as Whelan left.

Outside the bus, Whelan gratefully filled his lungs with the acrid air of Maxwell Street, smoke, onions, burning rubber, and all. He walked back to Fourteenth and bought some tamales from a pair of young Mexican women and a can of pineapple juice. The tamales were good, a little light on the meat but the real thing, and the salsa took layers off the inside of his mouth and probably years off his life. As he ate he walked through the rainbow of buyers and sellers. Mariachi music fought with rhythm-and-blues, and people haggled and bargained and lied to one another.

When he could think of nothing more to eat, Whelan made his way back toward his car. At the very end of the long lines of food vendors, a pair of men, one black and one white, sorted rapidly through a trash can. As far as Whelan could tell, each man was oblivious of the other. They nibbled at the cast-off produce they found, and the white man soon came across the remains of a sandwich. He was in his fifties, five-nine or five-ten, with dark hair and a heavy shadow of beard. He wore a dirty gray hooded sweatshirt, and as he ate he watched the street around him. The other man was much older, perhaps late sixties, and paid attention to nothing but his search.

When he was finished with the sandwich, the white man in the sweatshirt suddenly spotted Whelan. He froze for a moment, and Whelan found himself looking directly into the man's eyes. They held an impersonal kind of fear that Whelan knew would be directed at anyone who seemed to be watching the man or spoke to him suddenly. Whelan turned away, and when he looked back the man had gone. They could disappear, these men who lived on the street; they could slip into the cracks in the broken sidewalk. And if a man like this wanted to hide, he could stay hidden for a long time.

The muddy lot was nearly full of cars now. Whelan got into his and left Maxwell Street. So far, he knew only a couple of things with certainty: that people didn't have a lot to tell him about the missing street vendor, and that he wasn't the first white man to come looking for Sam Burwell. And though he couldn't be certain, he didn't think he'd find this man on Maxwell Street anymore.

FIVE

DAY 3, SUNDAY NIGHT

Dinner was liver and onions, and the liver was tough and gristly and he charred the onions.

Calcified meat and burned onions—great dinner, Whelan, he told himself.

When he was finished he tossed the dishes in the sink and covered them with soap and warm water. He'd often wondered what it would be like to cover a sinkful of dishes with gasoline and toss in a match.

He had no idea what to do with himself. He thought of mustering a bit of extra nerve and driving down to the little grill on Rush Street to see Pat. He considered it for a moment, and the idea grew on him.

Here I am. I want to see you. I have reviewed the facts impartially and have come to the conclusion that my rival is an asshole.

Why not? Toss the ball into her court, put on a little pressure. No, a little pressure was the last thing she wanted. Last thing he wanted, as well.

He spent the rest of Sunday evening with the papers, occasionally glancing at a football game. The Bears had a late game on the Coast with the Forty-Niners that became a rout before halftime and threatened to spoil his dinner. Around eight he was thinking of going out for a beer when the police came to visit.

There were two of them on his doorstep, a tall sandy-haired

one in his thirties and a thin dark man of average height. The dark man nodded slightly and said, "Whelan."

"Durkin."

The man half turned and indicated the taller man behind him. "This is Detective Krause. We need to talk to you, Whelan."

"Sure." Whelan hid his surprise and stepped back to let them in. He looked at Durkin. "I heard you were down at Area Four. When did you transfer up here?" As soon as the question was out, an answer came to him, and the little glimmer of amusement that came into Durkin's eyes told Whelan he was right.

The detective shook his head and gave Whelan a half smile. "I didn't. I'm still out of Four. Violent Crimes. We need to ask you some questions."

Whelan heard the emphasis on "questions" and stared at Durkin for a moment. Mark Durkin in his house. A bad day.

"Come on in. You want a cup of coffee?" He looked from one to the other.

Durkin shook his head. Krause said, "No, thanks."

They sat down, and he noticed that they spread themselves out. He'd have to turn from side to side to address their questions. Solid technique, a couple of pros, even if one of them was Durkin.

"So what can I do for you?"

"Some information, like I said. Seems you been down in our neck of the woods, Whelan. You getting tired of the North Side?"

"Not yet. Go ahead."

Durkin doodled on a notebook and pretended to have trouble reading his own writing. "Sa-mu-el Bur-well. You know him."

"No."

"We have—uh, information to the contrary."

"No, you don't."

Durkin shrugged. "I say I do."

"Show me."

Durkin's dark face got a shade darker. The doodling became

scribbling. He was careful not to look up, and Whelan watched his face go taut with suppressed anger.

Krause leaned forward in the chair to Whelan's left, elbows on his knees and hands clasped loosely together. "We are aware that you've questioned several residents of his neighborhood about this man. You're investigating Mr. Burwell. That's right, isn't it?" He gave Whelan a frank, friendly look, all blue eyes and pale blond hair. He had slightly crooked front teeth that gave him the air of a plowboy asking for directions.

"Not exactly. I'm trying to find him."

"How come?" Durkin shifted on the couch and looked at him. "How come you're looking for him?"

"I've been hired to find him."

"By who?"

Whelan resisted the temptation to correct Durkin's grammar. He could tell at a glance that not much had changed since the old days in this intense, angry man, and this would be no time to make fun of him in front of another officer.

"That is information I can't give you."

"Privileged information," Krause said, as if reciting.

"Yes. My client hired me to find Samuel Burwell for him."

"You find him, Whelan?"

"Not yet."

"Where'd you look?"

"Projects where he used to live, a couple of places on the West Side. Maxwell Street."

Durkin nodded as though approving and looked at Krause. "That's where *we* found him. Maxwell Street." He turned back to Whelan. "You ain't gonna find him, though. He's dead."

I see trouble coming, Whelan thought. He sighed. "Where?"

"Under a sidewalk."

"What?"

"Under one of those, you know…" Durkin shrugged and gave up on his vocabulary.

"Vault sidewalk," Krause added.

Whelan nodded.

In the 1850s, much of Chicago had rested on a swamp,

making the city a crowded, filthy, disease-ridden maze of narrow streets and rickety buildings. To combat the deadly conditions, the city had enlisted the Army Corps of Engineers to pull off a dazzling but simple change: to get the city up from the swamp by lifting it off the ground. For the next year, block by block, building by building, the city had been jacked up off its foundations and resettled at a new height some eight feet above the old level. New streets and sidewalks had been laid, creating little underground caverns between the new street level and the old one. Most of these tunnels and caves had been removed over the ensuing generations, but in a couple of the town's oldest and most impoverished neighborhoods, the so-called vault sidewalks still existed, dark, dangerous little niches below the rest of the city. Kids played in them, the homeless camped out in them, dogs rooted around in them for food, and vermin staked out a permanent claim.

"Where was this?"

"Just north of the viaduct on Fifteenth Street," Durkin said.

Whelan didn't ask whether Sam Burwell had been murdered. If two Violent Crimes detectives come to see you, the guy didn't die of exposure.

"How was he killed?"

Krause opened his mouth but Durkin silenced him with a look.

"Couldn't tell you. We haven't heard from the ME yet," he said, still looking at his partner.

"Come on, Durkin, if you don't know anything, then you don't know it was homicide. So why are you guys in my house?"

The other man stared at him for a moment, daring him to let the moment escalate. This was the Mark Durkin he remembered, a man of constant anger, a man who nurtured his injuries and eventually managed to make all of them personal.

Whelan turned to Krause. The younger man was watching his partner in obvious discomfort. "Relax, Detective. Durkin and I go way back. We always got along like this." He looked at Durkin. "So the years have really mellowed you out, huh, Mark?"

Durkin smiled slowly. "I'm as mellow as I need to be."

"So let's try it again. What killed this man?"

Durkin made a pistol with his thumb and forefinger. "Bullets. Bullets killed him. Couple of 'em, it looked like. Body wasn't in too good a shape. Dogs or something been at it."

"When was he killed?"

"Like I said, when we talk to the ME—"

"Give me a ballpark time, okay?"

"Oh, a while." Durkin smiled and Whelan knew he wasn't getting anything else.

"And I'm a suspect."

Durkin pursed his lips. "If you were a suspect, we'd have you down at Area Four. We're here for information. You don't give it up, we'll take you home with us and you can ride the Halsted bus back to the North Side when we let you go around three in the morning."

"I'll give you what I can."

"Oh, you bet you will. So who's your client?"

Whelan hesitated and Durkin leaned forward, pointing a dark tobacco-stained finger.

"Come up with a name this time. It's an open case. You got to cooperate or your license will be in the shitter."

"He's an attorney named David Hill. He hired me to find Samuel Burwell on behalf of a client."

"You know the client, Whelan?"

"No."

Durkin looked at him through half-closed eyes. "Know anything you can tell us?"

"Nope. The attorney doesn't think it's any of my business. I think it's somebody out of state. A 'relative' is all the man told me."

"So he hires you to go prowling around the West Side, huh? Afraid to go out and look around himself, huh? Afraid of the brothers." Durkin smiled.

"He *is* a brother, Durkin."

"A shine lawyer, you're workin' for?"

"Hardly anybody calls them that anymore. Except you."

Whelan waited for another question.

"Okay, this soul brother hires you to find this guy. Then what?"

"Then nothing. I hadn't found him yet. I spent some time talking to people that knew him, but I never got close."

"Never, huh?" Durkin looked at his nails. "Whelan, you're supposed to be pretty good. How come you didn't find him?"

"I just started looking a couple of days ago. I got the impression his friends didn't want me to find him."

"Why would they? White guy come lookin' for one of the brothers, nobody's real eager to give it up. And they all made you for a cop, Whelan, you can count on that. You never lose that look or that walk. You ask questions the same way…"

"No. Asking questions is something I do my own way. And I would've found this man eventually."

Durkin looked at Krause and made a little snort. "Always gets his man. He's a Mountie, this guy. Is that it, Whelan?"

"Have your fun, Durkin. I find them often enough that I'm not out looking for a regular job. I would've found this guy."

"Yeah, well, somebody else found him. And now he's dead. And we found him, too. Puts you in third place. So we're gonna go through the people you talked to and get it right. Starting with this lawyer."

It took half an hour for Whelan to run down all the people he had spoken to or questioned. When he was finished, they stood. Krause nodded and said, "Thank you," and Durkin just nodded. Whelan shut the door after them. He put on a record, an old one, Bill Evans. His room filled with the plaintive, haunting sounds of a piano man long dead, and he found himself thinking of a dead peddler he'd never even seen.

I'm out of this one, he told himself.

Monday brought a gray morning with a little bite in the air, a lake breeze filled with water smells, and the promise of cold weather. Football weather, night fishing weather. The street seemed quieter. The street people huddled in doorways or on staircases and waited for the sun to make an appearance.

He called David Hill, but the attorney wasn't in yet. After ninety minutes in his office Whelan had had no visitors and his phone had rung only once, a salesman attempting to convince him to buy magazine subscriptions. At ten-thirty he went out for a cup of coffee and a short stroll around the neighborhood.

A group of young black kids stood outside the pool hall across the street and watched him. His corner was getting to be a little bit tougher with the appearance of these kids, from the subsidized high-rises just to the north that had created a larger black pocket in Uptown to go along with the dozen or so other population groups.

When he got back to the office, he decided to get aggressive. He pulled out his new Rolodex and was about to start calling legal firms he'd done investigations for to see if anyone had any work for him. As he picked up the phone, he heard a faint shuffling sound outside his door. He stopped and listened but heard nothing. The noise came again as he started to dial, and this time he put down the phone quietly and walked quickly across the office to the door. Someone moved slightly, just outside his office door.

Whelan waited for a ten-count and then yanked the door open.

O.C. Brown stood in the hall with one hand in his trouser pocket and a navy blue fedora in the other. He wore a dark blue suit with acres of lapels, and a white shirt that had been starched and ironed the old way, and a bright blue-and-white tie just wide enough to have gone in and out of fashion at least twice. Light reflected off the glassy shine of his narrow-tip black oxfords. Whelan thought Brown must have cut quite a figure when he was twenty-two.

"Mr. Brown. Hello."

O.C. Brown straightened, grasped one wrist with the other hand, and nodded.

"Morning, sir."

"Come on in," Whelan said, and stepped aside to allow the older man in. He led Brown into the inner office and offered him a chair, then went around the desk and sat down.

The sounds and smells of Lawrence Avenue rushed through the half-open window, and Whelan became conscious of the noise and the cold north wind that was beginning to make the old shade flap.

"Should I close that?"

"No, no. Feels good."

"How about the noise?"

Brown smiled. "I run a tavern for twenty-six years, sir. Noise is part of my life. I hear it when I'm sleeping. I wake up in the middle of the night, and I hear people banging empty glasses on the bar and calling 'O.C., hey, O.C.' "

As Whelan took out a notepad and a pen from the center drawer, he watched Brown take in the barren office with its sparse and largely unmatched furniture.

"Probably not what you expected."

Brown glanced at him, slightly embarrassed. "It's just fine. You're not an office man, probably don't spend much time here. You're a man of the streets."

"How do you know that?"

"Knew it soon as you come into my place. I could see by the way you looked at us, how you carried yourself."

"You sure it wasn't just my cop walk?"

Brown pursed his lips. "No, you got that, all right, but you didn't act like no po-lice."

Whelan studied the older man for a moment. There was a slight stiffness to Brown but he was fighting it. He looked from wall to wall as though something might catch his attention, then forced himself to look Whelan in the eye.

"What can I do for you, Mr. Brown?"

He took out a cigarette and shot an ashtray across the desk. The old man relaxed slightly, took out a pack of unfiltered Chesterfields, and shook one out. When they had both lit up and colored the air smoky, Brown cleared his throat.

"I wanted to talk to you about Sam. Sam Burwell. The police—"

"I heard. I talked to them. And I'm sorry about your friend."

Brown gave a little shrug and seemed to be looking at his

shoes. "We went way back. Way back."

"The police probably told you a little more than they told me. Like when he was killed."

"They didn't know, but"—he shot Whelan a slightly guilty look—"nobody'd seen Sam in a couple weeks."

"When did the police come to talk to you?"

"Sunday. Late Sunday. Sam had one of my matchbooks in his pocket. That and his driver's license, only things he had. I think they come by my place first, 'cause Sam's driver's license didn't have a—you know, a current address."

"Did he have one?"

"Yes, sir." Brown puffed on his Chesterfield and then ground it out, wasting most of it.

Whelan sighed to himself and looked out the window. Sometimes you had to pry things out of the old ones, even things they wanted to say.

"You wanted to talk about Sam, you said."

"Yes, sir. I'd like to do something."

"What do you mean?"

"I'd like to do something about this. About him dying like…like that. I'd like to help."

"I'm afraid I'm not going to be involved in that, Mr. Brown."

Brown looked down at his hands. He wore a large gold ring on his right hand. It had seen rough usage, the hand: the little finger was permanently curved and the nail on the middle finger was shattered. Whelan's father had had a nail like that; once smashed so completely, the nail would never grow again.

Whelan watched the old man and felt oddly embarrassed. "It's not…it's illegal for me to become involved in an open police case. They'd have me out of business for that."

Brown nodded. "That lawyer that you were working for, he know?"

"I haven't been able to get hold of him, but by now I assume the police have informed him of Sam's death. I'll give it a couple days, then I'll talk to him, just to wrap things up."

"They didn't tell you nothing, the police?"

"No. You know the way it is. They're not in the habit of

offering information to begin with, and one of the investigating officers is…somebody from the old days."

Brown raised his eyebrows slightly and looked interested. "You don't get along, huh?"

"We're not fishing buddies. I'm the last person he'd tell."

"They told me it was robbery. Couple of little boys."

"Did they say why they thought it was robbery?"

"They said he didn't have any money on him."

"He doesn't sound like a man who walked around with much."

"No, sir, but he'd have had some. He made a few dollars down on Maxwell Street. Made some money in the neighborhood, haulin' things. He had an old Ford pickup. Good with cars, too, and he helped me out now and then. He wasn't no bum, Mr. Whelan."

"That's not how I meant it."

"And his ring was gone too. Had one of those silver Indian rings. They took that too."

"How little were these little boys?"

"Fifteen, sixteen."

"Do they have a particular reason for suspecting these two kids?"

Brown shrugged. "Been a lot of trouble with some boys down on Maxwell. Bunch of young boys been robbing folk, waiting around late in the day when people packing up they goods. They beat one man 'cause he wouldn't hand over his watch. The po-lice think maybe these boys waited till Sam was loading up to go home and killed him."

"Did they find his truck?"

"No, sir. Seems to me whoever killed him probably took the truck, drove Sam to this place where they found him, and…" He made a little wave with one hand.

"And you don't think it was the kids."

Brown looked at him. "I didn't say that."

"Yeah, you did. You were talking about these boys and you switched to 'whoever killed him,' which means you're at least entertaining the possibility that the police are wrong."

Brown shifted in his chair and studied Whelan.

"Seems to me you like to put words in other folks' mouths."

"I never heard it put exactly that way, Mr. Brown, but, yeah, that's one of the things I do. Sometimes it helps people come to the point."

Brown mumbled something to himself, and Whelan could make out "telling me I can't come to the point." Then he put his head down and gave it a little shake. Whelan could see where the gray hair was starting to thin near the top. "Want to talk about 'the point'? I'll tell you 'bout the point. The *point* is that these boys knock folk upside the head, but I never heard anything about them shooting anybody."

"And what do you plan to do about it, Mr. Brown?" Whelan asked, for he saw what was coming.

Brown slapped his hands on his legs and glared at Whelan. "What do I plan? I plan to hire you, sir. What you think I come all the way here for? 'Cause I like riding the bus? Spent half my damn life ridin' buses. Rode a bus *up* here with my folks. Damn Halsted bus don't even come all the way here. Had to walk more than a mile—"

"Take it easy."

"Don't you be telling me how to act. I'll tell you something, Mr. Whelan. You one patronizing young man, you hear?"

"Maybe I am. It's not intentional. Go ahead."

Brown straightened out his tie and cleared his throat again. He didn't appear the least bit mollified, but eventually he went on.

"I'm not comfortable with all this here."

"I understand that."

"It seems to me there's all kinds of other information here that somebody ought to look into. Seems to me somebody ought to be asking a few questions on the street—"

"What kind of information?"

"Sam thought somebody was followin' him. He told me somebody been following him around. Watching him."

"Where?"

"Down there, Jewtown." Brown shot Whelan a quick look.

"Maxwell Street. Sam always called it Jewtown. That's what we called it in the old days, Jewtown."

Jewtown. There'd been a time when every neighborhood, every group in Chicago had a nickname, and the names ranged from the slightly disparaging to the outright racist. It was the city of Jewtown, Buffalo Town, Bucktown, Chinatown. City of Sheenies and Micks and Loogins and Ricans and Coons and Krauts and Polacks and Dagoes. You could still hear the names in the saloons: nothing had changed but the scope of things you could call a member of another group in public.

"He said somebody'd been watching him. Said he could feel it."

"Did he ever actually see anybody?"

"One time he said somebody followed him in a car."

"On Maxwell Street?"

"No. Down Ogden, this was. Followed him down Ogden."

"Got a description of the car?"

"Naw."

"And the other times, when he felt someone watching him—this happen on Maxwell Street or in the neighborhood?"

"Couple times on Maxwell." A curious look came into the old man's eyes. "Couple times up here."

"Up here?"

"Sam stayed up here, Mr. Whelan. In Uptown. Had a woman he was seeing. White lady, this was."

Whelan struggled for a moment with the image of a gray-haired man O.C. Brown's age calling on a lady. He stopped when he realized that Brown was watching him with a sly smile.

"You never lose *that,* son. Not completely. You think when you get a little gray, you're gonna die? You think your thing gonna fall off when you get old?" He was grinning now, and Whelan was genuinely embarrassed. "An old man, he gets a little bit now and then. He gets a little." Brown gave him an amused look and then his facial expression changed again. "Couple of folks in the neighborhood told him people been looking for him, too. White man, one of 'em was."

"Before me."

"Yes, sir."

"I heard that too."

"You heard it where, Mr. Whelan?"

"A blind gentleman in the projects over on Racine."

"Mr. Ellis. You were talking to Mr. Ellis."

"Right."

"I knew Mr. Ellis in the old days. Schoolteacher, he was. Smartest man I ever met." Brown took out another cigarette and lit up.

"Did Sam have an idea who that man might be?"

Brown appeared to hesitate, then shook his head. "No."

"What about the driver of the car that followed him? Was it a white man?"

"No. He said that was a brother."

"Nothing else?"

"That's it."

Whelan thought for a moment. "What else have you got, Mr. Brown? I think there's something else."

Brown didn't answer for a long moment. He puffed at his Chesterfield, studied it as though he'd never seen one before, set it down in the ashtray, and looked down at his hands.

"I got one other—you know, one other item. One other thing."

"Want to share it or do I have to guess?"

Brown shot him an irritated glance. "That lawyer, the one says he's working for Sam's kin. What exactly did he tell you?"

"Just what I said, that a relative was looking for Sam. Didn't say who or how many or where they lived. He let it slip that the relative was a woman. Somewhere east, is my hunch."

"Sam didn't have nobody out east, Mr. Whelan. Only one Sam got left was right here. His son, and that's all."

"I didn't know about the son."

Brown made a little shrug. "Wasn't anybody else I ever heard him speak of. I'd like to have a little talk with this lawyer, just him and me."

"Why?"

"Something funny there, that's all."

"Why don't you look him up? I don't think he's going to tell me anymore than he has already, but he might say something to you, since you were a friend of Sam's. Maybe this person who hired him would be interested in talking to you."

Brown pursed his lips and gave a short shake of his head. "I don't want to talk to no lawyer."

"You wouldn't like him anyway." Whelan sat back and wondered if there were a simple, painless way to tell the old man that this wasn't a job for a private detective. He decided to buy a little time.

"Can you think of anybody who would be nervous if somebody came looking for Sam now?"

"What you mean?"

"I got a phone call Friday night that told me a number of things, not the least of which was that I'd get my ass kicked if I came back to the West Side."

O.C. Brown looked out the window; his face gave nothing away. After a moment he picked up the dwindling remains of his cigarette, flicked a long column of ash into the ashtray, and took a puff.

"I don't know who that would be. What'd he sound like?"

"I think he was young, that's all."

Brown shook his head.

"Did you mention any of your suspicions to the police?"

"They got their own notions about things, sir."

"That's not the point."

Brown fixed him with a sardonic expression. "Look here, Mr. Whelan. These po-lice detectives come to my place with their own ideas about what happened, and an old saloonkeeper, a black saloonkeeper, tells them these stories about strange white men looking for Sam. Oh, I told 'em, all right. And that dark-haired one—"

"Durkin."

"Yes, sir. That boy's trouble. Looked a little crazy to me."

"He is."

"I wasn't gonna do no good, talking to him. He thought he was downtown at the drunk tank listenin' to some ramblin' old bum. Which is what he thought of Sam, I could tell that, too." Brown said a "Hmmmph" and shook his head. "Could smell the liquor on *him*."

"Mark Durkin's a man on the edge of life, Mr. Brown. I'm surprised he's made it this far. So, how much of this *did* you tell Durkin and his partner?"

"I told them Sam thought somebody was followin' him, and I told them about you. That's about all."

"Okay, now give me something you didn't give them. Like the name of the white man Sam thought was following him."

"He didn't tell me no name."

"But he probably knew."

"Don't mean I did."

"But you could probably guess."

Brown sat back in the guest chair and gave Whelan a sardonic look.

"Only white men I knew were saloonkeepers and a couple musicians. They all long gone. Don't know any white men now, Mr. Whelan. I live on the West Side. I know the white priest at Saint Anna's and the white man that fixes my teeth. And now I know you." He smiled. "Look here, Whelan, how many black men you know?"

Whelan shrugged. There were blacks in Uptown, a lot of them, poor like most of the people in Uptown, but they tended to live in little pockets of the neighborhood. There was Sonny Riles, the fight trainer, and a little man named Cherry, one of the street people. And J.B., the security guard at the Salvation Army, and a neighbor across the street whom he had never spoken to, and the mail carrier. This was Chicago: just under half the population was black, but white people lived with whites, blacks with blacks. There were exceptions, in the upscale neighborhoods where young singles and people with a little coin mingled better, but those places remained oddities.

"Not many, Mr. Brown."

"Y'see what I'm saying here?"

"I guess so, but let's look at it from another angle. A friend of yours is killed, and the police have a couple kids in custody who have been preying on Maxwell Street. They never actually killed anyone before, but there's a first time for everything. This time they crossed the line and now they're a different kind of criminal. It's not such a long stretch, Mr. Brown. I'd hate to be the PD assigned to defend these kids."

Brown gave him a skeptical look. "All I know is, a white man come lookin' around for Sam. Little bit later, Sam say a black man been looking for him. Then this lawyer hires you, says some relative looking for him, some relative Sam never had. All these people be looking for the man, and then he's dead. Don't sound like nothing to do with no little bad-ass boys and robbery to me. No, sir."

"A lot of people would tell you it's just all coincidence."

"I don't believe in coincidence."

Whelan smiled, remembering the many times Detective Albert Bauman of Chicago's Finest had said that. "I know another hardcase always tells me the same thing."

"I'm not a hardcase."

"Oh, I think you are. Anyway, I was in your position once. A friend of mine was killed and the police wanted to make it a simple robbery, and I couldn't see it. It seemed to me there were other more likely possibilities. So maybe you're right, and maybe I have just a tiny prejudice in your favor. I still don't see what I can do about it. It's an open case, and I can't get involved in it."

O.C. Brown tilted his gray head to one side and squinted slightly. For a moment, Whelan thought Brown had some private knowledge of him, that he could see right through the professional excuses. That he knew better.

"Seem to me like you can get involved in anything you want, Whelan."

"Not if I want to continue to live in all this splendor."

Brown made a little shrug. "What if I hire you to look into this relative? What about that? And this lawyer."

"You can't. I can have more than one client, but I can't have a client hiring me to investigate another client."

"Why not?"

"Because I'm required, ethically, to preserve a certain

amount of client privacy."

"You never had a client you thought smelled a little funny?"

"Sure. Those ones, you turn over to the police. And the police already know about the lawyer."

The old man ground out his cigarette and sat for a moment with his palms on his thighs. Old men showing their manners. Young ones never sat this way anymore. They sank back in their chairs and crossed their legs and stared belligerently around. Whelan felt sorry for him.

"I wish I could do something. And…who knows? Maybe I'll be in a position to help a little bit later. Let's just wait and see what the police do."

"The police. You sure that's what it is?"

"What do you mean, Mr. Brown?"

"Maybe you just can't see a young fella like yourself workin' for some…old man from the West Side."

Whelan knew he meant working for an old *black* man. "I'd do something for you if I could, Mr. Brown."

Brown nodded and got to his feet. He held out his dark brown hand with its busted nails and knuckles and Whelan shook it.

"Give you a ride home?"

"Got here by myself, I can get home by myself."

"It'll give me an excuse to get out of here."

Brown smiled. "I told you you weren't an office man."

"Thank God for that."

Six

DAY 4, MONDAY

It was nearly 80 degrees, and Whelan put on some jazz and drove with the windows down.

"You like jazz, Mr. Brown?"

O.C. Brown looked at him as though he'd said something wonderfully funny. "Whatcha say, do I like jazz?" He laughed. "Man wants to know do I like jazz. Yeah, Mr. Whelan, I like jazz. I used to play a bit."

"What did you play?"

"A little cornet. Some trumpet."

"Any good?"

"Pretty fair."

Brown fell silent and Whelan decided to leave him alone. Whelan saw him straighten slightly and look around.

"Where you taking me, Mr. Whelan?"

"Home."

"Lake Shore Drive is faster."

"Yeah, but I like to drive through neighborhoods. If you can't look at the neighborhoods, you might as well not be in Chicago. You in a hurry?"

"No, that's fine. It's your time."

As they cruised up Ashland, Whelan went over what Brown had told him and had to admit there was a lot of room for doubt here. Maybe Sam Burwell had been killed by a couple of teenagers looking for pocket money, but other people, several of them, had gone to a great deal of trouble to find the old peddler, and someone had already threatened Whelan.

"I'll see what I can do."

"What?"

"I'll see what I can do."

"You're gonna look into this?"

"I guess I am."

"This gonna make trouble for you, Whelan?"

"Wouldn't be surprised." He smiled at Brown. "Trouble is my business."

The old man laughed at that. "I can pay you."

"It's not a case yet. I just said I'd look into it."

"What the hell's the difference?"

"I'm not sure, but I'll let you know if and when we need to talk about money. So tell me this: Why did you look me up if I was one of the people trying to find your friend?"

Brown looked out the window at the Mexican restaurants clustered around Division and Ashland. "Nobody seen Sam in two weeks. The police wouldn't say much, but they said he'd been dead awhile. I think my boy been dead at least since last Saturday or Sunday. He was supposed to come by, have a drink with me. We were gonna fish one day last week. Gonna go down to Lincoln Park, we had this spot at the lagoon there. He never showed, he never called me. Not that he always called folks or kept his appointments. But I think he'd have called me sometime during the week, to tell me what happened. So…" He shrugged with one shoulder. "I think he was already dead, and you didn't know it when you come lookin' for him."

"I think that's why the police haven't seriously considered me, too."

"And like I said, I could tell some things about you when you come into my place. I can tell a little bit about damn near everybody comes into my place."

"Sounds like folklore to me."

"Call it what you want, young man, but a saloonkeeper can tell a lot from the way a man carries himself in a tavern. Also, you got your own little way of talking to folks, the way you ask questions. I figure you're an honest man, Mr. Whelan. You gonna give me an argument?"

"Not about that."

Brown nodded. He looked out the window and began drumming with one hand on the doorframe. After a moment he stopped and looked at the radio.

"Hear that boy right there? That boy on the alto sax?"

"Sure."

"That's Lester Pettis. I played with him. He could play, Lester. Played with Bird, Coltrane, Dizzy, Ornette Coleman, Miles Davis, all of 'em. Was a time you couldn't cut a record without Lester Pettis sitting in. Used to drink in my tavern when he was in town. Dead now. Most all my friends are dead, Mr. Whelan. The ones that aren't, at least the ones from the old days…Fella I used to tend bar with on Forty-seventh Street, he's in a home. Can't walk, can't nobody take care of him. Got a friend I go see about once a month, out in the VA hospital. Emphysema. Always says he feels better, but I know he ain't never coming out. Another fella, white fella we knew, he was a drummer. Now he's living on the street down there on Maxwell, callin' himself a 'picker.' Sam told me he sees this fella diggin' through the dumpsters down there for his supper." He looked out the window again and shook his head.

"I'll look into it," Whelan repeated.

"Good."

Whelan waited a couple of beats, then started. "So tell me about Sam Burwell." He spoke casually, looking straight ahead. "You knew him a long time?"

He could see Brown studying him. "Thirty-eight years. More than that."

"You didn't grow up together, then."

"No. Neither of us come from Chicago. I come up from Mississippi, Sam was from Georgia. Both of us come up during the war."

Whelan smiled. The war. To this man's generation, there was only one, no matter how many times the community of nations decided to square off.

"I stood up at his wedding."

"What happened to his wife?"

"Erma passed. She passed a long time ago. Wasn't but forty-two, forty-three years old."

"And the son you told me about? You know where I can find his son?"

Brown seemed to hesitate for a moment. He frowned. "I suppose you can find Sam's boy. He live on the West Side, I don't know where exactly. Wouldn't be much help. Him and Sam... you know how that is, Whelan."

Whelan was about to pursue the question, but a note in Brown's voice told him this was a stupid idea, a dead end, at least for the moment. He tried another angle. "Seems to me you got involved in this pretty quickly. Most people would've waited awhile, maybe a few weeks, to see what the police investigation turned up."

"Maybe. Maybe the *police* can prove those little boys did it. If they can't, maybe the one that killed Sam will be gone by the time they start lookin' into it again."

"Gone where?"

"I don't know."

"Did Sam tell when it started? When he first felt he was being watched?"

"Yes, sir. First couple times were about a year ago."

"Around when the white man came asking questions, the one who talked to Mr. Ellis."

"That's right."

"And that was the beginning?"

"Yeah, that's when it started."

"And then?"

"Again in the spring. Back up there, Whelan, where you live."

"And the man in the car?"

"Summer. July, August. 'Bout then."

"So, last fall and then during the spring and summer. Was there anything unusual happening in his life then? Was he involved in anything—"

"Involved in what? He was down on his luck, Whelan, he wasn't no crook."

"That's not what I meant. The first thing you have to look

at is whether he gave anybody a reason to be looking for him. And I don't know anything about this man yet. You don't give up much, Mr. Brown."

"Got nothin' to give up. I'm the one asking you to look into this, Mr. Whelan. What kinda sense does it make for me to hold things back?"

"I didn't say you were doing it intentionally. People tend to be protective of their memories of the dead. I'm just trying to see if anything stands out as an obvious motive."

"If there is, I can't see it."

"If there isn't, the police are probably right. Those are your choices, Mr. Brown. Either his killing was random, related to robbery, or it was planned, by someone who knew him and had some grudge." Whelan watched the traffic, but he could feel Brown's gaze on him. "I know Sam left town for a time when he was younger. What can you tell me about that?"

There was a pause, and then Brown spoke slowly. "How you know that?"

"The lawyer told me."

"How *he* know about that?"

"I gather the client told him."

"He say where Sam went when he left town?"

"No. He didn't seem to know that."

Brown nodded. "Well, all right. If he knew that—well, that would be something, 'cause Sam didn't talk about it. I still think there's somethin' real funny about this 'client,' Whelan. And about this lawyer, too."

"You won't think he's funny when you meet him. Anyhow, what about those times? Why did he leave town?"

Brown gave his head a little tilt and looked straight ahead. "Wanted to make himself a dollar, I guess. Everybody wanted to make a dollar. Wasn't no different then than it is now."

Whelan took his eyes off the road to glance at his passenger. The old man sat stiffly, still staring straight ahead, fighting any eye contact. "And maybe he was in trouble, Mr. Brown."

Brown shot him a quick look, direct and resentful. "Yeah, he got himself in some trouble. Mostly, he let other folks get him in trouble." Brown looked away and made it clear that this avenue of approach was closed.

"You don't want me to know about it because you're afraid it will color my impressions of your friend." He sighed. A driver cut in ahead of him and Whelan took a whack at the horn with the heel of his hand. "And even if it does, it won't make me look any the less hard. This is what I do, Mr. Brown. You either have confidence in me or hire somebody out of the Yellow Pages. There's a real hotshot outfit on River Road, they'll show you machines and gadgets you thought only James Bond had."

"Listen here, nobody insulted you. Calm down, young man."

Whelan stopped for a red light and took his hands off the wheel. "Okay. I'm calm. I'm doing deep breathing. Talk to me."

"He got himself into some trouble, like I said. But it was thirty years ago and it wasn't with the law. Got nothing to do with now. Somebody killed him *now,* Mr. Whelan. That's what we got to look at."

"You're right." The light changed, and the guy in the car behind them leaned on his horn. Whelan waited a beat, looked at the other driver in his rearview mirror, and then pulled slowly into the intersection.

Brown took a quick look at the driver behind them. "That boy look about sixteen. You messing with his mind there?"

"Just trying to teach him Zen. So when did Sam come back to Chicago?"

" 'Bout nineteen sixty."

"But he didn't like to talk about it."

"That's right. It just didn't work out for him. Told me he made some money pretty fast—Texas, this was—and lost it just as fast. Didn't say how. I just don't think he did himself any good." Brown turned an unlit cigarette over and over in his fingers. "I know it didn't do *him* no good."

"What do you mean?"

Brown gave a little shrug. "When he came back, he was thirty-three, thirty-four years old and he looked fifty." He looked at Whelan and raised his eyebrows. "That drink. That's what it was, that drink. He always liked his drink. Couldn't nobody drink like Sam, couldn't nobody keep up with him. Never seemed to give him any trouble. You know how it is with some folk. But when he come back, he wasn't the same."

"He was an alcoholic."

"I don't know. That's a doctor's word, Mr. Whelan. I don't know what they mean by it. All I know is he had himself a real problem with the drink. He hit it real hard. Drank a lot, you could smell it on him. Had that cigarettes-and-whiskey smell. But that might've been because he was broke. Things just didn't work out for him, and when he come back he didn't have anything. And you could see it in his eyes; he didn't think things were gonna change much."

"You must have some idea where he'd been. Something must have come out in casual conversation."

"He went all over. Went up to Detroit for a while, went out west, got as far as Phoenix. Down to Texas, like I said. Just moving wherever he thought there was work, wherever it looked like a black man might be able to make hisself a dollar. Which wasn't every place."

"I know. It was the fifties."

"That's right. He even went down to Mexico for a time. That's what he told me, anyhow. Mexico." The way Brown said Mexico, he might have been talking about Sumatra.

Whelan drove past Douglas Park and took a quick glance at Brown.

"You going home or to the bar?"

"The bar. If I leave the hired help in charge long enough, I won't have no bar."

A moment later Whelan pulled up in front of the Blue Note and parked. He turned off the engine but left the radio going. He lit a cigarette and looked at Brown.

"I still feel like I'm just looking at pieces. I need the whole picture."

"What do you need?"

"I'd like to know why this man left town."

"They's lots of folk leave town, Whelan. Happens all the time."

"And if I was trying to find out why one of *them* was killed, I'd want to know why he left his hometown to bum around for four or five years. Doesn't sound to me like a man who left willingly."

"How do you know that? Maybe he—"

"Because he came back. He came back home, O.C."

O.C. Brown studied the front of his tavern and then looked at Whelan. "Sam had himself a run of trouble. Money, most of it. And women. Women loved Sam, Mr. Whelan, but they give him a world of trouble."

"What was the money trouble?"

"He liked the horses, got into the habit. Even started running a little book out of the place where he worked, lounge over on South State—the King's Ransom. Big place. So he was layin' money on a lot of things and he started to lose, and word got around that Sam owed money to some people you didn't want to owe money to."

"Was it true?"

"Oh, coulda been true. It was a real wide-open place, all kinds of people went there. White people too, to dance and hear the bands. I never did find out if what I was hearing was true, 'cause right after that, some other things happened and Sam left town."

"What other things?"

"Place got hit. Somebody broke in on a Sunday night after closing and took the safe, just took the whole thing out. There was talk on the street later on about who hit the place."

"And people thought it was Sam?"

"Had to be somebody inside. Most folk thought it was a couple boys from over on Forty-seventh Street but everybody figured they needed somebody inside to set it up."

"Anybody ever find out?"

"Not for sure. One of these men got himself killed in a fight in a tavern up on Wabash. Couple years later, this was. The other one, he spent some time inside for something else, but he got out eventually. Name was Covington, George Covington."

"Like the ballplayer."

Brown smiled. "You remember him, Wes Covington?"

"Oh, yeah. I remember him with the Sox, but mostly I remember him with the Phillies, hitting a frozen rope over the right field bleachers in Cubs Park once to end a game. The thing never got more than twenty-five or thirty feet off the ground. George Altman thought he was going to catch it."

"Well, this Covington fella, he used to gamble. Used to lay it down pretty heavy. I'm pretty sure he's the one that hit the King's Ransom."

"Did Covington ever give Sam any trouble that you know of?"

"No. But he was inside when Sam come back."

"Sam ever say anything about Covington?"

"No. But he remembered. Covington's name come up one time, and Sam got real quiet."

"And Covington's still alive?"

"Last I heard. He was livin' over on Polk. Big yellow building on Kedzie and Polk."

"Do you think Sam was involved in this robbery?"

Brown tilted his head and squinted. He opened his mouth but nothing came out, as though he couldn't bring himself to speak. Finally he shook his head. "Naw. He wasn't a thief."

"Okay. Still…it might have had something to do with his leaving."

"Hell, Whelan, everything in the man's life had something to do with him leaving. His book went bad on him, the place he worked at got robbed, he had woman trouble—"

"There were problems between him and Erma?"

"Yeah, but nothing like that." Brown looked away for a moment. "That was one sweet woman. I had a little thing for Erma myself. But she wasn't interested in me. She liked Sam. She was also seeing this other fella, name was Ray Booker. I think Sam was the one she really wanted, but this was a serious woman, you understand what I'm sayin'? She didn't want no life hanging around in clubs and listenin' to jazz. That's no kind of life for a woman. And Sam wasn't about to settle down. So there was some trouble there. After Sam left, she married Ray

Booker. Ray was about twenty years older than Erma. Didn't last long, though. He died. Lung cancer. Took a lot of folk I know." Brown shook his head.

"But Sam married her when he got back."

"Right. And for a time he was keeping it together. He give up all that stuff from the past. Even tried to—you know, get past that drink." Brown gave him a shy smile. "I didn't see him much in those days. He was a married man, he was a settled-down man. I was a tavern owner. Had my saloon by then."

"And they had a child, and she died."

"Right. She had a stroke. Young woman like that, dying from a stroke. This was about twelve years ago."

"And since then? These past years, what's he been doing?" He couldn't have been making a living down on Maxwell Street."

O.C. laughed softly. "No, man, you don't make no kind of money down on Maxwell unless you got something special to sell—nothing regular, anyhow. Sam just set up on Sundays, most of the time. Once in a while on a Saturday."

"How did he get by?"

"Odd jobs. Worked as a house painter sometimes. Did some work for me around the tavern, carpentry and electrical. He picked up a little of everything along the way, Mr. Whelan. Wasn't anything wrong with his brain."

"Where did he live?"

"After Erma died, her sister took the boy and Sam stayed with different folks for a while. Then Sam had a room someplace on Madison."

"And lately?"

"Last time I saw him, we had a drink together in my place. Said he had him a new place up north."

"Up north? With the woman you mentioned?"

"No. His own place. He was feeling pretty good about that. He had himself a little apartment up there. Man that's been living in a little room gets himself a real place, it does him some good."

"You have an address?"

"No. I know it wasn't far from this woman. Let's see. Had

a used tire shop downstairs of his place, and he said there was a Salvation Army place up the street where folks lined up for food."

"I know where that is. Anything about the woman? Like a name?"

"Mary, he told me once. She was white, like I said, and 'bout Sam's age. Waitress in a little coffee place underneath the El tracks."

"Which station?"

"That big one, the one's all marble out front."

"Wilson Avenue. Got anything else?"

Brown pursed his lips and shook his head almost imperceptibly, as if reluctant.

"And as far as you know, there was nobody Sam had a problem with lately."

"No."

"White *or* black."

O.C. Brown studied him for a moment. "It was a white man came looking for him."

"And it was a black man that followed him."

"That could've been a whole 'nother thing."

"It could have, but I'm betting it was related. And the man looking for him doesn't have to be the man who actually killed him. One of these men could have been someone hired to find him. Like me."

Whelan watched the street traffic and realized the old man was staring at him.

"I know; it could have been the man who hired me."

"I didn't say that."

"No, but you wanted to. I just said it for you."

"Come on inside, Mr. Whelan, and have a cup of bad coffee."

"I can still feel the last one I had in your place," he said, but he got out anyway.

He wound up spending more than an hour in the Blue Note, sipping O.C.'s horrible black coffee and shooting the breeze with O.C., an old railroad man named Harris, and O.C.'s porter, Winston, who handled the bar in the morning.

When he left, O.C. walked him to the door. "You let me know if you find out something. Hear?"

"Sure."

"You need some money for expenses, right?" O.C. pulled out a roll of bills.

Whelan patted him on the back. "Calm yourself, and put your money away. We'll talk about money some other time."

"You ain't no businessman, Whelan."

"Nicest thing anybody's said to me in ages."

On the way back to the office, he drove by the Subway Donut Shop, a busy steamy collecting point for half the street people on Wilson Avenue and anybody who liked strong coffee and good doughnuts. He took a long look at it and reminded himself of one of his oldest beliefs: that there's something wrong with everyone's story. So far there was something wrong with everybody's story in this one, even O.C.'s. Whelan had bought coffee at the Subway an average of four times a week for the past seven years, and the waitress there was seventy-one and named Ruth. She had been the waitress there since the beginning of time, the only waitress. There was no waitress named Mary.

In the afternoon, he tried to reach David Hill and was told the attorney was in court. The young woman he spoke to said that Hill would be in court most of the next morning as well.

"Is he ever coming back?"

The young woman giggled. "He'll be in the office late in the afternoon, sir. Do you want to leave a message?"

"No, thanks. I'll surprise him."

SEVEN

DAY 4, MONDAY PM

Whelan parked down the block, then walked back up to the little office complex on Clark that housed David Hill's office. The building was of very recent construction, which meant it had gone up in a month and a strong lake wind would knock it over. On one side of Hill's office there was a record store and, on the other, an eye care center that promised two pairs of glasses for the price of one. One or the other would be gone inside of six months. Things didn't last long here. This was New Town, once the trendiest neighborhood on the North Side of Chicago, still one of the most crowded, with enormous high-rise apartment buildings and four-plus-ones on narrow streets never meant for automobile traffic, and a hundred places where young singles could grab fast food.

Hill's office was in the middle of the building on the ground floor. It said so on the window, in large gold and black lettering: LAW OFFICES OF DAVID C. HILL.

Whelan nodded. A couple of months in town, and David Hill was already writing his name on windows and paying lots of rent.

He pulled open the door and heard music, sleepy music, the kind called soft rock, makeout music for preteens. A young singer whose voice hadn't changed yet was telling his love that he couldn't live without her.

Inside, a young Mexican-looking woman was sitting at a large oak desk and proofing something she'd just typed. She shook her head.

"Could be worse," Whelan said. "I could type it, and then you'd really be shaking your head."

She held up a left hand with a badly swollen middle finger. "My fingers don't work anymore."

The nameplate on her desk said she was Pilar Sandoval. The clutter on her desk said working for David Hill was no walk in the park. There were piles of typescript, a well-used shorthand pad, a dictaphone, and half a dozen letters ready to be mailed, all of them on a smooth ivory stationery bearing the name DAVID HILL, in large sepia letters.

The young woman put down the page she was reading. "May I help you, sir?"

"I need to see Mr. Hill."

"Do you have an appointment?" Her voice said she knew he didn't.

"No, and I don't think he wants to end his day by seeing me, but I think he will. My name is Paul Whelan. He knows me."

"You're the gentleman I spoke to earlier."

" Right."

She glanced at the phone buttons. "He's on the phone. Will you have a seat?"

"Sure."

Whelan dropped himself into a steel-and-leather chair that smelled like the inside of a new car. He picked up a newspaper and stared at it. A moment later he saw Pilar Sandoval pick up her phone. She spoke briefly, then listened for a moment. When she spoke again she looked flustered but determined to be heard.

"Yes, sir," he heard her say. "I know that. The gentleman said you know him. I can send him away if that's what you want, sir. His name is Paul Whelan."

Color appeared in her cheeks. She set her jaw and waited for his answer. David Hill had pissed off his secretary.

"Thank you, sir." She replaced the handset on the receiver. "Mr. Hill will see you now, Mr. Whelan." Her face was fully flushed, but there was a little gleam of triumph in her eyes.

"Thanks. I hope I didn't cause you any trouble. But if I did, I think you can handle it."

"I can." Her voice said she'd handled much worse. She indicated Hill's office door with a little nod of her head. As Whelan passed her desk, she added, "You were right. He doesn't want to see you, but he's seeing you."

Whelan stepped inside Hill's office and closed the door behind him. David Hill sat holding a letter to the window light, away from his face. His face was compressed into a combination squint and frown as he struggled with either the typing or the message. He was in shirtsleeves, in a shirt starched marble-hard, and the cloth stuck to his back despite the comfortable temperature in the room. A cigarette was burning itself up in the ashtray.

Portrait of an impatient young man.

Hill put down the letter and shot a grimace in Whelan's direction. He indulged himself in a hard stare for a moment, and Whelan was surprised to see genuine dislike there.

"Mr. Whelan. What brings you here? Is this about your fee?" He stressed the last word with distaste, and Whelan laughed.

"An attorney who doesn't want to talk about fees. It's a topsy-turvy world, isn't it? No, this is not about my fee, and I'm sorry to bother you." Hill continued to stare. "For starters, why don't you show me the courtesy I showed you in my much humbler office?"

Hill blinked. "Of course, forgive me. Please have a seat. I'm just in the middle of some rather draining negotiations and I..." He shook his head distractedly.

Whelan took a chair across from him. "And you've talked to the police."

Hill shot him a look from under his brows. "Yes. I wasn't at all certain why they would want to talk to me, till they mentioned getting my name from you."

"Any reason I shouldn't have given them your name?"

"Of course not, but the point of asking *me* about a man I never even met—"

"They were interested in the fact that I was wandering around Maxwell Street and roaming the West Side looking for a man whose body they found stuffed into a cave under the sidewalk. They were curious about that, Mr. Hill. It didn't look real good for me, so I had to tell them why I was there."

He noticed Hill's face change slightly while he was talking. The lawyer looked just past Whelan, as though preoccupied.

"Well, from what little they were willing to tell me, you're off the hook. The officers I spoke to informed me that they have suspects in custody already. A group of your city's fine young people."

Whelan nodded. "Durkin and Krause? Is that who you spoke with?"

"Yes. Officer Durkin seemed to take an instant dislike to me and to my office. He kept looking around as though he couldn't quite bring himself to believe that he was talking to a black man behind a desk."

"Oh, he believes it. He just doesn't think it's right. And how did your client take it?"

Hill frowned in irritation. He seemed to study Whelan for a second before answering. "As well as could be expected, Mr. Whelan. How would you feel if you were searching for your last remaining relative and learned that he had recently died a violent death? I'm afraid I had given the client to understand that we were...close to finding Mr. Burwell."

"I'm not sure that was wise."

"I didn't ask you. Now, as to the purpose of your visit—shall we finalize our transaction?"

"Actually, I was hoping that since the case is finished, you could see your way clear to giving me a little more information."

"Information?" Hill squinted. "What kind of information?"

"About Sam Burwell."

Hill stared at Whelan as though trying to see inside his skull. Then he gave a little irritated shake of his head. "How would these matters concern you, Mr. Whelan?"

"I've spent the last three days digging up information about this man, and now I find out that he's dead. I just...I don't know, there's an unfinished feel to it." He shrugged.

"I'm sure there is, but you told me yourself that you've looked for people and found that they were dead. I'm sure those cases had an 'unfinished' feel as well. I'm sorry, Mr. Whelan, I can't disclose anything further. Now, if we could, I'd like to deal with the matter of our account. Three days on the case at two-fifty per day, minus the retainer of five hundred. So there is a balance due you of two hundred and fifty dollars plus your expenses."

"Forget the expenses."

"That's not how I do business."

"But it's how I do business, Mr. Hill. You owe me two and a half and the courtesy of some answers to my questions."

Hill shook his head. "You have a basic misunderstanding of our agreement: I owe you money, nothing more. We have concluded our business, and I see no point in discussing this case any further." Whelan marveled at the way Hill maintained the dispassionate tone of voice while his body language said he was thinking of coming across the top of the desk at him.

The lawyer went through the elaborate little display of his fine pen and his lovely checkbook with their ornamentation of deceased reptiles. All his movements were now carried out at high speed, to leave no doubt that he was a very busy man. He made hurried little scratching sounds on the check and tore it loose with a sharp movement of his right hand.

"There you are, Mr. Whelan."

Whelan took the check and inserted it in the chest pocket of his vest without looking at it. As he got to his feet, Hill stood and offered his hand. They shook.

"Thank you for your efforts, Mr. Whelan. I won't hesitate to recommend you in the future."

"You're welcome. Please convey my sympathy to the client about Mr. Burwell's death."

"I will do that."

"And let her know she is free to contact me at any time."

Hill looked amused. "I'll make the client aware of that, Mr. Whelan," he said in a monotone.

"Good. The thing is, I may have uncovered information that would be of interest to her."

"Such as?" Hill raised his eyebrows.

Such as, he thought, the fact that Sam had a son here. Whelan shook his head. "Sorry. I guess you were right. Our business is concluded."

At the door, Whelan turned and nodded to Hill. The attorney was watching him with an unmistakable look of confusion.

In the outer office, Whelan waved to Pilar Sandoval.

"Good-bye, sir. I hope you enjoyed your interview with Mr. Hill." She grinned.

"Oh, I don't know if you could say either of us enjoyed it, but I think I liked it more than he did. I tend to leave people confused after they've talked to me."

The visit to Hill had clarified things and satisfied hunches. There was nothing unusual about a lawyer withholding information about a client, but they didn't normally do it with the intensity of Mr. David Hill. Whelan remembered Hill's description of Sam Burwell and understood now why it had struck him as odd.

On the corner of Wrightwood and Clark there was a restaurant with classic 1960 Chicago decor, a masterpiece of imitation pine paneling and Formica countertops and Naugahyde stools and booths. The door opened and the morning smells of bacon and sausage and eggs fried in butter wafted out in the chill air. The restaurant beckoned to him with a paper sign that claimed BREAKFAST ANYTIME.

What the hell, he thought. It's been a productive afternoon and I got paid and I never had a proper breakfast and I missed lunch entirely. He went into the restaurant and slid into one of the green booths. A middle-aged woman with badly dyed black hair pushed herself off a stool near the register. She approached and raised her eyebrows.

"Coffee?"

"Sure." He pointed at a sign for a three-egg special. It showed a mound of scrambled eggs and a pile of sausages. "I'll have the cholesterol plate."

• • •

He stopped on the way back to the office and grabbed a quick cup of coffee. At his office he tossed the windows open and let the warm air in. He could smell the onions grilling at the little basement greasy spoon down the street. He took a sip of his coffee and got on the phone.

At Area Four Violent Crimes, a Detective Ryan told him that Durkin and Krause were unavailable, so he left a message for either one to call him.

Time to live dangerously.

At Area Six, he was told that Detective Bauman was on furlough.

"God help us all: Bauman with free time. Do you guys think that's wise?"

The detective on the other end chuckled. "I take it you are—uh, familiar with Detective Bauman's habits, sir."

"Yeah. We're almost friends."

He put down the phone and tried to imagine what the obsessive Bauman would do with enforced free time. When Whelan had first made the belligerent detective's acquaintance two years earlier, someone had told him that Bauman's nickname was "the Constant Cop." A brusque, difficult man, Bauman spent his off-duty hours haunting the streets and nosing around into old unsolved cases. He was hostile and argumentative, lived alone, drank prodigiously, suspected everyone, and delighted in jerking the chain of whatever unfortunate soul was partnered with him. These days, he shared a gray Caprice with a perfectly put-together young detective named Landini, who owned a rainbow of knit shirts, wore medallions, and apparently started each morning by diving into a pool of cologne.

The building at Kedzie and Polk was indeed yellow, and stood out from among its gray limestone neighbors like a hooker drumming up trade. Men on stairways watched Whelan get out of the car, checked him out, checked out his car, and then studiously ignored him.

The building manager was a shriveled black man with a shaven head, and he remembered the tenant named Covington.

"Covington's long gone."

"He moved?"

"Had to move. Couldn't pay no rent no more. He's gone."

"You know where?" The man shrugged his narrow shoulders and Whelan added, "I'm not a cop."

"Look like one."

Whelan gestured to the rusting bones of his car. "That's what I drive."

"You right. You ain't no cop. But I don't know where he at. None of my concern. I got to take care of *this*." He jerked his bald head at the building behind him, and the note in his voice made it plain that "this" was more than enough to keep any man occupied.

"How long's he been gone?"

"Couple years. Could be dead by now."

"Anybody in the building that would know him?"

The man pursed his lips and shook his head. "Wasn't nobody here he was friendly with. Covington kept to hisself."

Whelan handed him a card. " If anybody hears anything about him, give me a call. It's worth a couple bucks."

"All right, sir," the man said. When Whelan left, the man was still frowning at the card.

The place was called the Alley Cat, and Whelan had always thought it was named for those who drank there. It was on Lawrence just down the street from his office and he wouldn't have gone there on his own but Bauman had taken him there once when, like tonight, Joe Danno's was closed.

He pushed open the door and was greeted by the time-honored sounds of a bar fight.

Two men grappled against the bar a few feet from the door. They were both in their fifties or sixties, and it was more likely that they'd damage the decor than themselves. Each man had the other by the hair; one had a hand on his opponent's throat and the other had his fingers in his companion's eyes. The bartender, a bald, chubby man in a wrinkled white shirt, stood nearby. He watched them and shook his head in disgust.

At the far end of the bar, his broad back nearly blocking out the TV screen set at bar level, was Detective Albert Bauman, enjoying his furlough. He sat with his elbow on the bar, his face resting on one hand, and puffed at one of his nasty little cigars. There was a bottle of Beck's in front of him, and next to it an empty shot glass.

A few feet away from him, a man in a badly wrinkled brown suit lay facedown on the floor.

Whelan walked up to Bauman and put a hand on his shoulder. "Nice place. You bring all your dates here?"

Bauman looked around slowly. His cheeks were glowing—he had a slight buzz on—but his eyes were still clear: he probably hadn't been here more than a couple of hours. A smile tried to come out of its hole but retreated immediately.

"Hey, Snoopy. What brings you out? Sit down and have a cocktail."

"Don't mind if I do." Whelan pulled out a stool and dropped onto it. He looked over at the man on the floor as Bauman signaled the bartender.

"Hey, Ralph. We got new blood down here. How about a Beck's for this guy."

Whelan indicated the man on the floor. "Maybe we should pick him up."

Bauman snorted. "You fucking pick him up. I picked him up twice already. I set him on a chair and he fell on his face. He's safer where he is. Name's Gibby. He's got what you'd call a problem with liquor."

"Not like you, huh?"

The bartender brought Whelan's beer.

"Fuck you. No, not you, Ralph, this guy I'm with. Here. Take it outta here." Bauman shoved a pile of singles at the bartender.

Whelan ran the palm of his hand across the mouth of the bottle and took a drink. "Thanks."

Bauman nodded and sipped his from a glass. His eyes changed focus till he was looking directly past Whelan's shoulder at the two aging pugilists. He looked amused.

"Do you get the winner?"

Bauman smiled. "I keep thinkin' of callin' it in. One of the coppers out on the street tonight is this Hungarian asshole named Kovacs. Maybe I'd get lucky and Kovacs would get the call. He'd come in here like, you know, James Arness, and find these two old farts wrestlin' in the sawdust."

"And he'd see you, and he'd know who called it in. And that would make you happy." Whelan took a sip of his beer. "So you're on furlough. Having any fun?"

Bauman paused with his beer halfway to his mouth and shot a sidelong glance Whelan's way. "What do you think?"

"I think Albert Bauman with time on his hands is a dangerous thing for society."

Bauman fought off a little smile and drained the rest of his beer. He shrugged. "I watch TV, I have a few beers. I drive around. I took a drive out to the country yesterday, drove all the way up to Lake Geneva."

"What did you do there? Fish? Swim?"

Bauman grinned. "I had a few beers." He waved to the bartender, who was at the other end again, trying to calm down the fighters. The old men had at least separated and now leaned against stools and faced each other, red-faced and panting and looking in need of medical attention.

"Hey, Ralph. You come on down here and serve me, and I'll call the paramedics for Dempsey and Firpo there." He turned toward Whelan. "So what brings you to a sleazy joint like this?"

"Nothing better to do. I was gonna go out anyway, and I thought I might find you here. Guess who I ran into."

"The Pope?"

"Mark Durkin."

"Oh, there's an old favorite of mine. Thought he'd be in the joint by now."

"Not yet. I keep hoping, though. He paid me a visit at my spacious bachelor apartment."

Bauman frowned and let out a melodious little burp. "What kind of visit? Isn't he working out of Four?"

"The burp was a nice touch. Yeah, he's still at Four. He's working on a homicide, an old man down on Maxwell Street."

"What's that got to do with you? You selling your old furniture down there, huh? Selling the light bulbs out of your bedroom lamps?"

"Turns out the guy I was looking for was Durkin's homicide."

Bauman let out a little rumble of laughter and shook his head. " Leave it to you, Whelan. Leave it to you to be putting your nose in someplace where there's a stiff. So old Mark Durkin thinks you did this guy?"

"No. He just jumped at the chance to come hound an old buddy. He thinks he's got the thing in a package already."

"You two were romantically involved in the old days, huh?"

"We go way back. Knew each other in the Academy. We didn't like each other then, either. I knew he'd be a rotten cop, and that's how he turned out."

"So what's the skinny on this deceased client of yours?"

Bauman turned on an amiable smile. Whelan scanned his face quickly, then looked down at his beer. The dark red stain of broken blood vessels was spreading; little purple lines pushed their way across his cheeks like red lace. A furlough was no favor for Bauman. Free time was the last thing he needed.

"He wasn't my client. I was working for a lawyer, allegedly for a relative of this man. The deceased was a neighborhood handyman type and had a spot down on Maxwell, sold odds and ends. He was shot and killed, probably a couple of weeks ago. Durkin wouldn't tell me anything except that I'm probably not a suspect. He seems to think a gang of street kids pulled it off."

"And Whelan thinks it's more complicated." Bauman smirked and took another drink.

"I don't know. Maybe."

"And you're lookin' on your own. For your—ah, peace of mind?"

Whelan hesitated. There was no point in lying to Bauman.

Bauman laughed. "No, you're not. You got a client. In an

ongoing police investigation. Gee, what a surprise."

" I'm not investigating the same thing they're investigating. I'm not investigating this man's murder. I'm looking into something else."

"Oh, yeah? Now why do I think you're lookin' into this guy's killing?"

"Beats the hell out of me. You just have a suspicious nature."

"Okay, let's hear what you think you're investigating."

" I'm looking into something that happened before the man died. I'm trying to get a handle on someone I met who… has a connection with the dead man."

Bauman leaned his bulk against the backrest of the stool and laughed.

"You shoulda been a lawyer, Whelan. You can split hairs with anybody. Lemme see if I got it right: You're not investigating this guy's murder, you're investigating his *life*. And you're checking out somebody that knew him. Is that about it?"

Whelan kept a straight face. "Not bad. That's pretty much what I'm doing."

Bauman nodded. "If I was Durkin, I'd bust your ass. But you wouldn't be sticking your nose into *my* case, now, would you?"

"Nope. So, since you don't have any problem with what I'm doing, how about a little help?"

Bauman shook his head. "Nah. It's got nothing to do with me. You wanta fuck around with Mark Durkin, you got my blessing. Best thing could happen to us is if Durkin went over to the other side where he belongs. But I'm not gettin' tangled up in this shit, Whelan."

"All I need is for somebody to find out if Durkin's got the case he says he has. If he does, I don't have to continue poking around. You think I want to spin my wheels on this? I told someone I'd look into it, and that's what I'm doing. If there's nothing to look into, I'm out of it."

"Call Durkin."

"Maybe some day I'll do *you* a favor."

Bauman gave him a sly look. "Like finding some missing person for me, Whelan? For free? Like that?"

"Got somebody special in mind?"

"Oh, you never know. But right now I don't need no favors."

"I do."

Bauman drained his Beck's and put it down. He massaged his eyes with his fingers. "Awright, Whelan. I'll make a call over to Four."

"I knew you'd still have a following on the West Side, Bauman."

"I'm beloved everywhere I go."

Bauman looked around at the tavern and Whelan saw the boredom in his eyes. He saw Bauman look at his empty shot glass.

"How long you going to be off?"

"Another week."

Bauman's tone left no doubt that "another week" was somebody else's idea. Bauman started to raise the empty shot glass to signal the bartender, and Whelan tapped him on the shoulder.

"I didn't eat dinner yet. You want to go get some food in your stomach, so you can drink some more?"

"Get off my back, Mother Whelan." Bauman looked at his shot glass again and shrugged. "But yeah, I could eat. Nothin' bizarre, though, no Himalayan cuisine or anything."

"Your furlough has eaten away your sense of adventure."

"Adventure's fine, but I don't need no heartburn tonight, okay?"

"Okay. How about a greasy burger and grilled onions?"

"There you go, Whelan. There you go. A no-nonsense American meal."

"I'm hurt." The man called Gibby had managed to pull himself up to a sitting position.

"Look, he's alive."

The man sat hunched over and made loud belching sounds.

"Easy there, Gibby. Don't wanna get the floor messed up—you might have to sleep here tonight." Bauman got to his feet. "Come on, Whelan. You can drive."

• • •

They hit a White Castle, and Whelan watched Bauman tear through a half dozen of the odd little burgers known as "sliders" in ten minutes. When they were finished, Bauman wanted to go for a ride. In minutes they were cruising the Outer Drive at sixty and Bauman was giving directions.

"Speed limit's forty-five, Whelan."

"Yeah, but I don't care."

To their left, a cold wind was churning up the lake, and whitecaps came crashing against the shore in wall after wall. The water climbed high up the rocks and threatened to reach the very edge of the roadway.

"So where are we going?"

Bauman grinned. "Where the sunlight never shines."

In the very bowels of the city, under the Michigan Avenue Bridge, ran a surreal tunnel of a roadway that snaked beneath the city for several miles without seeing the light of day. Small green overhead lights every ten yards or so lent the place a garish touch, like Oz gone wrong. Half a mile to the east was the lake. A fishy smell betrayed the proximity of the Chicago River a few feet to the west. Whelan parked behind a loading dock.

A pair of homeless men crouching down against the concrete wall of the tunnel gazed at them for a moment and then looked away.

"Why are we here?" Whelan asked as they walked.

Bauman grinned and suddenly looked much more sober. "Let's have an adventure."

Oh-oh, Whelan thought. "Not me, Bauman. I still have pain from the last one."

"Aw, come on, Whelan. You're no fun anymore."

Whelan thought for a moment. "You wanted to come down here to look for that guy. The crossbow guy." For the two years Whelan had known Bauman, the detective had been obsessed with hunting down a man who had used a crossbow to kill a homeless man not far from where they were.

Bauman shook his head, blew out his cheeks till he looked

like a red-faced Dizzy Gillespie, then sniffed. "Nah. That guy, you know what I think? I think he knows."

"That you're looking for him."

"Right. I think he's in—uh, semiretirement. But I'll get him someday."

One of the homeless men suddenly materialized at their left, as though emerging from the wall of the tunnel. "Excuse me, gentlemen," he said, stopping in front of Whelan.

"What's up, Moe?" Bauman moved up till he was almost nose to nose with the man.

The man gave Bauman a doubtful look and his eyes moved to Whelan. "I need a dollar and thirty-seven cents."

Bauman nodded. "What are you, an accountant? What do you need a buck thirty-seven for?"

"I want a cheeseburger and fries from McDonald's. That's what it costs with tax."

Bauman stared at the man and screwed his red face into a frown. "I don't think that'll do it, pal. I don't think you can buy anything for a buck thirty-seven. Wait, you mean one of the little cheeseburgers?"

The man nodded.

Bauman turned to Whelan and made a little measuring gesture with his thumb and forefinger. "He means one of those little fuckers where the meat is the size of a half-dollar. I just ate half a dozen of those."

"Eight," Whelan corrected.

"No, man, you don't want one of those kiddie burgers." Bauman fished in his pocket and pulled out a handful of crumpled bills and change. A dollar fell out, and a couple of pennies, as well as lint and what appeared to be a yellow dry-cleaning receipt.

"Here, take this," he said, handing the man a ten. "Buy a—whaddaya call it? A Big Mac. Buy your buddy one too."

The man stared at the ten and looked wide-eyed at Bauman. "Thanks, mister."

"It's okay, now get outta my way." Bauman looked over at the second man and grinned. "Your buddy's got a sawbuck.

Don't let him tell you it's a single."

The two men hurried up the stairs to the McDonald's on Michigan Avenue, where a sawbuck might just barely get the two of them a meal.

Bauman marched ahead. "C'mon, Whelan."

"Why? Why are we walking through the only underground street in Chicago? Let's go up aboveground where there's fresh air."

Bauman mumbled something that sounded like "I hate fresh air" and continued on his way. Up ahead, where the tunnel became Lower Wacker, there was a late-model car parked with its hazard lights on. A man poked his head out the driver's side window and peered around in the darkness. Bauman said something to the driver and Whelan saw the man pull his head back inside like a nervous turtle.

When Whelan drew closer to the car, he saw it had Indiana plates. Bauman was asking the driver what he was doing parked there. The man gripped the steering wheel tightly and stared till Whelan stuck his head in. The driver leaned back from the window.

"What's wrong?" Whelan asked.

The man opened his mouth and nothing came out. He was sweating and his face was red, and he had a bug-eyed look to him.

Whelan nodded. "Been having a few cocktails?"

The man looked from him to Bauman. His eyes widened and he quickly glanced back at Whelan. His breath came noisily through his mouth; Whelan wondered if he were about to hyperventilate.

"What *is* this place?"

"What?" Whelan looked at Bauman. The cop was grinning.

"What is this place? Where's…I was driving through Chicago, and all of a sudden…"

The man stared around him at the dank wet walls of the tunnel and the dark staircases that led up to the surface world, where people could see the moon. He leaned with his head against the steering wheel and mumbled something.

"What did you say?" Whelan asked.

"I wanna go home. I just wanna go home."

Bauman snorted. "Home's in Indiana, huh? Bet they don't have nothing like this in the Hoosier State."

Whelan watched the man for a moment, noted the unusual brightness in his eyes. "Been doing a little blow there, huh? A couple of beers, a little toot." He looked at Bauman. "He's really disoriented."

"Hallucinating," Bauman said, barely mouthing the words.

"You think you've entered the Twilight Zone, right?" Whelan smiled, feeling sorry for him.

The man stared at him and shut his mouth tightly, unwilling to speak his deepest dread. Then he looked down at the steering column and said, "I want to be in Chicago. I just want to be in Chicago."

"You're in Chicago. This is Lower Wacker Drive. It's a little spooky, but it's just a street that runs through a tunnel under the rest of the town."

The man winced. "Under the town? I'm *under* Chicago? Where the…the giant rats are?" He looked as though he were about to cry.

Whelan patted him on the arm. "You're all right. There are no giant rats anymore. They're all dead or in the City Council. You keep on this street for a mile, not even that, and you're out in the fresh air again; then you keep going south and eventually you get to Indiana."

At the mention of his beloved state, the man seemed to relax. "This goes to Indiana?"

"You bet. Can I give you a little advice? Stop somewhere and get some coffee. Give yourself some time to calm down and sober up."

The man nodded, then shrank back as Bauman pushed Whelan aside and filled the window.

"And here's some more advice, there, Opie. What line of work you in?"

"I sell office furniture."

"You wanna keep sellin' desks and filing cabinets, you lay

offa that shit you put up your nose, hear? Or you'll be sellin' down here in the underworld."

At the mention of his worst fear, the man blinked, turned, and nodded. Then Bauman flashed his detective's shield and let it hang down in front of the man's face.

"Oh, shit."

"Now go home." Bauman straightened up and the driver started his car. They waved as he drove off, his headlights off and his hazard lights still flashing.

Bauman hitched his pants up over his big hard belly and looked at Whelan. "See? Nothing like a nice walk after a good meal."

They resumed their stroll through the tunnel and didn't speak. Whelan shot a quick look at Bauman and tried to put himself in the position of the inebriated salesman from Indiana. This was the stuff of nightmare: a green-faced giant in the tunnel that runs under the city.

"You do this often, Bauman?"

"What, come down here? No. You mean roam around the city at night? Yeah."

A block farther, Bauman stopped, shrugged, and looked at Whelan. "Okay, let's go up to the bright lights and look for girls."

Bauman had no more to say aboveground than he had below. They walked back up Michigan Avenue, crossing the bridge, and neither man spoke. Whelan watched his companion, who was studying the buildings as if seeing them for the first time.

"I used to like it down here." Bauman turned to see if Whelan was listening.

"Who wouldn't?"

Bauman shook his head. "No, I don't mean I walked around lookin' at the buildings and shops. I used to hang out down here."

"Doesn't seem like your style."

Bauman gave him a quick look, amusement mixed with irritation, and then said, "I was going out with somebody down here."

"Oh," Whelan said, suddenly speechless.

"Waitress," Bauman said. A half block farther, he pointed to a building across the street. "She worked there."

Whelan looked where Bauman pointed. On the second floor, above a swank women's shop, was Changsha, a Chinese restaurant known as much for its elegant service and decor as for its Hunan food. Whelan had been there once.

"Chinese?"

"She was Vietnamese. Chinese parents."

Whelan waited for more information and soon saw that none was coming—or would be coming in the foreseeable future. Evidently Bauman had exhausted his conversation on all other subjects as well, for he said nothing more till Whelan dropped him off at the Alley Cat.

"Thanks, Whelan. Stay outta trouble—if that's possible for you."

"What about you?"

"I'm just a quiet guy on furlough." Bauman hitched up his pants and went inside the bar for a nightcap.

As he drove back to his house, Whelan thought about Bauman's cryptic reference to the Vietnamese woman and realized there was no one on the planet who knew the man's private thoughts.

What a way to live.

His thoughts turned to this case that might not even be a case, this favor for an old man that was taking him into places he didn't know. Once or twice before, his work had sent him into neighborhoods that were alien to him, rich people's communities where the mere sight of his rusted-out car would send people to their phones. This case was different. He was going into places where he wasn't welcome. There was nothing new in that: he'd experienced it before, even in Uptown. But this was different, the differences were more fundamental.

He wasn't even sure where to go next on O.C. Brown's case, but he was certain that someone would give him a nudge. He half expected that it would be David Hill.

EIGHT

DAY 5, TUESDAY

There was a FOR RENT sign on the glass of the door to his office building. It claimed that two "spacious offices" were available on the first floor. Good news and bad news. The good was that maybe they'd let him move down where there was still life, where PAUL WHELAN INVESTIGATIVE SERVICES wasn't the only occupied suite on the floor. The bad was that two more businesses had left the North Side's least promising professional location, and the death of the building couldn't be far behind.

He expected no one and didn't look up till he heard the scraping of feet against the marble floor. Then he heard the rustle of thick leather, and a dark shape separated itself from the shadows at the top of the staircase. He sensed movement in his direction.

Whelan was still several steps short of the landing when the visitor addressed him. "You Whelan?"

"Yeah." Something in the man's monotone told him this wasn't business. "Can I help you?"

His caller stood on the top step and blocked Whelan's path, a black man in sunglasses and a Bulls cap. Whelan wondered whether the visitor was the man who had followed him in the white Ford. Whelan figured him for early twenties, with close-set eyes, small features, and close-cropped hair. He was five-nine or five-ten and slender, and his movements showed tension. He removed the sunglasses and tucked them into his jacket pocket.

"No, man, but I'm gon' help you." And Whelan recognized

the voice.

Whelan was just setting his front foot on the landing when the man threw a punch. He moved his head slightly to the left and the first one whizzed past his ear, but a second punch caught him on the bridge of the nose. It was a good shot; an inch up or down and it would have broken his nose. As it was, he saw bright colors and odd shapes and needed some time to right himself. He backed away to get his balance, blocked another punch, and landed a straight left. It caught his assailant somewhere on the mouth and made him grunt but didn't stop him.

The other man threw a right and then brought his foot up in a sweeping arc that caught Whelan just below the ribs. He fell against the banister and caught himself with one hand as the man came at him.

Whelan ducked another punch and grabbed the other man's jacket. He used the man's lunging motion to swing him off balance and threw him into the far wall. The Bulls cap came off and went sailing down the stairs.

The other man pushed off the wall and cocked his right for another punch. Whelan could hear him breathing heavily.

"I told you I'd kick your white ass if you came back."

Whelan looked up and saw the man staring at him, fists clenched at his sides. His eyes bulged in rage and he ignored the blood that seeped from his lower lip and stained his teeth.

"I should fuckin' kill you, man." The man breathed through his mouth. Then they both heard the street door open and the sound of someone coming up the first flight. The young man turned and ran down the stairs, taking them two at a time.

Whelan stood slowly, put his fingers to his nose. There seemed to be a trickle from the nostrils but nothing dramatic.

A nice morning workout. Now, off to work.

He let himself in and wet a handkerchief at the spigot to his water cooler. He'd been in the office four minutes when the phone rang. He picked it up to the sound of laughter.

"Hi, Mr. Whelan. Think I got your patterns down, baby?" Shelley laughed delightedly into the phone. "You sound out of breath."

"I keep thinking I have to hire a more professional-sounding answering service."

"Uh-uh, sweets, then you'd have to start keeping professional habits and working hours. You'd have to come in at nine when you say you'll be in at nine."

"So I'm ten minutes late. I—uh, ran into an acquaintance."

"My ma used to say, 'How would you like to hang for ten minutes?' Anyhow, you already had a client call. A Mr. Hill. Said he'd be in to see you around ten."

"I thought I'd be hearing from him. Something good has to happen today." He patted the bridge of his nose and wondered if it would swell and leave him looking like a red-haired Jake LaMotta. "Anybody else? How about Detective Bauman. Remember him?"

"I remember all my nightmares, hon. No, he hasn't called."

"And a Detective Durkin?"

"So many cops. No, not him either."

"Thanks, Shel."

"Toodle-oo," she piped, and hung up.

I have an answering service. My answering service consists of a little man from India who finds English a constant struggle, and a lady who laughs at me and says "Toodle-oo."

David Hill arrived exactly as the hour hand on the office clock crawled to the ten. Whelan suspected Hill had been out in the barren hall studying his watch.

"Come in, Mr. Hill, and have a seat."

"Thank you." The lawyer flashed his lizardly accessories and lit up a cigarette. He looked around the office as he exhaled.

"What can I do for you?"

Hill smiled. "I have another business proposition to put to you."

"I can hardly wait."

"I conveyed your message to my client."

"And?"

Hill raised his hands, palm up. "There is a certain amount of interest in your information, but I myself have reservations."

Where did they learn to speak like this? "What kind of reservations? I don't understand."

"Quite frankly, Mr. Whelan, I think my client is going through a very vulnerable period. This is a time when anyone might grasp at straws to get information about a deceased relative. You must understand that."

"You think I might take advantage of your client when she's not thinking things through clearly."

"I wouldn't accuse you of anything like that. But my client's emotional well-being is of great…personal concern to me."

Whelan nodded. "The client is a personal friend."

"I didn't say that either, Whelan. But I will tell you that the client is someone I've known for a long time. And I have rather rigid views of an attorney's obligations to any client, let alone one with whom he has some history."

"I respect that, and I have no intention of taking advantage of your client. I have my own interests in this case, though. I thought by sharing some information I've come across, I might gain some understanding about the situation. You showed no interest in giving me information about the dead man."

"It's not your business!"

Whelan shrugged. "I told you it was. I told you I needed to know a little more, and I think your client might be more inclined to share it with me than you are."

"There will be no contact between you and the client, Mr. Whelan. I can guarantee you that."

"Then you came to my grungy office for nothing. The local kids have probably stripped that Buick of yours by now."

"I am in a position to pay you for whatever you wanted to share with my client. And as you've probably guessed, the client is not without means."

"Oh?"

Hill made a coy little sideways nod. "We can negotiate for your information, Mr. Whelan. There is no problem whatever with that."

"Okay. Make me an offer."

"For what?"

"For information I've discovered."

Hill sighed. "Of what nature?"

"That I must keep under my hat. But it's something your client should know."

Hill blinked and then gazed at Whelan for a moment, eyes moving rapidly across Whelan's face. Then Hill shook his head, rubbed the bridge of his nose and looked at Whelan in distaste.

"I really don't enjoy this sort of thing, Whelan. If you have something my client needs to know, you are bound to tell me. If your information is worth something, you'll be compensated."

Whelan shook his head. "I'm not working for you anymore. Tell you what I think, though. I think your client probably needs to know exactly the kinds of things I've been finding out about the deceased. I think she'd be better off with me than she is with you." He leaned back and studied the lawyer.

Hill watched him for a moment, eyes wide, then gave him an incredulous smile. "Funny thing, Mr. Whelan: I mention that my client is not without resources and suddenly you want an introduction. Happily, that decision is still mine. And you are wasting my time."

"*You* came to see *me*."

Hill got up to leave. "Yes, but I thought you had information of a different nature. *This* nonsense about secret discoveries is unlikely to be of any interest at all to my client."

"If that's so, I'm sorry to have inconvenienced you."

Hill gave a short nod and left the office.

And I'm sorry I met you, Whelan said to himself.

Whelan was coming back from grabbing a quick cup of coffee and ran up the last half flight to catch the phone. It was Bauman.

"Hey, Whelan, I'm disappointed. I was hopin' you'd be out and I'd get to talk to that broad that answers the phone."

"We sent her to a convent. Got something for me?"

"Yeah. I made a couple calls, so you owe me. And I don't mean lunch."

"Fine, what did you get?"

"Sounds like old Durkin's got himself a case. They found a gun in the bushes down there. Clean, though."

"Which makes it just a gun. Besides, you know any kids that wipe and toss the piece after they use it? Kids fall in love with guns. Sounds like a dead end to me."

"Yeah, well, they found the guy's truck, this Burwell."

"So?"

"So these little shits that Durkin picked up took the truck. They admitted it. And anyway, their fingerprints are all over it."

"Where'd they find it?"

"There's an abandoned factory—on Sixteenth, I think it was—just south of the tracks. It was there. They drove it there, took out the battery and the radio." Bauman laughed. "They took out an *AM radio* to sell on the street. Stupid little fuckers. That's all they got out of it. An AM radio and a battery and whatever pocket change this picker had on him."

"Do they know how much that was?"

"Nah. The kids are all sayin' it wasn't them, they just took the truck, they don't know nothing about no stiff. But there's the truck, and they can put these guys together on a couple other armed robberies, and one of 'em's got a genuine sheet, so I'd say they're in deep shit. Especially with Durkin on it. He'll either plant evidence or force a confession. And if he don't fuck it up, he's got his case."

"What if I told you I didn't buy it?"

Bauman chuckled hoarsely into the phone. "You wouldn't be Whelan if you did. You never want anything to be simple." And he hung up.

The obituary was small and marked by an American flag to indicate the death of a veteran. It gave the skeletal details of Sam Burwell's passing and the particulars of his wake and funeral. The wake was to be held for one night, at the Porter and White Funeral Home on South Kedzie. There was one other detail in the obituary, a detail Whelan had hoped to see. The obituary said that Mr. Burwell was the "loving father of Perry." Whelan put down the paper and wondered if David Hill's client was reading the same notice.

• • •

Whelan pulled into the parking lot of the funeral home and found a spot in a far corner of the lot, away from the rows of cars already there. He sat in the car for a moment with the radio tuned to a station that played old jazz for twelve hours a day and then went off the air by ten. He had no clear idea why he was there. He acknowledged a curiosity about this dead man whom he'd never even seen in life and a professional interest in the people who might show up at his wake. But the more he turned it over in his mind, the better he realized he was here simply for O.C. Brown's sake.

A steady stream of mourners entered the funeral home; he wondered if they were all there for Sam Burwell. The jazz station gave him a tinny-sounding recording of an obscure jazz quartet led by a saxophone player, and he listened to the sax wailing and had a cigarette. He waited vainly for someone he recognized to go into the building and then gave it up.

Inside, he found a sign, white plastic letters on black, that told him there were four visitations in progress. Samuel Burwell's was in Chapel C, and an arrow pointed him to the rear of the building.

Whelan walked in the direction of the arrow and paused at the entrance to Chapel B. It was a tiny room dominated by a plain brown casket. Overhead in the doorway a smaller version of the previous sign told the onlooker that this man's name was Harold Melton. There were four chairs in a little row just before the casket, but they were empty. Without knowing why, he stepped into the room. The casket held a small black man in his sixties or seventies. The funeral home had been powerless to disguise the fact that this man had been emaciated: the man's shirt collar was at least a size too large and the ancient-looking wool suit had been bought for a heavier man.

Whelan looked at the man's face and wanted to leave. Instead, he found himself saying a short prayer for this old one who had died without enough mourners to fill a small room. The last of his family, perhaps, a man who had outlived all those around him. He finished and made the sign of the cross, then left, half embarrassed by his own intrusion, half hoping someone would come by and see that Harold Melton had a visitor.

Samuel Burwell was not alone. There were already fifteen or twenty people in the chapel, but he recognized none of them. Most of them turned to watch Whelan when he entered but no one stared for more than a second; this was a man's funeral.

He walked to the front of the room and stood a few feet away from the casket to see this man he'd never met in life.

The body in the casket was that of a tired-looking man, a tall, thin man with a mustache gone gray and silver in his hair. A scar had torn a whitish path through one eyebrow, and the skin around the eyes was deeply wrinkled. Whelan said a brief prayer and then moved away.

He took a seat in the back of the chapel and looked around. The Porter and White Home had been a part of the community for generations and, like the rest of this old and battered neighborhood, was showing its age. Cracks spidered their way across the ceiling and down walls; the carpet, once a dark rich wine color, was faded and threadbare in several places.

The room began to fill up, and a number of the newcomers were women, their perfumes mingling with the pervasive aroma of the carnations and roses around the casket. Whelan saw well-dressed black couples in middle age, old ones whose threadbare clothes told of their fortunes in a society that shelves its elderly, and good-looking younger men and women who made a startling contrast with the faded man in the casket.

One of the later arrivals was a skinny little white man in a baggy suit who entered crushing his cloth hat in his hands. Whelan recognized him as one of the vendors from Maxwell Street, the man who'd tried to sell him a flashlight. A few moments later a middle-aged Mexican couple entered, said a prayer at the casket, and then found seats near the back of the room, where they huddled together.

Whelan studied the people around him and wished he hadn't come. The depth of his discomfort surprised him. Many times he had been the outsider in a group of people, people of another race or ethnic group, and it hadn't bothered him. He had in fact usually found it interesting. This was different: this was a gathering on the most profound level, and his presence seemed an intrusion.

After twenty minutes that seemed like three hours, O.C. Brown entered. He had an entourage of sorts: two old men Whelan didn't recognize were with him, as was his porter Winston, Mr. Wells from O.C.'s building, and an elderly black woman.

He scanned the room again and realized there was something missing, or at least odd in the gathering. Finally he understood: there was no central group in this room. At the front of the chapel, where a family would have bunched in a tight little knot, greeting people as they arrived, there was no one. As though to acknowledge this difference, the mourners had left the front row empty, so that the closest people to the casket were eight or ten feet away.

None of these people belonged to him, Whelan thought.

Whelan thought about going over to speak to O.C. Brown and then decided not to call attention to himself. He folded his arms and stared down at his shoes and took in snatches of the many conversations around him. A slight lull in the volume caught his ear and he looked up.

Standing in the doorway to the chapel were two men and a woman. The first man was undoubtedly the funeral director, an imposing man, easily the tallest person in the room, and broad at the shoulders. He was extremely light-skinned, almost white, with a tiny, perfectly trimmed mustache, and his manner was solicitous but professional.

Whelan knew the woman, knew her name as well: Willis. He had questioned her on his first visit to the West Side, an irritable young nurse on her way to work.

The third person in the group was by far the most interesting. He was a slender young man of average height and very dark, with close-set eyes that looked almost black. He listened to the funeral director and nodded, and there was a tension to his body, a tightness to his back and shoulders and neck, as though he were about to lash out at something. Whelan had already seen him lash out once, in the hall outside his office.

He could not keep his eyes off his assailant. After a moment the funeral director excused himself. The young man stepped into the room with the woman and they greeted the people nearest the door. The woman did most of the talking, and the young man's eyes scanned the faces in the chairs. His gaze met Brown's a few feet away, and they nodded to each other. The young man continued to survey the room, nodding a couple of times and once raising his hand in a halfhearted wave. Then he saw Whelan. The young man blinked in spite of himself and made a little half turn as if to say something to the woman, then caught himself. He stared at Whelan and seemed to be about to approach him when the funeral director reentered the room and took him aside.

Whelan was watching their conversation when he heard the voice beside him.

"Kinda far from home, there, Whelan." O.C. Brown stood over him, smiling. His eyes had a little gleam to them, and Whelan realized the man was genuinely glad to see him. They shook hands, and Whelan patted the seat beside him.

"Take a load off."

"All right." O.C. sat with a slight groan and tilted his head to one side as though listening. He caught Whelan watching him and said, "You get old, you make a lot of noises when you sit down."

"I'm almost there myself. Not a bad crowd," Whelan said, just to be saying something.

O.C. looked around slowly and nodded. "Pretty fair. Pretty fair. Would have been a big crowd when he was young. Had a lot of friends then, knew everybody on the street. Not just black people, neither. Knew a lot of white people. Wouldn't have been able to use this little bitty chapel." He paused. "You checking out his people? You thinking maybe something interesting is gonna show up here?"

Whelan shrugged. "Maybe. But, no, I didn't come to observe these people or anything like that. These are his friends.

I just came…it seemed like something I should do. I feel like you've gotten me involved in his life."

O.C. studied his face and then nodded. He seemed pleased.

"I just hope it doesn't offend anyone for me to be here."

"Nobody gonna be offended because you come to pay your respects."

"Well, I don't know about that, O.C. The young man over there by the wall, I can just about guarantee he doesn't want me here."

O.C. looked over at the man who had assaulted Whelan. "Perry? Perry Willis? The boy say something to you?"

Whelan remembered the obituary. He studied his assailant for a long moment. "So that's his son. Yeah, he said something to me. Once on the phone—the call I told you about."

Brown nodded. "That was him?"

"Think so. And then in person, this morning. He was waiting for me outside my office. He punched me and told me he should kill me. He didn't say what for, but I've got a pretty good idea."

O.C. looked from Whelan to the young man named Perry. He frowned and shook his head. "He thinks you had something to do with all this here?"

"Yep. That's what he thinks."

"Well, look here, Whelan, I'm sorry to be causing you trouble. I'll have a talk with the boy. But you got to understand how he feels. He's not himself. He's not thinking clear."

Whelan nodded, still looking at the young man. He remembered the man in the baseball cap who'd tailed him on the West Side. "Does Perry drive a white Ford?"

O.C. snorted. "No, he got him a red Thunderbird somebody oughta put out of its misery. Need new shocks, new paint, new transmission, new oil pan." He interrupted his catalog of the car's injuries and looked at Whelan. "He didn't say who he was, huh?"

"He was too busy swinging."

The old man nodded at Perry. "Yeah, that's Sam's boy."

"And the woman with him is his wife?"

"Danielle, yeah. Ain't been married but six or seven months."

"I think I ought to hit the road, O.C."

O.C. put a hand on his leg. "No, sir. You come to pay your respects and nobody's gonna say anything to you. I told you I'd talk to the boy, and I will." And before Whelan could say anything, Brown had lifted himself up off the chair and was moving determinedly in the direction of Sam Burwell's son.

Whelan saw him grab the younger man by the upper arm. He could see O.C.'s knotty fingers squeezing Perry through the cloth of his black suit and almost smiled when a look of pain came into the young man's eyes. Perry said something and O.C. just shook his head, ushering the young man out into the hall.

When O.C. came back, his face wore the look of a man who knows he has taken control. He glanced at Whelan, made a curt nod, and went over to join a group of older men standing near the casket. Perry entered a moment later, appearing sullen and hostile. He let his eyes linger for a moment on Whelan. Then he turned away.

A moment later a Catholic priest entered the chapel. The priest was a white man in his late thirties, with a red Irish face and a wide nose, and he seemed to know most of those in the room. Whelan saw him put a hand on Perry's shoulder and say something. The young man nodded and glanced over at the casket.

Whelan decided not to stay for the prayers. He got up and made his way toward the door and was just about there when Perry cut him off.

"O.C. thinks he needs your help, but I don't."

Whelan looked at him and said nothing.

Perry stepped closer. "I say I don't need your help."

"Then I won't offer it. I'm working for Mr. Brown."

"Don't nobody here need your help, man."

Whelan checked the clock in the back of the chapel and said nothing to Perry.

"Got nothin' to say?"

"It's a funeral, friend. There's a certain way I behave at them."

Perry seemed startled. He was about to say something, then just stared at Whelan for a moment before walking away. Whelan turned to wave to O.C. Brown, and the old man broke off his conversation to join him.

"What's the matter there, Whelan? You leaving before the man says the prayers?"

"I think it's time for me to go."

O.C. glanced over to Perry. "Don't pay him no mind, Whelan. The boy's got a lot of things to deal with here. Him and Sam, they had their trouble. Most of the time, they didn't even speak. I know he's thinking 'bout that now."

Whelan nodded. "In some ways, I'm sure that's harder than if they were close. But he seems like the kind of man who brings himself trouble when nobody else gets around to it."

"Yeah, you got that right." O.C. seemed about to say something else and then nodded to someone behind Whelan. Whelan turned and saw a tall muscular black man in a white sergeant's shirt.

The police officer came over and shook O.C.'s hand. "Hey, O.C." He nodded in Whelan's direction. His brass nameplate said BELTON.

O.C. clapped the taller man on the shoulder. "How you feel, Ed?"

"I'm all right. I was real sorry to hear about old Sam. I know you were tight."

"That's all right. Listen here, Ed, this is a friend of mine, Paul Whelan. Used to be one of you." O.C. pointed to the tall cop's badge.

Sergeant Belton gave Whelan an interested appraisal. "That right? Where'd you work, Mr. Whelan?"

They made cop talk for a moment before the sergeant moved on, and then Whelan saw David Hill enter the chapel. Hill had removed his glasses, and his eyes took on a wide-eyed stare that made him look like a college student. Hill stared a moment when he saw Whelan, a look that seemed to mix discomfort and hostility.

Whelan returned the stare until the attorney broke off.

Hill glanced for a moment at O.C. Brown and then scanned the room. He tugged at his collar, brushed the front of his jacket, then went to the casket, where he stood with his hands clasped in front of him. As Whelan watched, Hill took out his glasses and put them on again. Hill stared at the body for a long moment and then walked away. He spotted a seat at the far end of a back row and made for it.

O.C. watched him and said nothing for a moment. Then he turned to Whelan. "I noticed you were watching that fella in the blue suit."

Whelan felt himself smiling. "That is the honorable David C. Hill. The man who hired me to find Sam."

"Well, I'll be damned. What's he doing here?"

"I don't know," Whelan said, and then realized that he'd been hoping Hill would show up with someone else. Something else the older man had said earlier now ran through his mind. "O.C., you mentioned other trouble Sam had just before he left town. You said his book had gone bad."

"That's right. But he paid off everybody. Didn't nobody come looking for him, talking about him owin' money or anything like that."

"And woman trouble. You said he had woman trouble. Tell me about that."

"Not much to tell. You been in woman trouble, Whelan, I know you have."

"Yeah, but I haven't left town because of it yet."

"Sam was seeing a lot of women, including Erma, who he eventually married later on, the one I told you about. And he was seeing a white girl for a while, *young* white girl."

"Young enough to send somebody to jail?"

"No, not that young."

"What kind of trouble?"

"Just that some folk noticed he was seein' somebody wasn't his color. Give people something to talk about. This was a little girl he knew at a club on South State; she worked there. Waited tables. Once in a while she got up on stage and sang with the band. Wanted to be an actress but she shoulda been a singer.

Turn out she was twenty."

"Let me guess: Daddy come looking for him."

"No. Didn't last that long. The girl and Sam, they were just foolin' around. Then she started seein' this trombone player, white fella played in the clubs. That was the end of show business for her. Family made her come back home, to Springfield or someplace, sent some people out to put the fear of the Lord into the trombone player." O.C. thought for a moment. "But if the girl hadn't been white, it wouldn't have been no big thing. Sam had lots of women around then."

"Anybody that was special?"

O.C. nodded slowly. "It was another woman back then, real light-skinned girl named Mamie. Now Mamie *got* to Sam, Whelan. I'll tell you that. She got to him. She was a beautiful woman. Kinda olive skin, big dark eyes, wore her hair real long. All the girls were straightening their hair, but Mamie liked to wear it over one eye, like a black Veronica Lake, Lauren Becall, you know what I'm saying? You know that look?"

"I still see it in my dreams. What became of her?"

"Chicago wasn't big enough for her. She had ideas she was gonna be a movie star. She went out to California."

"About the same time Sam left?"

"He didn't go to California." Whelan said nothing, and the older man thought a moment before shaking his head. "No, she left town after he did. Maybe a year later. And she didn't have no time for Sam, Whelan. He run taverns and shot craps in back rooms, and this was a lady with—you know, ideas 'bout herself. They had a thing going for a long time. You know, off and on. But Mamie, she wasn't gonna stay around here. She was goin' to Hollywood. Some folks thought she'd go out there and pass. She was light enough."

"It would help if I could talk to one of these women."

"You out of luck there, Whelan. The little white girl, she got killed in a car accident."

"What about Mamie?"

"Like I said, she went out to California."

"Did he ever hear from her again?"

"Didn't nobody ever hear from Mamie again."

"It was just a thought."

O.C. sighed. "Old Sam, he had an eye. Color didn't make no difference to him. For a while back there, he was takin' out this Chinese girl. And I told you about the woman he was seein' up north by you."

Whelan nodded. He surveyed the room once more. David Hill sat back in a folding chair and gazed in the general direction of the casket.

Whelan patted O.C. on the back. "I'm taking off."

"Drop by my place or give me a call."

He nodded. "Good night, O.C."

"Night, Whelan. And thanks for comin' out."

Nine

DAY 6, WEDNESDAY

O.C. had given him the block and the approximate location on it, so it didn't take long the next morning to find the place where Sam Burwell had lived. It was on Broadway, across the street from a tired-looking supermarket and a few doors down the street from the Salvation Army building at Broadway and Sunnyside. Storefronts lined the block, some of them occupied, others empty and with meager prospects for ever being used again. There were a pair of down-at-the-heels businesses on the ground floor of Burwell's building: a tire shop with a group of men standing in front and a video shop that boasted triple-X rated movies and action films in three languages.

The door to the second floor stood between the shops. There were four names taped to the doorframe below the bells: SANCHEZ, HALEY, ROGERS, and PITTS, and an empty space where a piece of tape had recently held a fifth name. A little star had been pasted next to HALEY. No mailboxes. Whelan tried the door, gave it a little push, and went inside. The hall was dark and a little pile of mail cluttered the bottom step. He bent over and spread the envelopes and fliers out: several for Umberto Sanchez, one letter from the VA hospital addressed to James Pitts, but the majority for Mrs. Violet Haley.

He inhaled the smell of rotted wood, old linoleum, plaster gone to powder. The banister was gone, so he put a steadying hand on the wall as he went up. Paint and plaster came loose at his touch and fell to the stairs with a skittery sound.

The second floor appeared to be divided into five tiny

apartments, and the first one had a dull brass star on the doorframe. He knocked.

"Who's that?" A woman's voice, low and flat, bereft of emotion.

"Mrs. Haley?"

"What?" the woman said aloud, then lower, to herself, "What now, for chrissake."

Whelan stood in the hallway and heard nothing; she wasn't coming to the door without a good reason.

"Mrs. Haley, my name is Paul Whelan. I'm a private investigator and I need some information. Can I talk to you for a moment?" He could hear her moving around inside. She muttered something and then she was quiet.

"Mrs. Haley, I can pay for information."

He was surprised when the door opened slightly—she'd been standing next to it. She was squinting at him through tinted glasses that distorted her eyes and made them look sleepy.

Three inches of cheap door chain separated them, an illusory security. Anyone could put a shoulder into the door and tear the chain in half.

She puffed at a cigarette and blew her smoke through the opening.

"You don't look like no detective."

"Here." He held open his wallet and showed her his license.

"Hold it closer. I can't see so good."

Whelan thrust the license closer and saw her nod. The door closed briefly, the chain rattled off, and she swung it open. He could see just over her shoulder into a small, neat apartment. To the left, he caught the merest glimpse of the bedroom. The bed was made, covered with a taut beige bedspread.

Mrs. Haley blocked his way. She wore her bathrobe, a peach terry-cloth robe out at one elbow. Her gray hair hung over her forehead and into her face.

She smelled of coffee and a thousand cigarettes and mildewed cotton, but she straddled the doorway like a guard and he had a feeling this was one old woman who could handle herself on the street.

"What do you want?"

"A man was living here, named Sam Burwell."

Her mouth tightened and she thrust her chin toward the last door in the hall. "Him. The colored one."

"A tall thin black man in his late fifties."

She nodded.

"He was found murdered down near Maxwell Street."

"I know. The cops was here already. Before you." She seemed pleased to be able to tell him he wasn't the first.

"When?"

She shrugged. "I dunno. Yesterday or the day before. So what do you want to know?"

"I was wondering if I could have a look around in his apartment."

She frowned. "I don't think I'm supposed to be doin' that."

Time to gamble a little. "The officers investigating this, detectives Durkin and Krause—those are the ones you spoke with, am I right?"

"Yeah."

"Well, you can call them if you want official permission. I can wait. They already consulted me about this on Sunday."

She looked confused for a moment, then shrugged, as though it were all part of her routine.

"Don't make no difference to me anyways. Come on."

She moved past him, padding down the hall in blue canvas men's shoes that showed the joints of her toes. In front of the last door, she fished in the deep pockets of her robe and came up with a ring full of keys, then went through them one by one till she found one with a strip of blue tape on it.

She put it into the lock and opened the door.

"This is it. It's a mess, I'll tell you that. This ain't how I rented it to him. I ain't had no chance to clean up in here."

"Your building?"

She frowned as if the question were ridiculous. "No. I'm the manager. The owner, he lives out on the Northwest Side. Polish fella. Speaks English, though. Don't have no accent." She looked questioningly at Whelan. "So go on in if you want."

"Thanks," he said, and went inside. When she continued to stand in the doorway, he smiled. "I'll probably stop by and ask you a few questions before I go. Is that all right, Mrs. Haley?" She opened her mouth to speak and he added, "Your name's Violet, isn't it?"

"Yeah, Violet. Vi. People call me Vi." She frowned slightly. "How'd you know my name?"

Whelan shrugged. "First thing an investigator learns. You don't go into a place without knowing the names of the people in charge."

A faint smile worked at the down-turned corners of her mouth. She gave a little nod. "I'll be inside. You stop by when you're done here. Just pull the door shut—it locks itself."

"Okay, Vi, and thanks again."

She shuffled off in her men's shoes, leaving the scent of cigarette smoke behind her, and shot the quickest look at him over her shoulder as she entered her apartment.

Whelan took a long first pass around. It was really just one long rectangular room divided into different living areas by the paint on the walls and the type of furniture.

Sam Burwell's last home had been a barren place to settle for, but it was no worse than most of the apartments and rented rooms Whelan had seen in Uptown and better than some. It had glass in all the windows, for starters, a rug on the floor of the area that served as both bedroom and living room, and a tiny refrigerator that sat atop a homemade counter in the shallow nook that passed for a kitchen. The door, once white, had gone beige with age and grease, and there was a dark, permanent mass of fingerprints around the handle. Inside, Whelan found a hard little loaf of sandwich bread, a package of salami darkening at the edges, and a bottle of ketchup.

There was a beer can in the sink and the tray from a frozen dinner, with a fork in it, but there were no other dishes around. He opened the cabinets above the ancient sink: they were empty except for a little black scattering of mouse droppings.

Recessed into the back wall was a sort of closet made by hanging a blue cotton curtain across the angle where two walls met. A handful of men's clothing items hung there, and a faded blue canvas bag with a United Airlines logo lay on the floor. The bag was empty.

The countertops bore nothing but ashtrays, all but one empty. The last one sat in the corner of the kitchen close to the apartment's only window. It faced the alley and the backside of another flyblown apartment building where Whelan could see an old man sitting out on the fire escape and sipping at a Pepsi. The ashtray held a couple of unfiltered Camels, both smoked down to the end, still bearing the marks where he'd held them pinched between a thumb and a fingernail. Whelan leaned against the counter and pictured a man standing in front of the window, smoking and watching the alley or the people in the next building or the sky.

He opened the drawers of the bedside table, looked inside. One was empty. In the other, he found several pairs of boxer underwear, three pairs of socks, and a blue bandanna handkerchief.

The bathroom was little more than a toilet and a face bowl. A makeshift shower had been installed in a corner of the tiny room, with a ceramic basin hastily laid in the floor to catch the overflow from the shower. One towel hung limply over the shower curtain. There was a small bar of soap on the sink but he saw no toilet articles.

The bed went with everything else: a soft skinny mattress on a folding spring with some casters so that it could be wheeled into a corner and free up some space. The bed looked slept in but clean, and there was no ashtray near it.

Whelan moved to the center of the room and surveyed it from one side to the other, moving slowly and trying to miss nothing. When he was finished, he sat down on the little two-seater couch that constituted the living room and had a smoke, trying to force himself into the picture he was getting.

It was all here, the clothes, the meager food in the cooler, the cigarettes, the can of beer. There was nothing actually wrong, but no matter how Whelan added it up, he could not produce the image he was looking for. He looked around and shook his head.

He didn't live here.

Whelan closed the door behind him. Down the hall a door made a delicate click and he smiled. He walked down to Violet Haley's apartment and knocked once. The door opened immediately, and Mrs. Haley stood in front of him, giving him a wide-eyed look meant to convey surprise.

"Yeah? Oh, you're back. Find what you was looking for?"

"Uh, no, can't say I found a whole lot at all. I wonder if I could ask you a few more questions."

She shrugged. She'd made a valiant but unsuccessful attempt to put herself together. The robe had been tossed—literally, onto the couch, from where it could be seen sliding slowly down onto the floor—and replaced with a yellow housedress with a floral print and one button missing in the middle of the stomach. She hadn't brushed her hair, opting instead for a hairnet to keep the chaos confined to the top of her head.

Mrs. Haley thrust her hands into the pockets of the housedress and stuck her chin out. "So ask."

Something tells me I'm not going to be asked in for coffee, Whelan thought.

"Okay. How long had Sam Burwell lived here?"

"I dunno. Couple months, three months." Whelan nodded. Maybe Bridgeport, the accent. Mrs. Haley said "tree" instead of "three" and had a number of other speech mannerisms that put one in mind of the late Richard J. Daley, who had made the Bridgeport accent a national landmark.

"Can you tell me anything about his habits? What he did, any visitors he had?"

"Don't know nothing about him. Kept to himself, I'll say that for him. Wasn't noisy, 'specially for colored. Not like some of the others, not like this guy," and here she cocked her head to the left to indicate the apartment next to hers. "That's Sanchez. He's Mexican." She shook her head. "They're noisy people, your Mexicans. Like to play that horn music all the time, drive me nuts. And they talk real loud, they kinda chatter, all at the same time, and I—"

"Did Sam Burwell have visitors?"

She shut her mouth abruptly and gave him a look that might have been irritation, but he couldn't be sure through her dark glasses.

"No. Well, not usually, anyhow."

Not usually. Time to play hunches. "How about the lady?"

Mrs. Haley pursed her lips and gave a little shake of her head. "I figured you knew about her. That kinda thing, that ain't none of my business. People wanta carry on like a couple teenagers, that's their business."

She was staring at him, and he thought he could see the traces of a smirk, of inside knowledge.

"Tell me about the lady."

Mrs. Haley made a little hissing sound out the side of her mouth and nodded. "I could tell you about that one, all right. Her and all the other ones like her. Tell you one thing, that one, *she'd* never get a place here. I wouldn't have her under my roof." Mrs. Haley nodded slowly, having suddenly become the property owner as well as guardian of the public morality.

"Let's see if your description matches what I've got."

A pair of high arching eyebrows shot up from behind the glasses. "Well, she was one of *them.*"

Whelan tried to conceal his surprise.

"She come to see him in his flat. But you know what she was, don't you?"

"You think she was a prostitute."

She shook her head at Whelan's stupidity. "Well, whaddaya think?"

"I don't know what to think. You tell me."

"Well, I know my way around, and I can tell one of them when I see one. Don't matter *how* they're dressed. That's somethin' you can't hide, you know what I'm sayin'?"

"How was she dressed?"

"Like somebody with money, that's how. She had her hair done up fancy and she wore, let's see, one time she wore a blue dress, real tight, and another time she had on a green skirt and a white blouse like somebody that worked in an office."

"What else can you tell me about her?"

Mrs. Haley's face took on the look of insider knowledge. "Let's see. She was pretty light-skinned for colored, and kinda tall. Tall and skinny, had her hair dyed red, wore short skirts tryin' to act like she's young. And she wore those spiked heels, made this goddamn clicky noise up and down the hallway, she might as well've made an announcement. I'll tell you somethin' else, too." She bent forward, warming to her subject. "She couldn't walk in those things. She damn near fell one time."

"You watched her."

Mrs. Haley's mouth opened in confusion. "Well, what's that mean? Yeah, I like to know what's goin' on in my building. This whole building is my responsibility. Something goes wrong here, and it's my neck, so, yeah, I watched that one. You bet. You woulda watched her too. Acting like she's some kinda young kid and she's probably older than me." Mrs. Haley gave him a smug smile and shook her head at the other woman's folly.

"Anybody else come to see him? How about a young black man? Tall, wears glasses, very well dressed."

She gave him a blank look for a moment, then shook her head.

He thought of Perry Willis. "How about a shorter guy, also a young black man?" Another shake of the head, irritated this time.

Whelan stared at the woman. She seemed uncomfortable, and he realized she wanted him to leave. A new idea struck him.

"You've been in there since the police came, haven't you?"

Her mouth opened and she shrugged. "I manage the building. I had to go in, see if there was anything else goin' on there."

"In a dead man's apartment? What would be going on there?" He wondered whether she'd taken something from the apartment, something that would give him information. "Mrs. Haley, I need anything anybody can tell me about this man. If you took anything from the apartment that might give me information, I'd pay you for it and nobody would know about it."

She gave a little shake of her unwashed hair. "I didn't take nothing. I ain't a thief."

"All right. Thank you for your time."

She opened her mouth quickly, and he realized she was worried about the money.

He pulled out his money clip and handed her a ten. "That's for your trouble."

She smiled slightly, folding the ten and jamming it into one of the pockets of her housecoat.

"You come back if you need any more information or… you know, anything."

"Thanks, I might do that."

She nodded and shut the door.

Up the street they were beginning to line up for the next meal at the Sal Army, where there was a new officer in charge. His friend, the delightfully independent Captain Wallis, had been transferred. Whelan wondered if the new officer would be as streetwise and resilient as Wallis and decided it wasn't likely.

In front of the tire shop, a pair of black men in their forties were examining a set of used tires. Whelan approached and nodded when they looked at him. They nodded back and said nothing.

"You fellas know any of the people upstairs?"

The older of the two men shrugged. His companion shook his head.

"I'm interested in a tall thin black man who lived there. Name was Sam Burwell."

The older man looked at him. "The one that got killed."

"Right."

"Didn't see no badge."

"I don't have one. I'm retired. Did you know Sam?" Whelan dug his cigarettes out of a vest pocket, shook one out, and held out the pack. The men each took a smoke and Whelan lit all three.

The older man said, "The man just came and went and didn't speak. Didn't bother nobody, just kept to himself. Got killed for a few dollars, that's what I heard."

"Yeah. That's what I hear. So you can't tell me anything about him."

The man shook his head, blew out smoke, looked away.

"I'm trying to track down any relatives he might have had and any close friends. Ever see him with a young black man, a little on the thin side? Looks like he's angry."

The older man laughed. "Mister, they all be looking angry now."

"Lot of angry folks on the street." The younger one spoke for the first time. "Everybody trying to survive."

"You haven't seen this guy, though."

Both men shook their heads. Whelan thought of the woman Sam had told his friends about and the one Mrs. Haley had described.

"Have you ever seen a tall well-dressed black woman go upstairs, an older woman, maybe in her fifties, light-skinned?"

The young man shook his head and looked bored. The older one shook his head but grinned. "Sound like my type. Good-looking woman in her fifties be fine with me."

"How about a white woman, about the same age?"

The young one looked back at Whelan. "You mean the one from Public Aid? That one? Man, she ain't no fifty." He nudged his friend. "He's talking 'bout the lady from Aid. The caseworker."

The older one gave Whelan a sardonic look. "Naw, she ain't no fifty. You gettin' me all excited there, man. Talkin' about women in they fifties. That lady about forty-five. Maybe a little older, but she ain't seen fifty yet. Not bad-looking, though."

"She was this man's caseworker?"

"Not him, the Mexican. It's a Mexican family up in there, the man can't work. Can't walk, so the lady, she come out to get his forms and check things out."

"The Mexican family." Sanchez, Whelan remembered. He fought an impulse to go back upstairs and ask them their caseworker's name. It wasn't something you'd tell a stranger knocking at your door. "And you never saw her talking to the other man."

"Nope," the older one said. He thought for a moment. "Wait, I saw the brother with a black lady. She wasn't tall, though."

"What did she look like?"

He shrugged. "Skinny woman. Old, wore a kinda baggy coat."

"You know her?"

"Naw. Didn't see her but once or twice."

Whelan thought for a moment. It wasn't getting any simpler. "Okay, thanks."

Back at the office, he got on the phone. Tracking down a client on General Assistance was no trouble, but trying to identify a caseworker from a client's name, particularly a common name, proved to be a little trickier, requiring him to speak with several people and ask them to go backwards through lists and records. Eventually he had a name: Sandra McAuliffe.

Ms. McAuliffe wasn't in at the moment, and it took several other calls to reach her. When he did, he regretted it almost immediately. A conversation with Sandra McAuliffe was, apparently, a minefield.

"Sandra McAuliffe," a voice said into the phone. It was a voice with sand and edges to it, a voice that had taught itself to sound tough, the voice of a female street cop or the principal of a school for preteen homicidal maniacs. It was a voice that had little time for him, a voice that brooked no nonsense, took no prisoners.

Whelan explained who he was and what his interest was and what he wanted to know from Sandra McAuliffe, and she didn't buy any of it. She gave him one-syllable answers and made little snorts into the phone and eventually cut him off in mid-question.

"Let me save us both some time, Mr. Whelan. I think what you really want to know is whether I knew this man who was killed. I didn't. I remember seeing a tall thin black man, fiftyish, maybe older. I saw him once or twice. I know the landlady there, who is basically a bag lady with an attitude. And I know the Sanchez family. There's nothing I can tell you about your client that will justify our talking any further."

"All right, just let me ask—" He was going to ask if she'd ever seen a young man fitting Perry Willis's description in the building when she hung up in his ear.

It's always best to make a good first impression, he told himself.

He redialed and got the receptionist, who told him that the office was open till four-forty-five, and that Sandra McAuliffe got off then, as did all the caseworkers in the office.

"Listen, I tend to get my clients confused. Is Sandra McAuliffe tall, about fifty, with reddish hair and—"

The receptionist laughed. "Ooh, don't let *her* hear you say that. She's in her forties. Blondish hair, but yeah, she's tall." She was still giggling when she hung up the phone.

TEN

DAY 6, WEDNESDAY

He went out and picked up a paper from the Pakistani news vendor at Wilson and Broadway.

"Why are you always happy, Hafiz?"

The little man grinned and shook his head and shrugged. "I am not always happy," he said happily.

"Maybe it's Chicago. You like Chicago?"

The little head bobbed and nodded and Hafiz rolled his eyes. "Oh, I am liking Chicago, yes."

The lunch crowd was forming in the Subway Donut Shop, and Spiros, the young Greek behind the counter, was jumping. He had four burgers going on one side of his grill and a ham steak and a pork chop sizzling on the other, and he was shaking the little omelet pan around in the center. Piles of hash browns had been pushed to the edge of the grill, and half a dozen plates were lined up waiting to receive the food. The counter along the street-side window was filled with tired-looking street people and a pair of young black construction workers.

A short sardonic-looking woman in a green dress appeared in front of him at the counter. She had gray hair going white and tinted glasses that made her look like the Last Hippie. She looked fifty but Whelan knew she was seventy-one.

"Hello, Ruth."

"Hi, Mr. Whelan. What'll it be?"

"Coffee and a Denver omelet sandwich on whole wheat, to go."

"Why don't you just say the usual?"

"If I did, you'd act like you didn't know what I was talking about. What's new?"

She gave him an impish smile. "I'm going to college." She nodded in the general direction of Truman College, half a block away.

"What are you taking?"

"Business writing and Spanish." She beamed.

"Good for you. I keep saying I'm going to take Spanish someday."

She turned and poured his coffee into a brown ceramic cup. A shriveled old black man came to the counter holding out his cup, and she gave him an irritated look.

"You gonna ask or you just gonna wave your cup in my face?"

"Can I get some more coffee, please?" the old man said.

She looked at Whelan and grinned. "Hear that? Somebody said 'please.' All right, sir, anything for a man that says 'please.' " She glared at the other patrons in the smoky room. "The rest of you hear that?" she bellowed. "This man said 'please.' Make a note of it." The construction workers laughed, and a tall thin man in coveralls muttered something inaudible and shook his head.

"Burgers up," the Greek said, and Ruth quickly took the four platters from the side of the grill.

"Burgers!" she yelled, and four men approached from different directions.

When she was writing up Whelan's ticket he leaned forward.

"I also want to ask you a couple of questions."

She looked up from behind the tinted glasses. "You want my phone number?"

"I know where to find you."

"My old man will be a problem." She winked. "But it'll be worth your trouble."

"I have no doubt. Did you know Sam Burwell? Tall, pushing sixty, scar over this eye?" He pointed to his left eye.

"I know who you mean. That's the one that got killed. No, I didn't, not really. He came in here a few times but he didn't say much."

"Anything you can tell me?"

"Liked a lot of cream in his coffee. Liked to drink, but who doesn't, around here? Liked ham sandwiches on rye. I don't know what else to tell you."

"I was told he was seeing someone from here. A woman named Mary."

Ruth shook her head. "Don't know anybody named Mary. Had that little bag lady used to stand outside and sing for money, but she died."

"Did you ever see him with a tall black woman?"

"I saw him talking to a woman once or twice but she wasn't tall. She's just a little bitty woman. Light-skinned, kind of. Name's Mattie. Haven't seen her lately."

"Do you know where she lives?"

She shook her head. He handed her his card. "Call me if she comes in. I need to talk to her."

She nodded and tucked the card into the pocket of her apron; then her boss yelled that the pork chop and the omelet were ready.

"Pork chop up! Omelet!" she bawled out to the crowd.

Whelan strolled back up Broadway toward the office. He waved at the two Iranians inside the House of Zeus, who beckoned madly until he held up his lunch. They shrugged and grinned.

He was just sliding into his chair in the office when the phone rang.

"You got busy, hon."

"Hello, Shel. Anybody calling to offer me money?"

"Didn't sound like money to me, baby, and I'd recognize it. You had a call from some old guy, sounded like he was dying."

"Dying?"

"Oh, he wasn't really dying, he was just real hoarse—like Mel Torme with tonsilitis." She laughed.

"Mel Torme with tonsilitis, huh? What did he say?"

"He said he needed to talk to you about some things you

were asking him. He didn't say who he was, and he didn't say what it was about. Helpful, huh?"

"Maybe. Did he say he'd call back?"

"No. I couldn't hear him very well. He talked real low, and there was all kinds of traffic going by."

"Pay phone?"

"Sounded like it. Know who he is?"

"I think so. I just didn't expect him to call me."

"See? Life is full of surprises. Also, you had a call from O.C. Brown. Said he had something interesting to tell you, so you should call him at his tavern."

"Thanks, Shel."

"Later, baby."

He ate half his sandwich and called Brown at the Blue Note. The old saloonkeeper picked up the phone on the second ring.

"Yeah?"

Whelan smiled into the phone. "Does somebody teach all tavern owners in the city to answer the phone the same way?"

O.C. chuckled. "Hey, Whelan. You got my call?"

"That I did. I understand you have something for me."

"Yeah. And that girl who answers your phone, ain't she somethin'."

"That she is." He could sense O.C. wrestling with the purpose of his call and decided to help him out. "How did the funeral go, nice turnout?"

It was pretty fair, Whelan. Sam was well-liked. Lot of folk there, lot of folk I hadn't seen in a long time. Couple of boys we used to run with in the old days. Buddy Lenz was there too. He's down on his luck now, but he was there."

"Buddy Lenz?"

"Yeah, he was the boy I told you about, white boy from the old days. Used to play drums in the clubs: good, too. Played with a couple of black bands and played with white groups, too. Sat in with Joe Witt, Floyd Garnet, Frank Rickert, all of 'em. Old friend of Sam's. Now he's a picker on Maxwell Street. I think he live on the street." O.C. paused.

"What does he look like?"

"About my height, kinda bushy black hair, need a shave. Need a bath, too. Showed up in a sweatshirt. I think it's all he's got."

"I think maybe I've seen him." Whelan waited a moment, then added, "Anybody you didn't know?"

There was a slight pause on the phone. "There was some folks from down there on Maxwell Street, people that knew him from there. Couple old men, they work down there, I guess." O.C.'s voice dropped slightly. Whelan could picture him turning his back on his customers and hunching down over the phone.

"Now I didn't see nothing else, Whelan. But my man Winston say he saw a couple women there, keeping to themselves at the cemetery."

"You didn't see them?"

"Naw, I was up front by the casket. I was a pallbearer."

"Did he give you a description?"

"He didn't get a good look. But he said they were white."

Whelan thought for a moment. For the first time all week, he thought of the pair of women he'd talked to on Maxwell Street.

"Thanks, O.C. Listen, does the name Mattie mean anything to you?"

"Nope."

"Okay. And O.C.? Did the lawyer you saw at the wake show up at church?"

"No, not the church. He come to the graveside, Whelan. When we come out of the little chapel there at the cemetery, I saw him. Standing back where nobody could talk to 'im. Like he didn't want nothing to do with nobody there."

"That part's probably true."

"Don't know why he bothered to come."

"And there was nobody with him?"

"Nope. Nobody."

Whelan shook his head. There was no reason to be surprised. It had been, after all, a long shot; there was no reason to believe Hill's client was actually here in Chicago. Whelan thought for a moment, then said, "O.C., you said Sam roomed with somebody for a while, before he could get his own place.

Henry something."

"Yeah, Henry Bridgeman."

"I'd like to talk to him. Got a number for him?"

"He don't have no phone. I can tell you where he live though. Down the street from the church there, Saint Anna's."

"What's the address?"

O.C. chuckled. "Don't need no address to find Henry's place, Whelan. Only green house on the block. Damnedest color for a house I ever seen. He lives around back on the first floor."

"Well, I'll drop by and see him tomorrow."

O.C. laughed again, this time a delighted cackle. "Good luck, Whelan."

"What for?"

"Old Henry deaf as a stone, babe. He can't hear my jukebox when he sitting next to it."

"Great." O.C. was still chuckling when he hung up.

The second call would have to be returned in person; the caller lived in a blue bus on Maxwell Street without a phone. That one could wait. The gentleman on the bus wasn't going anywhere. Whelan went through the week's mail and decided it was probably time to pay a few bills. It was nearly four when he finished.

He drove south on Halsted through early rush hour traffic. At the intersection of Milwaukee, Grand, and Halsted, there was a gaper block as traffic from six directions slowed to watch two motorists rain punches on each other. Their vehicles sat a few feet away on Milwaukee—a rusted-out Mustang with its front end jammed into the side of a Chevy. The Mustang looked like a piglet attempting to nurse.

When he got to Halsted and Roosevelt, he made a right and turned on Morgan. He pulled into the dusty vacant lot behind the police station and parked. A pair of old black men were going through a dumpster. One of them looked up at him briefly and then went back to sorting through the refuse.

Whelan walked east to Halsted. The sky was already a dull

purple, and behind him the sun had passed from view behind the buildings to the west.

At Halsted and Liberty a generic fast-food place was still alive with late-afternoon business. According to an orange and white hand-lettered sign out front, the place sold burgers and Polish as well as fried chicken, ribs, rib tips, and hot links. The dumpsters behind the building lay on their sides and the dark, damp contents had spilled out into the open, drawing the year's last dark cloud of flies. The culprits in all this merriment stood a few yards away from the restaurant, a trio of small black boys, giggling and hooting and convulsing one another with what passes for wit when you're ten. They looked eagerly at passersby, hoping for recognition, some acknowledgment from the adult world that they'd caused irritation for somebody.

The chain-link gate to the tire yard was slightly ajar, as though to reassure him. The man and boy he'd spoken to the weekend before were long gone: they'd sell no tires tonight. Whelan walked in and looked around. Not the place he'd want to have for a front yard, but few people got to choose where they lived. In a city, your choice of neighborhood was largely an illusion. In Chicago, that choice was a joke: you picked your neighborhood on the basis of your race and your money. Even the rich were restricted by the demands of place, position, and image to a handful of communities.

If you were a Maxwell Street picker in your seventies, having long since outlived family and friends, the long back seat in a blue bus was still a lot better than the alternatives. At least Nate didn't live in a doorway or an appliance carton. The ones Whelan had just seen scouring the garbage for their next meal did not live anywhere. And according to an obscure but nonetheless binding law, they weren't even full citizens: they had no vote. No home, no vote. Whelan shook his head. Guys living in roadside ditches in Mexico had the vote, but America was a more complicated piece of work.

He walked quietly across the yard, past the black pyramids of used tires and the long sheets of polished hubcaps, to the bus and knocked at the opened door. There was no answer.

"Nate? You in there, Nate? It's Paul Whelan."

He heard a low grumble and realized that Nate had answered. Whelan grabbed onto the steel bars and climbed the high stairs into the bus. It was dark, and through the smells of grilled onions and cigarette smoke and sweat that he'd noticed before was a heavier, earthier smell: wood smoke. The smell of a man who has to warm himself over a wood fire in a steel drum. Cold was coming, the Hawk was blowing in, and men all over the city would soon have this smell to their clothing, their skin. Parking lot attendants and men who lived in doorways and the ones who stood in groups on street corners and construction workers on late-season projects: they would all smell this way.

There was a small light on in the back that went out as soon as Whelan began to make his way down the aisle. Nate sat in the same place Whelan had seen him before and watched his visitor approach. A newspaper was spread out on the card table. Beside it were the remains of a hamburger and a battery-operated radio, and the Coleman lantern that explained the light Whelan had just seen.

Whelan stopped a few feet from Nate and waited. The old man made the faintest nod and took a pull at a filterless cigarette. He blew smoke out the side of his mouth and glanced out the mud-streaked window next to him, and Whelan realized Nate wasn't going to speak first.

"You called me."

A purse of the lips, but Nate went on looking at the scenery.

Whelan dropped himself onto a seat and took out his own cigarettes. I've seen this movie, he thought, and when Nate stole a sidelong glance at him, he grinned. "We gonna talk, Nate, or just share a smoke together like army buddies?"

Nate looked up at him from under thick eyebrows shot with silver. "You the one needs information."

"Got some?"

Nate suddenly discovered that his cigarette was a thing of utter fascination. He looked for a moment at it, plucked a string of tobacco from it, then pulled a matching shred from his lip. He flicked ash into a Hills Brothers coffee can and peered into its depths. He pinched the wet end of the butt, put it back into his mouth, and puffed on it.

Props. Where would we be without props? All right, we humor him.

"Whatcha got, Nate? You must have something, or you wouldn't have called me."

Nate squinted at him. "Ain't gonna give it away."

"Nobody's asking you to." Whelan pulled out the money clip and took out a five. He folded it over and laid it on the card table.

Nate looked at it as if it were a roach. He looked at Whelan again, and Whelan dropped another five on top of it.

"That better?" Nate hesitated and Whelan could see him decide to play this out. "Because if it's not, I'm leaving."

Nate glanced at the money and then glared up at him. "You the one said you was interested in finding things out."

"Yeah, but I'm not the Bank of England."

The old man hesitated and then covered the bills with his hand. The hand spoke volumes: long and scarred and bony, and the last joint of one finger was missing.

"So what do you have, Nate?"

"You was askin' about anybody come looking for Sam."

"Right."

"Saw somebody with 'im."

"Who'd you see?"

"Somebody talkin' with 'im."

"Got a name?"

"Don't know everybody's name on the street."

"What did he look like?"

Nate shrugged. "White man. Think he had black hair. Mighta been a Mexican. He was wearin' a sweatshirt with a hood."

"Anything else you can tell me about him?"

"The man, he seem to want somethin' from Sam. Money, maybe. I see Sam give 'im some money. Look like he wanted to get rid of this man."

Nate took a noisy puff at the tiny cigarette butt. Whelan

wondered why he wasn't burning his fingers.

"Ever see anybody else talking to Sam—recently?"

Nate gave him a shrewd look and Whelan could tell he was trying to decide whether to hold out for more money. Then he said, "Saw a man watchin' 'im. This was a brother."

"Did he talk to Sam at all?"

"Naw. Watched him. Just watched him."

"A black man with glasses? Young?"

"The fuck I know if he was young?" Nate glared at Whelan and shook his head. He took a puff, blew smoke into the stagnant air of the bus, and gave a short nod. "Shades, though. He was wearin' shades."

"What else did you see, Nate?"

"Didn't see nothing."

Whelan nodded and stared at Nate for a moment and then decided to go fishing. "When's the last time you remember seeing Sam?"

"Don't know."

"They think he was killed two weeks ago on Sunday. Think you saw him that day?"

Nate seemed to chew on that for a moment, then made a little nod. "Maybe. That was that fire. It was a fire that day. Big one, whole lot of them tires."

"There's always a fire down here, Nate."

"Not like this one. This was a big one. 'Bout the end of the day. Everybody went on down to look at it."

"Including you."

Nate said nothing.

"And you saw Sam?"

"He was gettin' his stuff together, loadin' it into his boxes. Didn't pay it no mind, that fire."

"Anything else you saw?"

Nate shook his head.

"Anybody else around? Those kids, maybe, the ones the cops brought in for this?"

"Didn't see no kids. Everybody was goin' the same way. Goin' on down to look at that fire."

"When you came back, was Sam still there?"

"No. He was gone. His boxes was gone. Table was still there, though. Don't know why he lef' his table."

Whelan studied Nate for a moment. "Do you think those kids killed Sam?"

Nate gave him a defiant look. "Maybe. They'll do anything. Those little gang-bangers be sneakin' around here all the time, stealin' and doin' shit to folks."

"Did you tell any of this to the police?"

"Didn't no po-lice come to talk to me."

Whelan got to his feet. He looked Nate directly in the eye for a moment, and the old man looked away.

"Got something else, Nate?"

"Already told you what I had." Nate glared. The interview was over.

"Thanks, Nate. If you think of anything else, or if you see either of those men again, give me a call. And I'll probably be back."

Since you've got something you're not giving up.

Nate snorted. "We talk about this shit again, it's gonna cost you more than ten dollars."

"I believe that," Whelan said, and left the bus. He stood on Halsted and looked south and thought of the dark-haired man in the sweatshirt.

The sky was a dull red now. Another week and Daylight Saving Time would be finished and darkness would come in around six or six-thirty. Up the street, a Korean businessman was putting gates across his windows; on the other side of the street a gray-haired black man did the same thing. The dinner crowd had appeared at Jim's, a couple of women and half a dozen men, all lined up waiting to be served a large Polish under a mountain of grilled onion.

Why not? Whelan thought, and walked over to take his place in line.

He could feel the waves of heat pulsing out from the little shack, and if he had any doubt about the temperature inside, he had only to look at the half-dozen wet-faced men inside, all of them humping to turn the onions and toss fresh sausages into the steamers and make sandwiches and take your money. Every one of them had perspired through his shirt, front and back. Whelan stared at the little hillock of limp onions resting at the back of the grill. There had to be something unhealthy about a pile of half-cooked onions sitting there for so long, but no one he knew had ever gotten seriously ill eating a Maxwell Street Polish. Rumors of people dying from the food down here were, as far as he knew, as unfounded as the frame that let Mrs. O'Leary and her cow take the fall for the Chicago Fire.

He got a Polish and a root beer, then found himself a doorstep a few feet from the corner on the far side of the street. Like all evil-smelling street food, the Polish was wonderful and the onions, for all their ominous aspect, done to perfection.

Artists. You were made by street artists, he said to his sandwich.

He was finishing his root beer when he saw a dark green Chevy pull up in front of Jim's. Durkin and Krause got out. The young cop was saying something to Durkin and appeared upset. Durkin waved him off and went around the front of the car to the curb, hitching his pants up as he walked. His front foot slipped when he stepped up onto the curb and he almost went down, stopping his fall with one hand. He got up red faced, glaring around him. Whelan realized Durkin was drunk.

Old habits die hard, Whelan thought, and got to his feet.

Durkin moved to the front of the line and said something to the nearest man behind the counter. The people waiting for service muttered to one another but seemed to understand either that Durkin was trouble or that he was the law. Krause shook his head and stood a couple of feet behind his partner.

Whelan came up quietly behind Krause and heard the young detective tell Durkin that he wasn't hungry.

"Evening, Detective," Whelan said. Krause turned. He had a worried look in his eyes.

"Hi, Whelan." He shot a glance over his shoulder at Durkin. The older man turned, gnawing on his Polish. When he saw Whelan, he stopped chewing.

"What're you doin' here?"

"Eating, for one thing. I just had one of those."

"Oh, yeah?" Durkin chewed slowly. His eyes had a wet gleam to them, and the pale skin of his cheeks was marked by high points of red.

"Got a load on, huh?" Whelan said.

Durkin lowered the Polish and glared for a moment. "Got a problem with that?"

"His shift's over, Whelan," Krause said, but it sounded like something he'd just come up with.

"Doesn't make any difference to me. I don't care what he does."

"That's good, 'cause I don't give a fuck what you like."

Whelan looked at Krause. "And he's got a nice personality."

"Like you don't drink, huh, Whelan?"

"Never lost a squad car, Durkin."

"Fuck you."

Whelan looked at him, then turned to Krause. "He ever tell you about that?" Krause shook his head almost imperceptibly. "Good, I will. When Supercop here was a street cop, he was assigned to cover the Bud Billiken Parade. You been to the Billiken?"

"I'm from the North Side," Krause said.

"So am I, but that doesn't mean we can't pick up a little culture on the side. The Bud Billiken Parade is this great black parade they put on in August every year. It's a big deal. All the black politicians and TV personalities and a lot of the white folks that want black votes: they all show up. All up and down King Drive, the black folk come out in force, and it's one big party. Pretty easy duty, especially if you like parades. Sooner or later somebody at the Bud Billiken Parade starts passing around a flask or a bottle of screw-top." Whelan glanced at Durkin and smiled. Durkin wet his lips and stared back. He was breathing heavily, as though he'd just come up a long flight of stairs, and his face was dark red.

"So, big deal," Krause began. "Every parade there's—"

Whelan held up a hand. "Right, at every parade there's liquor.

At the Saint Patrick's Day Parade half the crowd is smashed, people pass out on the corners; at the Gay Pride Parade they used to fall off their floats. And at the Billiken, sometimes the black folk are feeling so good because they've got their own parade and nobody's gonna hassle them today that they even offer the cops a little taste. And that's what happened on the memorable occasion of which I speak. Some friendly black guy watching the parade passed a jar of homemade corn whiskey around. And then somebody else came up with a bottle of Richard's, and some other guy whips out a half pint of vodka, and our man on the scene here, he dives right into the spirit of things, and before the afternoon's over, Officer Durkin is shit-faced. He and his partner, older cop named Wroble, another good-time Charlie, hit half a dozen taverns on the way home, and someplace between Forty-seventh and Cermak, our boys forget where they parked the squad car."

"That's bullshit," Durkin said in a low mumble.

Whelan ignored him. "They had to ride around the neighborhood in the back of another squad looking for their car. Took them two hours to find it." He looked calmly at Durkin. "And Durkin became a legend."

"So? Everybody drinks, Whelan," Krause said. He was sweaty and uncomfortable and kept running a hand across the back of his neck.

"Almost everybody, Krause. But most folks wait till they're through with work."

"Well, we're off now."

Whelan looked from one to the other and told himself this young cop wouldn't spend a minute longer with an alley rat like Mark Durkin than he had to. "I don't think so," Whelan said.

Durkin pointed a finger at him. "What are you doin' here, Whelan?"

"Looking around. I come down here a lot. I've been coming down here since I was a kid."

Durkin tried a smile but only half of it came to life. "You're down here 'cause of that old shine we found. That guy you were lookin' for."

Whelan shook his head. "No, I heard you got that one all wrapped up. Nice collar for you, I heard. Both of you," he said, with a nod in Krause's direction. The younger cop seemed to hesitate and then nodded.

"So what are you looking for, Whelan?"

"Runaway."

"What?" Krause looked confused.

Durkin snorted and wet his lips again. "It's what he does, this guy. He finds kiddies that run away from Mommy and Daddy, ain't it, Whelan?"

"That's about it, Durkin." He nodded to each of them and left. When he was halfway down the block, he took a quick look over his shoulder. Durkin was weaving slightly and staring after Whelan. Krause was watching his partner with a worried look.

Whelan spent the best part of an hour roaming the deserted blocks of Maxwell Street, and when he was through he'd talked to three men and learned nothing. Night had arrived, and the men in the jumbled lots who sold hubcaps and tires had started their fires, and the chill air had an acrid bite to it.

He was leaning against a wall across from the beef stand and had just lit a cigarette when he realized that he was being watched. He looked across the street, remained motionless, but let his eyes sweep the lots and passageways and doorways from north to south and saw nothing.

He took a long puff and glanced to his left. A car backed into an alley till it was hidden behind the beef stand. Whelan waited a moment, then ran across the street and around the beef stand. The car was a few feet ahead of him. It was an impressive car, more than a little out of place on Maxwell Street, and Whelan had seen it several times before.

He moved quickly up on the driver's side and knocked on the roof.

"Let me guess: you ran out of gas in the alley."

David Hill froze with both hands on the wheel and then shook his head, as angry at himself as he was at Whelan. He glared for a moment, then collected himself, and in a moment he was a lawyer again and at no loss for words.

"I saw someone I knew lurking in a doorway, Whelan—*you.* So I drove around the block to get a better look."

"Not bad. The truth would be a lot better, but it's not a bad story. You just happened to be in this neighborhood where you originally hired *me* to look for Sam Burwell. So all of a sudden you're streetwise enough to cover it on your own." He grinned at Hill.

When the lawyer spoke, he sounded serene, confident. "What I am doing down here, Whelan, is no affair of yours. But a good lawyer never passes up free information, and when I saw you I decided to see exactly what brought you here."

"Well, Mr. Hill, if you've been watching me march up and down these streets for the past hour, your patience has been rewarded, and you now know exactly what I know. Make a complete report for your client."

Hill turned the key in the ignition and pulled out of the alley.

Whelan waved after him. "It was good for me, too."

When he walked back toward his car they were still selling dogs and Polish at Jim's. A burly cabdriver with a crewcut leaned against his Checker and gnawed at a Polish. He was watching a business discussion: two young black men negotiating the price of a gold chain. Capitalism in its purest form. Whelan paused for a moment and looked around for Durkin and Krause, but there was no sign of them.

I run into all my best friends down here, he thought.

ELEVEN

DAY 7, THURSDAY

The house where Henry Bridgeman lived was indeed green, a memorable jade green, but Whelan had seen more outrageous painting—one of his neighbors had recently begun painting his house lavender and the porches and stairs violet. Bridgeman's was an old frame building that had once been something special, with a cupola to one side on the upper floor and a porch that appeared to go all the way around the building. The screening of the porch was patched in a couple of places.

Whelan parked in front, got out, and was halfway across the barren soil of the lawn when someone spoke to him from behind.

"Looking for Henry?"

He turned and saw a ruddy-faced white man in a neon-pink touring cap and a black shirt. It was the priest he'd seen at the wake.

"Yes. How'd you know?"

The priest pointed at the building and laughed. "Because nobody else lives there." There was an air of suppressed energy about him, and with his wide blue eyes and round pink cheeks, he looked like somebody's Christmas card.

Whelan walked over to him and extended his hand. "I'm Paul Whelan."

The priest shook hands. "Mike Brennan. Somebody told me you're a private investigator. I wanted to meet you at Sam's wake. Never met a detective before." He laughed again. "Everybody probably tells you that, right?"

"Yeah, but I don't mind. I'm popular at parties. Are you on your way to see Henry?"

The priest hesitated. "No. Actually, I was just walking back to the rectory and I saw you get out of your car. Henry's not there."

"Know when he'll be home?"

The priest squinted back in the direction of the rectory and shrugged. "Around dinnertime." He faced Whelan again and smiled. "How about a cup of coffee?"

Father Brennan seemed to be a man with something on his mind. If I have any more coffee, I'll float, Whelan thought. To the priest, he said, "Sounds good."

"Come on, we'll take my car," the priest said. His car was a rusting Ford wagon close to death. He saw Whelan studying it. "It runs and it has seat belts."

"I have one just like it."

"I know," the priest said. "I saw you drive up." He grinned as he got into the car. Father Brennan looked close to Whelan's age, and there was gray in the close-cropped hair. The blue eyes were just as lively up close, but Whelan saw that this man's face revealed nothing unless he wished it to.

They drove in a wide, lazy circle and the priest waved or spoke to dozens of different people, adults and children alike. He seemed to know everybody, and they all called him Father Mike.

"They like you."

"Maybe."

"You like them."

"You got that right." A moment later, he yelled something out to a group of boys playing on the sidewalk, then turned to Whelan. "People don't understand the lives folks lead here. They think people choose to be poor. You've seen the old Sears factory?"

"Yes."

"The day they pulled out, half this community caved in. It was the last major employer. You know why I'm driving you around?"

"You're giving me a tour."

The priest smiled. "Well, yeah, I am. But I'm also taking you to the nearest restaurant. The nearest restaurant and the *only* restaurant, Mr. Whelan. There are no businesses, no factories, no banks, no restaurants in this neighborhood. There's nothing but people: a lot of them out of work, most of them poor, most of *them* kids. The average age of a person in this area is twenty-two, and a lot of them won't hit fifty." He took his eyes off the road and smiled grimly at Whelan. "This ain't no Bing Crosby movie, baby."

"But you like it here."

"No. I love it here. They ought to let me stay here forever." The priest looked straight ahead as he spoke. Then he took a quick glance at Whelan and smiled. "I'd never ask them for anything else."

The restaurant was at Madison and Kedzie, just a long fly ball from Marshall High School, whose basketball teams had helped put inner city schools on the sports map back in the fifties.

The entrance to the parking lot was blocked by a garbage truck, so the priest backed out and pulled his car into a no-parking space. He put an EMERGENCY, PRIEST ON CALL sign on the dashboard and looked at Whelan.

"See why it's important to take my car?"

"Yeah, I don't have one of those."

They went inside the restaurant, and half a dozen black diners greeted Father Mike and nodded politely at Whelan.

"Welcome to Edna's," the priest said.

It looked very much like a thousand other neighborhood places in Chicago, with Naugahyde booths and Formica counters. To Whelan, the major difference was the color of the diners. He made a quick scan of the menu and looked up to see that the priest was watching him.

"You're thinking this is just like a white restaurant someplace else."

"Something like that."

The priest shook his head. "This is *Edna's*. We've only got one restaurant but it's special." He wiggled his eyebrows.

"I collect restaurants, Father. What do you recommend?"

"Everything. But you can't go wrong with the daily specials."

"I thought we came here for coffee?"

The priest gave him a blank look. "We did, but now I'm hungry, and it's not polite to let somebody eat alone."

The waitress came over and took their order, and Whelan asked for the leg of lamb. The waitress nodded. "Good choice," she said in a quiet voice. "Biscuits or cornbread?"

"What do you recommend?"

She gave him the beginnings of a smile and shrugged. "Both of them. I'll get you a half order of each."

Father Brennan ordered the roast chicken. "I don't eat lamb," he said.

"An Irishman who doesn't eat lamb?"

"These are changing times, Whelan. We've got a pope who doesn't speak Italian."

Lunch came on a crowded cart. Whelan's took up his entire side of the table: a huge piece of lamb, a side of homemade macaroni and cheese, mashed potatoes, a bowl of dressing topped with a thin slice of cranberry sauce, a plate of biscuits and flat cornbread cakes.

Whelan stared at the array of plates, matched by those on the other side of the table.

"Maybe I can take a room here," he said, and started eating.

When they were halfway through, the priest looked at him and said, "What do you think?"

"I think I'm in love with Edna." Then, as Father Brennan nodded happily, Whelan asked, "So why are we here?"

The priest looked up with a forkful of potatoes halfway to his mouth and smiled. "You first. Why are you here?"

"Ah. Why am I here? So that's what this is all about. I'm here because I'm on a case."

The priest shrugged, looked slightly irritated. This was no Bing Crosby movie. "What case? There's no case. Just a dead black male, a victim of violence. There are suspects in custody; there is no further investigation." He recited the facts in a rapid singsong and, when he was finished, fixed Whelan with a sardonic smile.

"That's right. There's no investigation, so I can look around."

"Why do you want to? What do you care?"

"I've been hired, Father. It's what I do."

"Hired by whom?"

"O.C. Brown."

Father Brennan nodded.

"You know O.C.?"

The priest grinned. "Come on, Whelan, I know everybody. But *why* do you want to work on this case? I'm sure people ask you to do things all the time that you turn down."

"That's true. I don't do certain kinds of work. I don't follow spouses and I don't work undercover in an office to see who's robbing the boss blind. And I'm not allowed to work on an open police case."

"I think you do anyhow. Just a feeling I'm getting."

"But I take on cases that I think need looking into, and I take things on for people I like. I've taken a liking to O.C. He really wants to do something for his friend. I think it's more of a gesture than anything else. I probably won't come up with anything, but at least he'll feel—" The look on the priest's face stopped him.

"You have something already, and you're sure the cops are wrong." Father Brennan flashed a cherubic smile. "I can see it in your face."

"I've got to work on that." He lit a cigarette. "So you're really trying to find out what I'm doing in your community."

"Something like that."

"Why didn't you just call O.C.?"

"Probably tell me it was none of my business. He's not a parishioner. I make it to the Blue Note more often than he makes it to church. He's not a member of any church that I know of."

"I knew a saloonkeeper once who thought his tavern was a kind of church."

"Maybe O.C. does too."

The young waitress brought the bill, and the priest grabbed

it. "I got this. Thanks, Brenda."

An older woman emerged from the back of the restaurant, a tall silver-haired woman, good-looking in an austere way. She made her way toward their booth but still found time to stop both her waitresses and give them instructions.

She approached the booth with her hand extended. "Why, hello, Father Mike. I didn't know you were here."

The priest indicated Whelan. "This is Paul Whelan, Edna. He's a friend of mine, a private detective. He's come to investigate your menu."

"Pleased to meet you, Mr. Whelan. I hope you'll be back."

"I think it's my destiny," Whelan said.

Outside the restaurant, Whelan looked at the priest. "Did I tell you anything at all you didn't already know?"

"Nope."

"You just wanted to check me out."

"Yep. Besides, Henry's old." The priest got in and slid behind the wheel.

"You told Edna I was your friend. Am I?"

The priest gave him a childlike grin that made his face glow. "Sure. Now that I know you're not an asshole."

Whelan laughed. "Okay, so now what?"

Father Brennan shrugged. "Now we go see Henry. He works at the rectory. He's the caretaker." He laughed, a deep, resonant laugh that filled the old rusted Ford and muffled its coughing engine.

"You play poker, Father?"

"They won't let me play anymore."

The parish rectory was a forgotten jewel, a dark, stately four-story mansion, top-heavy with age-darkened oak furniture and hand-carved moldings and banisters. It smelled like a home, a mix of soap, furniture polish, and cooking smells.

"I like your house," Whelan said.

"I do too," said Father Brennan. "Hope they never throw me out. It'd be tough finding another one like this."

They found Henry Bridgeman wrestling with a bucket that he'd somehow jammed under a table in the rectory dining room. He pulled at it with only his left hand. In his right, he held a large wet mop that he refused to let go. The mop was dripping gray water onto the magnificent parquet floor and the handle was inching closer and closer to a large statue of a saint, perhaps St. Anna herself. Whelan didn't think St. Anna would be able to duck.

The bucket wasn't coming out, and Henry apparently was willing to stay for the duration. He yanked at it, turned his spindly body one way and then another, dug his old black shoes into the wood, and strained, all the while emitting a low, grumbling stream of near profanity that was not so much an expression of anger as it was background music.

To his left, Whelan could hear the priest trying mightily to stifle his laughter. He looked at Father Brennan and saw tears forming in the boyish blue eyes. The priest took his eyes from Henry and looked at Whelan.

"I think we just saved you one question."

"Which one was that?"

"The one where you ask me why we keep Henry around."

Whelan grinned. "Is he always like this?"

"No." The priest pointed to a broken pane high in one of the living room windows. "Sometimes he's dangerous."

As if to punctuate this thought, Henry went into his finale. The bucket tipped over, and the old man went down on the seat of his pants; frothy wash water from the bucket flooded the dining room, and the handle of the mop bounced off St. Anna's patient forehead, caromed from there to a wall, knocked a small African carving off a sideboard, and, as it came back to earth from its long journey, whacked Henry in the back of the head.

The priest helped him up. "You all right, Henry?"

"Fine, fine. I'm fine, Father Mike. I slipped, is all."

"All right. Let's take a break." Under his breath, Whelan heard him say, "Give the rectory time to recover."

"Something wrong with that bucket," the old man said.

"Absolutely. We'll get a new one." Father Brennan pointed

to Whelan. "Got somebody I want you to meet. Friend of O.C. Brown."

Henry Bridgeman winced, shook his head and said, "What?"

Father Brennan nodded. "I keep forgetting." He repeated his introduction, much louder this time.

"Oh. Uh-huh," Henry said, giving Whelan a look that plainly said, "Since when does O.C. have a white friend?

"This is Mr. Whelan. He's a private detective, and I think he wants to ask you some questions about Sam Burwell." The priest nodded at Whelan. "*He* doesn't think those kids killed Sam Burwell either."

"No, I don't. Let's talk."

"You want me to leave?" Father Brennan asked.

"You can stay."

They sat in the reception room and Whelan half shouted his questions. Henry's responses consisted primarily of short shakes of his head. He and Sam Burwell had lived together for just under two years and during that time, as far as he knew, Sam had had trouble with no one.

"What about after he moved out, Henry? Did you keep in touch?"

Henry nodded. "Went to see the Sox couple times. Went fishin'. He liked to fish. Wasn't no good at it, though."

"And he never told you he was having trouble with anyone?"

"No."

"How about a man following him in a car?"

"Don't know nothin' about that."

"Ever hear him talk about a man named David Hill?"

Henry pursed his lips and shook his head.

"How about the woman he was seeing?"

"Name was Mary."

"I heard that too. What do you know about her?"

"I just know she live up north there."

"How about a woman named Mattie?"

"Mattie?" Henry scratched behind his ear and shook his head. "Never heard of no Mattie."

"How about anyone from the old days, people he might

have had trouble with in the old days, like George Covington?"

"Covington dead."

Whelan studied him for a moment. "Do you know when he died?"

Henry frowned and scratched his chin. "Can't say I do. Long time ago, though. Must be twenty years."

"I spoke to his landlord a couple days ago and got the impression Covington might still be alive."

Henry's expression suggested that Whelan was veering dangerously into the area of fantasy. He took a shot in the dark.

"How about…trouble with his son?"

Henry stared at him for an extra heartbeat and then quickly looked away, shaking his head. "No," he said, but he continued to look toward the window.

"I know he had some trouble with his son. O.C. told me that. A lot of men have trouble with their sons. Did Sam ever speak of it?"

Henry turned to the priest for help and Father Brennan leaned forward, politely waiting for Whelan to let him jump in.

"Father?"

"They had some trouble as Perry got older. Sam had a drinking problem, you probably know that. And after his wife died, he drank a lot harder. The boy was raised by Sam's in-laws because Sam didn't have a steady income. So there was some hard feeling there. And Perry's not the easiest person to get along with."

"I know. I've met him."

"Well, he doesn't drink or smoke or understand anyone who does, and as he got older he had more problems with his feelings toward Sam."

Whelan nodded and addressed Henry. "Did he ever speak about his trouble with Perry?"

"On'y time he ever said anything, he was, you know…he drank a bit one night, and he was sayin' things. Can't put no faith in what a man says when he drinks, Mr. Whelan."

"What did he say?"

"Said him and the boy probably kill each other one day."

The priest was shaking his head. "I can't imagine Perry hurting him."

"I need to talk to him, though. I need to talk to him and I think if I go to his house I'll get a door in my face. Maybe worse. Can you set something up?"

"He'll be here Saturday night for the Fall Festival." The priest smiled. "A Taste of the West Side. Seven o'clock till the food's all gone."

"And he'll be here? He's a parishioner?"

The smile took on new life now. "No, but his wife is, and if he wants to stay happily married, he'll be here. She's working at the festival."

"All right. A food fest, huh? Am I welcome?"

"Why not? We're not prejudiced."

In the late afternoon, Whelan drove up Broadway into New Town and practiced a little textbook surveillance on David Hill.

When he'd been sitting in his car for almost an hour, the young secretary, Pilar Sandoval, came out of Hill's office. Whelan had to wait another twenty minutes for the attorney to emerge. Hill walked south on Clark Street and turned at Wrightwood. Whelan started the car and drove up to the McDonald's, pulled through the parking lot, and came out the Drive-Thru lane. When he got to Wrightwood, Hill was just getting into the dark blue Buick halfway down the block.

He followed Hill to Halsted and then south, past Fullerton, to a strip of new taverns and restaurants. The attorney parked in front of a place called Grant's and went inside. Whelan stopped next to Hill's Buick. He could see clearly into the tavern, a long clean-looking room, well lit, with several rows of small tables parallel to the bar. Hill was sitting at the farthest table from the door, the farthest table from the bar and all forms of human contact, and the bartender, a bearded man in his thirties, came out to take his order.

Hill had taken off his suit coat. He sat with his chin in one hand, holding a small blue menu in the other. The rigid, arrogant posture was gone, the entire image, cultivated through constant attention to clothing and gesture and facial expression, had evaporated. A newcomer to this dark quiet bar would see someone far different, a tired man in a wrinkled white shirt, eating alone.

As an afterthought he stopped back at his office and checked in with Shelley.

"Some day you oughta stay in your office for ten minutes at a stretch, baby."

"I take it I have had calls."

"Two. Your beloved Detective Bauman. Sounded like he'd been drinking his lunch. He hit on me as usual."

"What did he want?"

"Didn't say. Just said he'd call you some other time."

"The other call?"

"That guy that sounds like he's calling from the grave. Mel Torme with a sore throat. That one."

"Actually, he sounds like Miles Davis. Did he leave a message?"

"Yeah, he said he had something for you. He sounded different from yesterday."

"Different how?"

"Like he was in a hurry."

"He smells money. Thanks, Shel."

TWELVE

DAY 7, THURSDAY

Clouds were moving in from the west, and the sun was setting in a wash of red. There was no light inside the blue bus, no sign of movement, and no answer as he paused at the step and called out Nate's name. He entered and moved carefully back through the bus, and as his eyes grew accustomed to the dim light within, he realized that he could hear his heart beating.

A few feet from Nate's makeshift table he stopped and held his breath and listened. When he was certain that he was alone on the bus, he moved forward. On Nate's table rested the remainder of a meal, a Styrofoam cup half filled with coffee and a beef sandwich with a few bites gone. Whelan touched the coffee, then the sandwich. Both cold.

He sat on the corner of the seat in front of Nate's living space. He could hear the traffic on Halsted and a pair of men arguing over money. Whelan looked at the old man's cot and easy chair and didn't like any of it.

He left the bus and looked around the yard, calling Nate's name. Dark had bled into the sky, and in a little while he wouldn't be able to see his way around the junkyard. He went out through the gate and stood for a moment on the broken sidewalk. There was a single tavern on this stretch of Halsted, a forbidding place with barred windows and a front untouched in thirty years by paint or soap or anything resembling a human hand. He went inside.

The bar was already lined with drinkers, some on their way back from work, others who'd been there all afternoon and would leave when the bartender decided he'd had enough of them. Whelan could tell the sober ones; they looked up when the door opened and took a moment to size him up. Most of the drinkers were black, a couple were white, a small group near the back of the place looked to be Latino, and they were all drinking beer from cans. Several of the men along the bar looked down when he met their gaze; it was easy to tell which ones could see cop in him. The bartender, for one.

Whelan took a stool near the door. In a corner to his right a young Latino in a leather jacket whispered and smiled into the phone.

The bartender was a middle-aged white man who took his time coming over. Eventually he got there. He sank back against a beer cooler and thrust his chin at Whelan.

"What's it gonna be?"

"I'll have a ginger ale."

The bartender packed ice into a plastic cup, poured soda into it from the gun, jammed a straw in it and set it down in front of Whelan.

"Dollar."

"I'm trying to get a hold of somebody who works up the street. Name's Nate."

The bartender pursed his lips and shook his head, then took one of the bills from Whelan's small stack.

"He works next door. In the tire place." The bartender was starting to shake his head when Whelan added, "The one that lives in the bus. Old guy."

He had the barkeep's attention now. The man looked Whelan up and down and made no secret of his distaste. "What you want with him?"

"I told him to keep an eye open for something for me—a little something for my car—and I think he came up with it."

"He don't come in here much."

"No, I guess he doesn't hang out anywhere except the bus. But he's not there. You seen him lately?"

"He comes in to use the phone sometimes. Came in today."

"He made a call?"

The bartender nodded.

"How long ago?"

A shrug. "I don't know. It was afternoon."

"Was he with anyone, or did he talk to anyone?"

"Mister, nobody wants to talk to him."

"Did he leave right after he made his call?"

"Wasn't any reason for him to stay. He smells. We don't need nobody in here smells like that." The bartender studied Whelan for a moment. "You plainclothes?"

"I'm not a cop. He called me, like I said. I think he had something for me, and now I can't find him."

The barman shrugged again. "You wait by that bus of his, he'll be back. He ain't goin' nowheres." Down the bar, a man tapped his beer can on the bar. The bartender gave the customer a sullen look, glanced briefly at Whelan, then moved away. Whelan took a sip of his ginger ale, left a buck, and went back out onto the street.

A chill had come into the air, and on the corner across from Nate's bus a group of men stood around a garbage drum and warmed their hands over a fire. They looked up in silent question as he approached.

Whelan nodded, and one of them moved away from the drum.

"Whatcha need, sir, tires? Got new Firestones, Michelins, give you a good price."

"I was looking for Nate." He gestured with his thumb in the direction of the bus.

"Ain't seen 'im."

"Seen anybody go inside the bus?"

"Don't nobody go in that bus." A couple of the other men laughed. "Ain't nobody goin' in that bus 'less Nate take a bath."

"It was another dude lookin' around that bus."

Whelan looked at the speaker, a tall, thin man with heavy-lidded eyes and a stocking cap. "When?"

The man made a little shrug and Whelan nodded. He pulled out a five and handed it to the man. "Nothing's free, huh?"

The man took the money and jammed it in the pocket of

his jacket. "'Bout a hour ago."

"What did he look like?" The man pursed his lips and shook his head. Whelan decided to fish. "Tall skinny white guy like me?"

The man shook his head. "Dude wasn't white." Then he became aware of the stares of his companions, self-conscious that he was offering too much information, and the well went dry.

"Okay, thanks." Whelan nodded to the men and walked up Halsted.

The streetlights had gone out on the west side of Halsted for a full block, so that people on the other side moved in a no-man's-land of shadow. Here and there he could see the flames of a garbage drum fire and a handful of dark figures moving about on the street.

Whelan stood in a doorway and watched the man in the gray hooded sweatshirt as he dug in a garbage container at the corner of Halsted and Maxwell for his dinner. The trash belonged to a sandwich stand called Matty's, a matchbox of a place that advertised Polish and kielbasa and dogs, and the stretch of Maxwell that ran behind it was little more than an alley. Whelan leaned against the side of the doorway until the man came up with something edible and began to eat.

He was across the street in seconds and positioned himself so that the man in the sweatshirt would have no clear avenue of escape.

The man ate greedily, noisily, focusing all his attention on the stale sandwich in his hand. Whelan could smell him from six feet away. Up close he was unshaven and ragged and filthy, with what appeared to be fresh stitches over one eye and a distended stomach that stretched the dirty cloth of his sweatshirt. There was something childlike in his posture and movements. Whelan watched him for a moment more and then moved quietly till he was just behind the man. He held out a bill till it dangled just to the left of the man's face.

"Ten bucks."

The man froze like a deer in the crosshairs. Then, as the

wondrous presence of the ten-dollar bill wore through his fear, he relaxed a little. He dropped the half-eaten burger in his hand and chanced a look at Whelan from the corner of his eye. His breathing came raspy and quick, through his mouth.

"It's okay, you can turn around," Whelan said, still holding out the bill.

The man turned and faced Whelan. His eyes widened slightly when he saw Whelan, and he wet his lips. Whelan could see him trying to see a way out of the little dead end he'd gotten himself into.

"You're not in any danger. I just want to talk to you, and it's worth ten bucks to me. You can get a hamburger that's still hot."

The man blinked, and some of the stiffness went out of his shoulders.

"You knew Sam Burwell." The man froze again. "You did, right?"

"I knew 'im."

"You know he's dead?"

The man nodded. "I went. To the funeral."

Whelan stared for a moment. "How'd you get out there?"

"Walked. I walked. I can walk all day, mister."

It's your whole life: you walk and you sleep in doorways, Whelan thought. "I'll bet you can," he told the man. "You know about the kids they brought in for Sam's killing?"

The man nodded. "Little bastards. I hate those little bastards. They shook me down. I smacked one of 'em in his mouth."

"They hurt you?"

"Busted up my eye. Cops took me to County for stitches. Ten stitches."

"Think they'd kill you?"

"Who knows? They're little animals."

"When they jumped you, did you see a gun?"

"No. Biggest one, he had a knife, like a butcher knife. Didn't have no gun."

"You're Buddy Lenz, aren't you?"

The man's eyes widened, but he shut his mouth tight. Whelan grinned and wiggled the ten again. The other man nodded, watching the bill.

"Okay, Buddy. My name's Paul. You used to play the drums in the old days." The other man shot him a quick, nervous look and Whelan added, "O.C. Brown told me about you."

Buddy seemed to relax. He nodded. "O.C. Brown. Played a good horn. Cornet, he useta play."

"Did you and Sam get along, Buddy?"

"Oh, sure. We went way back. We never had no problem. Musicians don't have no problem about people's color. I'm a picker, I sold 'im stuff. I sold stuff to a lotta these people down here. I'm good, too." He watched Whelan for any resistance to this idea. "You got to have a good eye about stuff. Lotta good stuff, it just looks like garbage, so you got to have a good eye. Sam useta be a picker but he wasn't feeling so hot no more, couldn't get out and look for stuff. So if I found something he could use, I sold it to him."

"You sold different things to different dealers?"

Buddy nodded. "Right. You got to know what each one sells."

"You stay down here, Buddy?"

A shrug. "Sometimes. I don't stay just in one place. I move around a bit."

"Were you down here the Sunday when there was a big fire? That's when they think Sam was killed."

Buddy Lenz looked away. "I was around. I didn't see nothin', though. I just saw, you know, the usual people and like that."

"I took you by surprise when I came up behind you."

"Yeah. You got to watch your back down here."

"Right. You seemed to recognize me, though. I thought for a minute it was me you were afraid of."

Buddy Lenz pursed his lips and shook his head but refused to meet Whelan's eyes.

"I get the feeling you know me, though. Have you seen me before?"

"Yeah. I saw you before."

"You saw me down here when I was asking people about Sam."

Buddy nodded.

"I'm a private investigator. Buddy. O.C. Brown asked me to look into Sam's death. He doesn't think those kids killed Sam, and I think he's right."

Buddy flashed him a sudden look, his eyes shining.

Whelan went fishing. "I wish I had you with me when I was talking to these people. I know somebody down here knows something. Probably somebody I've already talked to."

Buddy shuffled from foot to foot and moved almost imperceptibly a couple feet away.

"Buddy, maybe you saw me talking to somebody who knows something. Is that why I made you a little nervous? Who was it, Buddy?"

Buddy shrugged and scanned the street as if planning an escape route.

"Take the ten. Buddy. I'll be back, and maybe you'll be able to help me a little with this."

The drummer took the ten in dirty fingers and stared at Whelan openmouthed for a moment. Then he pocketed the bill and nodded. "That black one I saw you with, you oughta be asking him."

"The black man you saw me with—when?"

Buddy tried to look sly. "Last night. Right over there in the alley. I saw you come up behind him when he was in his car. He was watchin' *you.*" Buddy pointed a grubby finger at him.

"I know about him, Buddy. He was trying to find Sam before he died."

Buddy blinked, wet his lips. "He found 'im. He found Sam, mister. I saw 'im."

Whelan could hear his own heartbeat. "What did you see, Buddy?"

"That one that was followin' you, I saw him. He was standin' on the corner across the street from where Sam set up. Just watchin' 'im. He was watchin' Sam just like he watched you, only he wasn't sittin' in no car then. Just standin' there smokin' cigarettes and watchin' 'im."

"Did you see him here any other time?"

"Just that time." Buddy Lenz jammed the ten inside the waistband of his pants and nodded. "I gotta go."

"Thanks, Buddy," Whelan heard himself say. Buddy took one quick final look and then hurried off across Halsted. In a few seconds he'd disappeared into the blackness.

Whelan stood there for a moment and listened to the blood pounding in his ears. For just a fraction of a second he imagined himself wandering around, aimlessly searching through doorways, while another man stood a few feet away and laughed.

The Jet was the only vehicle left on a desolate stretch of Fourteenth Place. Whelan made a hurried check around as he opened the door. He got in quickly, turned the key in the ignition, and heard nothing. He pumped the gas pedal a couple of times and tried to start the car again but there was nothing. He knew if he sat here and gave it gas and turned the key in the ignition all night, the car would make no sound.

He sat for a moment in the darkened car and watched the street in his side-view mirror. A knot was forming in his stomach. With a quick glance around, he got out and looked at the hood. Where they had used the crowbar, the metal was puffed out, like a steel blister. He sighed and put the hood up and found exactly what he'd expected. The battery was gone.

And I was having such a nice day.

Whelan stood leaning against his car for a couple of minutes and had a cigarette. He could call for a tow, but it would be cheaper just to come back with a new battery and install it himself. The Jet was probably safe for the night; they'd already taken out the only piece of the car worth money.

Trying to shake the growing sense that he was not alone on the street, he headed back to Halsted.

He walked past the row of stores with their steel gates locked in place for the night and tried in vain to find a cab. When one finally materialized, the driver gave him an aggravated wave of his hand and shook his head, then slowed down a few yards away.

The cab backed up slowly and the driver, a burly man in a floppy Cubs hat, leaned out the window.

Whelan trotted over to him.

"I'm through for the night," the cabbie said, and gave Whelan a sullen stare. "You goin' north?"

"Yeah."

"How far?"

"Wilson and Broadway?"

The cabbie hesitated for a moment, muttered, "Fuck me," then said, "Get in."

Whelan slipped into the back seat and said nothing for a few blocks. The cabbie shot him an occasional look in the rearview mirror and broke his silence only to mutter curses at other motorists. Eventually he relaxed, turned off the dispatcher, and turned the radio to a jazz station. By Greektown he was ready to talk to his passenger.

"You work down there? Maxwell Street?"

"No. I was just down there to see somebody."

"Mister, that's a shit neighborhood to be walkin' around at night. Especially if you don't have no car."

"I have a car. I parked it a few blocks away, and somebody stole the battery."

The cabbie eyed the rearview mirror to see if Whelan was serious, then laughed. "No shit. They took your battery?"

"Yeah. And if I was a patient guy, I'd come down here on Sunday morning and somebody'd probably sell it back to me."

The cabbie shook his head and laughed again. "You see? I don't mean to make fun of you, mister, but see what I mean about that neighborhood? It's all boogies and bums down there."

Whelan let it pass. He studied the driver's cab license and the typical cabbie picture that made each driver look like something out of a lineup.

"You do most of your driving out south? Is that where you were coming from?"

"Nah. I try to stay north, or out by O'Hare or Downtown. Couple-three nights a week I pick up a fare from a saloon on La Salle Street. City Hall guy, one of these hotshots, lives in Bridgeport. So I take him out there and then I try to call it a night."

"Anybody important?"

The cabbie made a snorting noise. "He was important, he'd have his own limo and a driver. Wouldn't need no cab. He just wants to look like hot shit to his neighbors. He's a young guy, about thirty, some kinda assistant to the assistant deputy commissioner for something." The cabbie chuckled. He met Whelan's eyes in the mirror again. "You're a cop."

Whelan smiled. "I ask a lot of questions. But no, I'm not a cop anymore. I was just making conversation, actually."

"It's okay. What kinda work you do?"

"I'm a private investigator."

The cabbie grinned at him in the mirror. "No shit? I didn't know they were for real."

"I'm not so sure we are. Am I taking you far out of your way?"

"Nah, it's okay. I'm up by Diversey and Broadway." The tone of his voice said Whelan would still be standing back on the corner if it *was* out of his way. "You been in my cab before?"

"Could be. I take them now and then. Haven't been in one in about a year, though."

"You look familiar. Maybe I saw you somewheres else. Wilson and Broadway—you ever go in any of the joints up there?"

"Taverns? Not much. I go to a few places outside the neighborhood."

"Neighborhood? That's your neighborhood? Mister, you get to some interesting places."

Whelan smiled. "It's interesting, all right. I eat in a lot of places up there, though. I know a couple of cabbies that hang out in a coffee shop under the El tracks."

"The one right at Wilson and Broadway? Sure, I know that place. I been there a couple times."

The cabbie seemed satisfied that he had placed Whelan and fell silent. Whelan watched the dark streets pass and thought of the events of the evening: a call from Nate, the empty bus, a man seen leaving the bus, and Whelan's incapacitated car. He wondered whether the car had been a message to him or something more calculated, a way to strand him alone on a dark side street in a neighborhood where only the homeless lived. He thought of Nate again and felt a chill wash over him.

At Wilson and Broadway the cabbie pulled up to the curb and said, "Gimme five bucks and we'll call it even. I was goin' this way anyhow."

Whelan handed him a ten and said, "Keep it. Buy yourself a beer."

The cabbie looked at the ten and grinned. "Okay, buddy. Appreciate it. Hey, you ever need a cab at night, look me up. When I'm waitin' for a fare, I use a cabstand at Lincoln and Halsted."

"Up the street from the Biograph? Okay. Have a good one."

He got a dark Berghoff's from the refrigerator and turned on his stereo. Time for one more call.

"Blue Note," O.C. said in his best innkeeper's monotone.

"Paul Whelan, O.C."

"Whatcha need, Whelan? A good drink? Cold beer? It ain't but three customers here tonight."

"I'll take a rain check. Tonight I just need information. I found that old drummer you mentioned. Buddy Lenz."

"Where at?"

"Down on Maxwell Street."

"Poor old Buddy, he's half crazy. But I guess you found that out for yourself."

"He's about what I'd expect. Could be useful, though. You think he's worth talking to?"

"Hard to say."

"Did you ever hear of any trouble between him and Sam?"

"Naw, he hung around Sam a bit when Sam was, you know, down there selling. Thought he had some kinda talent for finding stuff. Sam give him a buck now and then to eat. Buddy wouldn't hurt nobody."

He remembered what Nate had said about Sam Burwell arguing with a man in a sweatshirt. Arguing over money, he'd thought. But this thing wasn't about money; none of it was about money. "That's pretty much what I thought, O.C."

He sipped at his beer and decided he needed to drown his sorrows in food. A late-night club sandwich, perhaps. He went into his kitchen and rooted around in the refrigerator. There was promise here: thin-sliced turkey, maple-cured ham, tomato, cheese. He piled meat and Monterey jack cheese on three large slices of rye and tossed it all in the toaster oven till the cheese was bubbling and threatening to go brown. He put on a couple of thin slices of one of the last of his own tomatoes, spooned on a little hot *giardiniera,* and cut it.

After a bite, he was already beginning to feel better. Then the phone rang. He crossed the room and picked it up to hear a man breathing heavily on the other end.

"Hello?"

"This is a friend," the voice rasped.

"Bauman. What happened, you lock yourself out?"

Bauman's hoarse laugh filled the phone. In the background, Whelan could hear country music and a man arguing in a loud voice.

"Okay, I'll wait till you can control your puckish sense of humor."

"Hey, Whelan, c'mon, you can take a joke. You're the great joker yourself."

"Where you at?"

"No fucking idea. But I got something for you."

"Let's hear it."

"You got a slight—uh, problem."

"How slight?"

"Mark Durkin. That's how slight."

No surprises there, he thought. Bauman was humming with the music.

"You like Patsy Cline, Bauman? Should have figured you for a Patsy Cline man."

"I like everything, Whelan. I'm just a happy-go-lucky guy.

So what'd you do to piss Durkin off?"

"Told embarrassing Durkin stories to his partner."

Bauman laughed. "You told him about the lost squad car?"

"Seemed like the proper thing to do."

"Oh, you're a bad man."

"So what did you hear?"

"I heard he's got a hard-on for you. I heard he wants a piece of you real bad. Don't know what he's got in mind. Sure you didn't do something else besides tellin' funny stories?"

"Can't think of anything else," he said, but he remembered the look in Durkin's eyes the other night. That look was about more than embarrassing stories.

"Better watch your back door, Whelan. He's a nasty prick. He ain't gonna do Marquis of Queensbury with you."

"Yeah. Thanks, Bauman."

Bauman laughed. "You can buy me dinner. If Durkin don't whack you." And he hung up.

Whelan put the phone back on the receiver and stood there for a moment. A cop could do a lot to a car, a cop could disable a car in a dozen ways and maybe make it look like kids. Any cop could.

Whelan sat in his darkened living room with the window open to let in the chilly air and its smells of coming winter. He thought of the cold silence in the empty blue bus, and he didn't want to think about what that meant. As he sipped his beer, he listened to a little jazz and then moved on to a rock station that played some early Bob Seger and Lou Reed. He thought of the people he still had to see and imagined that each visit, each interview, had an observer in the shadows, that everything he did was being watched. He had been ready to put a face and a name on this observer, but all that had changed. The watcher in this vision had no features, and Whelan could no longer tell even the color of his skin.

Thirteen

DAY 8, FRIDAY

He woke up early the next morning and sat for a half hour at the kitchen table with a cup of coffee, listening with one ear to the news and going over what had happened. It looked no better in the cold light of morning.

A fog had settled in during the night, and Uptown looked like London on a bad day. He walked to the office and called his service, and a fluted singsong voice greeted him.

"Hello, good morning, Paul Wee-lon Detective Sarvices."

Whelan sighed. When he least expected it, when his resistance was at its lowest, Abraham Chacko would unfailingly materialize on the other end of the phone.

He swallowed, remembered to speak slowly and carefully, took a deep breath and spoke firmly into the telephone. "Hello, Abraham. This is Paul Whelan."

There ensued the traditional moment of confusion, signaled by a long silence. Then, as Abraham sorted out the possibilities open to him, Whelan could hear the little Indian's fevered breathing, could almost feel the tension in his panic-stricken chest, could sense his fervent wish to be spirited away to Calcutta or Bangalore.

Just when it seemed that Abraham would be unable to complete the conversation, his cheery voice rang out. "Hello, good morning, sar. You are Mr. Whelan."

"I believe so. For a moment I thought you'd tell me I wasn't in."

Abraham laughed, a chirpy laugh. "No, no, sar, I know that

you are you and not someone who he is calling you. This much I know."

"You are a top-notch telephone operator, Abraham. Indispensable. Where is Shelley?"

"She is coming late."

"I see. Any calls?"

"No calls as yet, sar."

"Well, it was nice to chat with you, Abraham."

"Excuse me, sar. I wish to inform you that I am having the interview for a job today."

The morning was looking up. "So you might be leaving us?"

"Yes, sar. I am having the interview for the position of Chicago Police Dispatcher."

"God help us all," Whelan muttered.

"Excuse me?"

"I said God helps us all, Abraham. Good luck to you."

"Thank you, sar. Good-bye, sar."

Whelan sat holding the phone for a moment and a tremor went through his body. When the shudder had passed, he made a call he'd been wanting to make for days.

The call was to the New York Bar Association, and it disappointed him, for it told him that David Hill was indeed a member in good standing of the bar of the State of New York and had been for the past three years.

He killed the better part of an hour and a half getting a battery from an auto parts shop on Broadway and riding a cab down to Maxwell Street. When he'd installed the battery, he drove to within a half block of Halsted. He was walking to the blue bus when he came to a sudden stop.

A small crowd had gathered on the corner of Halsted and Liberty, and there were two police cars parked nose to nose a few feet from the corner. Beyond them he could see a dark blue Caprice with M plates. The uniformed officers were just visible a few yards past the bus.

Whelan parked and crossed the street. At the entrance to

the tire yard, a pair of young men were craning for a look at the police officers.

"What happened?"

They looked at him and one pointed to the bus. "They found some old dude back there."

"Dead?"

The speaker nodded. "Somebody wasted the dude."

Whelan moved past them and around the tire yard. Behind the bus was a vacant lot overgrown with tall weeds. A house had once stood here. Whelan could make out the sidewalk that had run up to the front and a section of concrete foundation that was still visible along one side. Now it was a receptacle for discarded things, a couple of wine bottles and a shot tire and a filthy denim shirt. And where the weeds met the back of the bus, three cops stood looking down at something in the grass and a fourth was on his haunches.

Whelan moved closer until he could see the body. The cop on the ground said something and one of the other cops shrugged, then turned slightly and saw Whelan.

"Back on the sidewalk, sir. Over there." He was a large man with a well-developed gut, and he was sweating in his leather jacket.

Whelan looked at him. "Can I take a look? I think I knew him."

The cop hesitated for a moment, then gestured for Whelan to come closer.

It was Nate, as he'd known it would be. He had been strangled with a dirty gray section of clothesline and the rope was tightly wound round his neck. The swollen, constricted face bore little resemblance to the old man from the back of the bus.

"Yeah," Whelan said. "His name is Nate. He lived in the back of this bus. I think he did some work for the guys that sell tires out of this lot."

"Know where we can find them?"

"No."

The cop on the ground straightened up. He brushed off his hands, hitched up his trousers, and squinted at Whelan.

"How do you know this guy? You work down here?"

"No. I talked to him a couple of times down here. I don't really know anything about him except his name."

"Pockets are turned out. Nothing on him."

"Robbery?" Whelan asked.

"We don't know yet, sir."

"Doesn't seem like it though, does it?"

The cop inclined his head slightly. "Why do you say that, sir?"

"I used to work out of Eighteen. I never heard of a robbery where they strangled the victim."

The cop seemed to relax. "Yeah, I'd say that's a new one on us, too."

The older cop studied him for a moment. "We might want to talk to you about this later. Got a number we can reach you at?"

Whelan fished out a card and handed it over.

The cop held the card out at arm's length and read it. He raised his eyebrows at the other cops. "Private investigator. Is that what's gonna happen to me when I get my twenty in?"

One of the other cops laughed. "You'll never get out: you're always gonna have half a dozen mortgages to pay off."

The cop who had been studying the body took the card. "You know anybody this guy had a problem with?"

"No. Like I said, I didn't really know him."

The cop nodded slowly and said nothing. Whelan started back toward the rear of the bus. Something made him look up. Mark Durkin was leaning against the rear bumper and puffing at a cigarette. He stared at Whelan for a moment, saying nothing. Durkin's hair clung damply to his forehead: a drinker's sweat. Like Bauman, he'd sweat in a snowstorm. In his eyes, there was an unnatural brightness that had nothing to do with drink. Whelan had seen eyes like Durkin's before, but their owners were usually wearing cuffs.

Whelan nodded. "Durkin."

Durkin moved his head almost imperceptibly and took another drag on his cigarette. As Whelan walked away, he could feel Durkin's eyes on him.

He spent a few minutes driving around the back streets on the off chance that he could find Buddy Lenz. At Fifteenth and Morgan he found a thin white man in a winter coat rifling through several boxes of discarded produce.

"Do you know Buddy?"

The man paused and looked at Whelan with a tomato in his hand. "Got a smoke?"

"I got a whole pack. I'm looking for Buddy."

The man approached the car and Whelan held out his cigarettes. "I ain't seen Buddy today. I seen 'im yesterday. Not today."

"Where does he stay at night?"

The man shrugged, then pointed toward the tracks to the south. "He flops under the viaduct there sometimes. Sometimes he goes down to the missions."

"Long walk."

The man shrugged. "He likes to walk. Always says that."

"Thanks."

Whelan made one pass through the viaduct, then back again, and checked another one a half block west. No one was sleeping in the damp tunnels. He left Maxwell and headed back to the office.

The sun had burned its way through the morning's fog and the day promised warmth and a soft southerly wind, but a man was dead and Whelan had seen that man's face. A man was dead and just hours before his death he'd called Paul Whelan. He wanted to believe Nate had had his own enemies, that Nate's death had nothing to do with him, but it wasn't a convincing argument.

As he drove back to the office, he punched buttons on the radio, trying to find music to take his mind off the dead man in the weeds, the look on the swollen face, but it was not a morning for music, and before he'd gone four blocks he had turned the radio off.

He grabbed a newspaper from the box on the corner and went up to the office. He made a quick call to David Hill's office and was greeted by the sunny voice of Pilar Sandoval.

"Is Mr. Hill in?"

"No, he is not," she said in her crisp manner. "He is in court today."

"Excellent place for him," Whelan muttered and the young woman laughed.

"Oh, Mr. Whelan. I didn't recognize your voice."

"Hello, Ms. Sandoval. You seem to be in good spirits."

"Of course," she said. "Mr. Hill isn't in!" She laughed. "Is there a message?"

"Just tell him I called. If he gives you a hard time, ruin his day: tell him I'll keep calling till I get him." After he'd hung up, Whelan spent a moment staring at the phone. He was wondering about the possibility of Pilar Sandoval sharing with him the names of Hill's current clients. He shook his head. Something told him that, no matter how irritating her boss was, Ms. Sandoval wouldn't divulge his private business.

He needed lunch. He needed lunch and cheering up, and there was but one place to go.

Half a dozen hard hats from the CTA yards already occupied the two best booths in the House of Zeus, and three kids with pierced ears and noses and hair dyed tropical colors shared an order of Greek fries, and a bag lady had either dropped off to sleep or died on a small table near the counter.

The floor show was already in progress when Whelan entered.

"I hope I didn't miss anything," he said to one of the hard hats.

The man smiled and nodded his yellow helmet in the direction of the counter. "Just started."

Three people stood at the counter holding little red plastic baskets and harangued Rashid about their contents. A few feet away, Rashid's cousin Gus stood with the air of a penitent and listened to an apparent lecture from a sickly looking man in a dark suit. Occasionally the man in the suit took his eyes off the list he was reading from and fixed Gus with a hard look. A young black man in a shirt and tie emerged from the kitchen shaking his head and said something to the pale-skinned man, who gave Gus a disgusted look and added an item to his list.

Oh, boy, Whelan thought: health inspectors. This should prove to be a test for both sides.

He took his place next to the angry customers: a short fat woman, a tall black man in his forties, and a young woman who could have been Filipino. Instead of dealing with each case individually and defusing some of the hostility, Rashid had elected to face all three of his accusers simultaneously, allowing them to unite and let their anger undergo some kind of mutation. He'd started out with three irritated patrons and now he had a lynch mob.

As nearly as Whelan could make out, the complaints were, from left to right, cold gyros on a stale pita, a hamburger burnt to cinders, and an Italian beef whose odd color matched its troubling odor.

All three customers were speaking at once, and Rashid held out his hands in the gesture of a politician calming his crowd and said, "Please, please, everything is okay. Everything is okay." He caught sight of Whelan out of the corner of his eye and burst into his wondrous white-toothed grin, an unlikely flash of ivory.

"Oh, Detective! Very nice, very nice to see you. My friend, he is detective. This man in my restaurant is detective."

The short chubby woman peered up at Whelan with distaste. "I don't care if he's the Pope. I want my lunch. And I don't want this."

"Little problem here, Detective, but nothing so bad," Rashid said hopefully. He favored each of his customers with his teeth again. "I will personally"—and here he slapped himself on the chest—"serve each one here."

"You the one served us in the first place," the man said. He looked at Whelan and held out his charred burger. "Look here, man. Look like it was in the Chicago Fire."

"I am waiting here the longest," the Filipino-looking woman

said. "Twenty minutes I am waiting. This beef, look at his color."

Rashid pretended to examine the beef and shrugged. "It is how it comes to us. From farms. In America," he added, hoping to share at least some of the blame with the embattled farmers of his adopted country.

The short fat woman was studying the menu. "I want that shrimp basket instead of this."

Oh-oh, Whelan thought. He looked at the woman, who squinted up at him and seemed to dare him to voice disagreement with her choice.

"I want the shrimp basket," she said to Whelan.

"I wouldn't do that," he muttered.

"What?" The woman gave him a sharp look.

"That'd be too many shrimp for me." There was truth in it. Twenty shrimp. Twenty deep-fried shrimp from a Greek restaurant in Uptown run by Persian snake-oil salesmen. Twenty shrimp that had lived in the gelid darkness of Rashid's cooler since Reagan gave up acting. Shrimp that Rashid and Gus had probably brought with them when they fled the health officials in sunny California. Whelan looked at the woman, who was still staring at him. "Twenty's a lot," he offered.

"I didn't have much of a breakfast."

Hope you have a good pharmacist nearby, he thought.

Rashid took the woman's order, put another burger on for the man, and refunded the Filipino woman's money, carefully forking the iridescent beef back into its container. He grinned at Whelan and rubbed his hands together. "You see, Detective? All taken care of."

"Right. Satisfied customers. I'll have a gyros to go, Rashid. Hold the onions. And cook the gyros," he added. Rashid winked and giggled and was turning the great cone-shaped gyros on its spit when the pale-skinned man approached.

"Mr. Abazi?"

Rashid pointed to his cousin. "He is Mr. Abazi."

Gus shook his head and pointed back. "He is too. We are both Mr. Abazi."

A faint spot of color came into the pale man's face. "You

can have your jokes now, my friends, but this is no joke." He held up a printed form with many lines for listing violations. Most of the lines were filled in a flowing script that hinted at the massive ego of the writer.

The pale man began his speech, summing up the violations and threatening to close the boys down. Whelan peered at the list but could make out only a few words: "cooler" appeared twice on the list, as did "freshness"; the word "unsanitary" seemed to be on every other line. Mr. Health Inspector held the list up and pointed to its contents as though lecturing schoolboys, and the two Iranians hung their heads and nodded.

The inspector paused at one point and nodded to Rashid. "Is that clear, Mr. Abazi? You, I take it, are the owner?"

Rashid jerked a thumb in the direction of his cousin. "He is the owner."

"No." Gus gave Rashid a sullen stare. "I own nothing. I work for this one, for no money at all. In Iran, I was professional man. Educated man."

Rashid showed fangs. "Educated man! Like what, like doctor? He is doctor, this one, this cleaner of toilets?"

"Hah, the poisoner, listen to him."

The inspector's eyebrows shot up. "Poisoner? What do you mean, poisoner?"

The cousins suddenly collected themselves and showed matching grins. "It is old joke," Gus said. "We are sorry about our poor restaurant."

"You may be a lot sorrier soon, sir."

Then, finished, Mr. Health Inspector collected his assistant and his briefcase and marched out onto Broadway. Whelan watched him with admiration: the unilateral malice of his performance had transformed him. No longer the bookish civil servant in need of a day in the sun, Mr. Health Inspector now resembled a bird of prey, a harrier looking for his lunch. As Whelan watched, the inspector consulted a notebook, said something to his assistant, nodded once, and was off in the direction of some other semi-hygienic Uptown eatery.

When Whelan turned back to the counter, the boys were

grinning at him. Rashid wiggled his bushy black eyebrows. "That was close one, eh, Detective?"

"We were hot potatoes, Rashid," Gus said. He gave his slender cousin a thudding smack on the back that earned him a halfhearted smile and hinted to Whelan of ancient boyish combats in the dusty streets of Tehran.

"Whew!" Rashid said, and grinned.

"Yes," Gus said. "Whew."

"I get the feeling that you fellows aren't taking Mr. Health Inspector seriously. These guys don't play around. They'll shut you down." Then, as Rashid started to protest, Whelan added, "Remember California?"

Gus nodded. "Yes, sure he does, the poisoner."

"This was unfortunate mistake, California. This was misunderstanding."

"Better be careful, guys. In California, they put you in jail for health-related offenses. This is Chicago: they'll take your money. All your money. They'll wring money out of you that you didn't know you had."

The boys exchanged a panicked glance and nodded. "Okay," they said together.

"Now how about my gyros?"

The Public Aid office was small, crowded, and badly ventilated. He crossed to the front desk and spoke to a receptionist sitting behind a little black sign that said INTAKE.

"I'd like to talk to Miss McAuliffe if she's in."

The receptionist made a little frown. "She's in, but—"

"I'm not a client. It's personal business." The receptionist looked over her shoulder and nodded in the direction of a woman standing with her back to them, bending over a desk.

"That's her in the blue dress."

"Can I just go back there?"

"I have to let her know you're here." The young woman picked up the phone, hit a com-line button, and waited.

"Someone here to see you…I know. He says it's a personal

business matter."

Whelan saw the woman straighten up, squint in his direction, and shrug. She said something into the phone and the young receptionist said, "Okay."

"She's coming out to see you."

"Okay," Whelan said. Right. She's not sure I should be allowed back to her office.

The squint seemed to disappear as Sandra McAuliffe crossed the room. Needs glasses for distance, he thought.

She was tall, and her pale blond hair was cut short and showed a delicate filigree of gray. She was big-boned with dark green eyes, high cheekbones, a wide Irish-looking nose, and full lips: a woman who had probably spent part of adolescence bemoaning her size and features and woke up one morning to the surprising realization that she was nonetheless good-looking, a woman out of a Willa Cather story. He felt foolish at his earlier notion that this might be the faceless woman in Sam Burwell's life.

"I'm Sandra McAuliffe. Can I help you?"

"I'm Paul Whelan. We spoke on the phone."

She sighed. "I thought we concluded our business, Mr. Whelan."

"People frequently announce to me that my conversations are over, but I'm a detective. If I let everybody tell me when I can ask questions, I might as well hang it up. No disrespect intended, ma'am, but I need information about the case I mentioned, and I think you'll agree it is not a trivial one, even if it has nothing to do with your caseload."

She opened her mouth to speak, shot a quick look at the receptionist, and sighed again. "I'm not here, Peggy. No more calls, no more visitors. If the *governor* calls, I'm out."

"I'm sorry, Sandy."

"It's okay. Come on, Mr. Whelan. Come back to my desk and we'll talk."

"You get a break, right?"

"Yes?"

"I could use a cup of coffee. Why don't we go down the

street to the place on the corner?"

She hesitated, clearly seeing necessary calls delayed, appointments missed.

"I won't keep you more than fifteen minutes, I wouldn't want to ruin your Friday. I'll even buy you ice cream."

She started to laugh, then shrugged. "All right. Let me get my desk put back together, and I'll meet you here."

They walked up the street to the twenty-four-hour grill on the corner of Sheridan and Lawrence, and Whelan waved to the little Filipino waitress.

"I take it you've been here before," Sandra McAuliffe said, as she slid into a window booth.

"Restaurants are my hobby. Good or bad."

"I've been coming here more lately. The one on the next block is going out of business."

"Yeah, but it's going to be reincarnated as a Vietnamese place." He wiggled his eyebrows.

She gave him a vaguely interested look. "You like Vietnamese food?"

"If there's a kind of food in Asia I don't like, I haven't heard about it yet."

She smiled and gave a little nod.

The waitress took their order for a coffee and a pot of tea.

"You had lunch already?" Whelan asked.

"Yes, thanks." She watched him without expression.

"I was serious about the ice cream. They have good ice cream here."

"Mr. Whelan, my body converts ice cream to fat cells inside of ten minutes. Thanks, anyhow."

When the waitress had served them, Sandra McAuliffe spent a few moments dipping her tea bag. Up close, she was a more complicated picture. Her age was more apparent, wrinkles beginning to appear at the corners of her eyes and more gray in her hair than he'd seen before: he put her somewhere between forty-two and forty-five. On the other hand, she had a splash of freckles across her cheekbones and the bridge of her nose, and the green eyes were something special. Good or bad, it was plain that Sandra McAuliffe accepted it all, for she wore no makeup.

He pulled the ashtray over and then caught himself. "Sorry, I forgot to ask. Mind if I smoke?"

"Doesn't bother me. I actually like cigars. I hate pipes, though."

"No pipes here." He lit up and was about to start on business when she spoke.

"I wasn't being intentionally rude to you before. I just didn't see…I don't know anything about private detectives, and—you don't have a badge, do you?"

Whelan was puzzled for a moment, then took out his identification. "Should have shown you this before. We don't carry badges."

She shot him a shy smile. "I know. My only previous contact with a private detective wasn't a pleasant one. We had a guy coming by and hassling a client whose ex-husband was suing her over a car, and this detective would march into our office and flash this badge in everybody's face and try to look tough. It was basically a toy badge. It said PRIVATE DETECTIVE."

Whelan smiled. "Blond guy, handlebar mustache, nice suit?"

"Yes, exactly!"

"His name is Ralph Budnik. He's sort of a curiosity within the profession. No one takes him seriously, but the rest of us all covet his cool badge."

"He's really a jerk. And I guess because of that experience, I couldn't associate you with a serious case."

"A lot of people think that way. They assume we spend all our time following unfaithful spouses. I don't do any of that kind of work."

"Have you ever?"

"Nope. I don't need the money that badly. Not that I make a lot, but I get by without having to do anything I don't want to do."

"And you're investigating this man's death, you said."

"Yes."

"Why?"

"A friend of his asked me to. I like the friend, so I said I would look into it."

"And aren't the police doing the same thing, with all their—you know, their resources?"

"No. It's pretty much a closed case. They think a bunch of kids did it. I don't think so."

"You have reason to think they're wrong?"

"Yeah, I do. Most of the time, they're right. This time, I don't think they are, partly because of the evidence and partly because I know the investigating officer."

She sipped at her tea and gazed out at the street for a moment. Then she put the cup down and looked at him. "What is it you think I can tell you?"

"Maybe nothing. I'm really trying to locate a woman who was seen going into his apartment, a tall black woman with red hair. I also have reason to believe the dead man had a relationship with a woman living in Uptown. I don't really have much of a description except that she was white."

Sandra McAuliffe leaned on her elbows, held the teacup in both hands, and looked at him over the rim. "And you thought I'd be able to tell you some…no, you thought I might be this woman?" She fixed him with an incredulous smile. A dimple that he hadn't noticed appeared in her cheek.

"Not exactly. I mean, the thought crossed my mind once, but this is just for information. Before I actually talked to you, all I had was the most general description possible: a white woman. And I knew there was a caseworker who visited that building." He shrugged. "It's all I had: a white woman. He was pretty secretive about it, and none of his friends ever met her. Don't be insulted. I'm trying to find out who murdered this man, so I can't be fussy about the leads I check out."

She sipped at her tea, put down the cup and added some more hot water, then took another sip. "You must have some theory if you're so convinced that the police have the wrong people."

"I do."

She sighed. "You're not particularly generous with information, Mr. Whelan. You drag me out of my office to see if I'm a potential murder suspect, but your case is still none of my business."

"That's one of the most impolite-sounding phrases in the language, but it doesn't really make sense to be talking to a stranger about these things. Why do you want to know?"

She shrugged. "I guess I don't, really. I was just curious." She took another sip of tea and looked down into the cup this time. Whelan realized he'd broken off a point of contact.

"His apartment," Whelan began, "was at the far end of the hall. He was a tall man pushing sixty and had a scar over one eye."

She nodded once. "I saw him. I know who he is…was. I know who he was. I think I told you that on the phone." She fought off a little shudder. "It's terrible to learn that someone you passed in the hall was murdered." She stared at Whelan for a moment as a new realization came into her eyes. "Maybe by someone else I passed in that building."

"No, I don't think so. I think his killing had nothing to do with his life now. Names keep coming up from the man's past, people he knew when he was a young man. I think he was killed by someone who had known him for a long time. Maybe even a family member."

"That's horrible."

"If it's true. All I'm saying is that I don't think his was a random killing, or that he was killed for money. And I don't think you'd ever have come in contact with the killer. If the killer had found him around here, Burwell would have been killed here."

Sandra McAuliffe discreetly checked her watch and gazed around the restaurant.

"I know. You have to be getting back. You don't remember ever seeing him with anyone? Anyone going into or coming out of that apartment?"

She shook her head. "Nobody. I saw him in the hall once, and I saw him coming up the stairs once. That's all. You've been in there, Mr. Whelan, it's a spooky building, and I saw very few people coming in or going out. And never a woman, of any color."

He nodded and took a last puff of his cigarette before grinding it out in the ashtray.

"It isn't very pleasant work you do."

"It isn't always like this. I don't think I could do this all the time. It would put a strain on my sanity. Most of the time I look for people who are missing, I'm working for somebody who wants to find a loved one." He remembered his first meeting with David Hill. "That's what I thought I was going to be doing when I took this one on. I was hired to look for this man, and I soon learned that no one had seen him in a week, and I started to get a bad feeling. Then they found his body and it became a whole new case. I can't say I'm enjoying it, but I'm going to finish it." He laughed, surprised at himself. "I've made too many new enemies to quit now."

She smiled. "You mentioned the officer in charge of the case. He's one of them? The new enemies?"

"He's not exactly new. But he's one good reason to believe this investigation has been mishandled."

She leaned forward now with her chin in one hand. "Do you make enough money on a case to make it worth your trouble?"

He smiled. "Sometimes. Other times, people come to you and you know as soon as you see them that they can't afford your fee."

"Why do you take them on?"

"It's not…it's not a business," he said, and was surprised at his own answer. "If they come to me with the kind of work that I think I should be involved in, I take the case and hope I make a few bucks somewhere down the line."

"Is this one of those cases?" She looked away quickly and shook her head. "I'm sorry, this really *is* none of my business."

He realized that she was genuinely embarrassed. A flush had spread over her cheeks and forehead. "It's all right, I don't mind talking about it. And, yeah, I'm afraid this is one of those cases. The man I'm working for has a little money, but not the kind he'd owe me if we agreed to my standard fee. He'll pay me something, but…I hadn't thought much about it." Whelan wondered why he was telling her all this.

Sandra McAuliffe seemed amused. "Mr. Whelan, you are an eccentric."

He thought about it and nodded slowly. "Maybe so. Maybe so."

She looked at her watch again. "Well…"

"Yeah, you have to get back. I was just about to ask how you got into being a caseworker."

"It's simple. I studied geology in college." She grinned, and he had a glimpse of a different person.

"Sounds like a story in itself." He caught himself on the verge of asking her to tell it to him another time and realized how that would sound. "I'll walk you back to the office."

She pursed her lips. "I'd rather walk back alone. People in offices talk," she said quietly. She stood and held out her hand. "I'm sorry I couldn't be of more help. Good luck in your investigation, Mr. Whelan."

"Thanks. I appreciate your time."

"And thanks for the tea."

"My pleasure," he said, but he was thinking, Maybe Vietnamese food sometime.

FOURTEEN

DAY 8, FRIDAY

Back at his office, he was sipping at a cup of coffee and paging idly through the newspaper when the phone rang.

"Paul Whelan."

"Mr. Whelan?" It took him a moment to place the woman's harsh voice. He heard muttered conversations in the background, and the clink of plates.

"Hello, Ruth. How're things in the doughnut business?"

"Aw, shuddup, you just ordered five minutes ago," she snarled. "You see I'm on the phone?" Then, softer, "Excuse me, Mr. Whelan. These people, they think I'm some kinda slave."

The Waitress's Lament.

"You can handle them, Ruth. What can I do for you?"

"She's here, Mr. Whelan. That Mattie. You said to call you if she came in. Well, she's here."

"Great. Thanks, Ruth."

In five minutes he reached the Subway Donut Shop. The air was thick with smoke and grease, and the long narrow counter that ran along the window to Broadway was filled with the shop's oddly varied crowd. In a far corner, her back to the room, sat a small spindly black woman in a green cloth coat. Whelan spotted Ruth, waited till she finished taking an order, and called her.

The waitress looked up with a frown, smiled when she saw it was Whelan. He indicated the woman and Ruth nodded. The woman raised a brown mug to her lips, and Whelan held up two fingers.

Ruth poured two cups of coffee and Whelan gave her a

buck and change, then carried the coffee over to the window.

"Excuse me, ma'am."

The woman looked up at him and then down at the stool beside her. "There's nobody sitting there."

"Is your name Mattie?"

The woman's eyes narrowed, more careful now about who she was inviting to sit next to her.

"Yes," she said calmly, and he realized she wasn't going to give away anything else. Her gaze flitted from Whelan to the others in the room, as though to reassure herself that she wasn't alone.

"My name's Paul. I'd like to talk to you about someone."

The woman grimaced. She was in her late fifties or early sixties, small-boned and light-skinned. The coat was clean but old, showing little pills of bunched thread everywhere. On the counter he noticed a small pillbox cap that matched it. She wore glasses with light brown frames, and the eyes behind the lenses told him he'd already underestimated their owner.

"Sir, if you want to talk to me, you best stop talking like you think I'm four. What is your full name, sir, and are you going to sit down? This doesn't look right."

"I'm sorry." He set the cups down on the counter and slid onto the stool. "My name is Paul Whelan, and I'm a private investigator, and the second cup is for you if you want it. And I want to talk to you about Sam Burwell."

She gave a little shake of her head and watched the foot traffic on Broadway for a moment. Just outside the window, a prim-looking young black woman had positioned herself a few feet from the restaurant and faced the passersby. She held a magazine in each hand. Whelan realized she was a Jehovah's Witness; she'd stand there in her rigid pose for hours, offering her publications to the pedestrians and saying nothing if no one spoke to her.

Mattie looked at Whelan. "I don't know anything about private investigators. I don't know what they do, but if you've come to ask anything disrespectful about that poor man—"

"Private investigators are like cops and bankers and

insurance people: some of them serve a basic function, and some aren't fit to scrub a sewer. I didn't know Sam Burwell, but a friend of his hired me to look into what happened to him."

"What friend?"

"O.C. Brown."

She shrugged. "I heard the name. I never met any of his friends from the West Side. Young man, what is it exactly that you want to find out about what happened? I assume you talked to the police."

"Yes. And I believe they know a good deal less than I do."

"Got a high opinion of yourself?"

"At times. I'm pretty sure I'm right about this. Mr. Brown hired me because he wants to know how Sam Burwell was killed. He doesn't think it had anything to do with the kids the police picked up, and neither do I."

"Why? Why does it have to be more…complicated than that?"

"Because several people had been asking about Sam or looking for him in the few months before his death. People came looking for him, and then he was dead." Whelan paused. "Maybe the kids did it, but it sure doesn't look that way to me."

Mattie stared out at the passersby and said nothing for a moment. Then a shudder seemed to pass through her.

"Are you all right, ma'am?"

"Whatcha mean, am I all right? You tell me somebody followed poor Sam around and killed him, and it's not supposed to scare me?"

"I'm sorry. I didn't want to upset you, but I guess it's unavoidable."

She sighed. "What do you want with me, young man?"

"I was told that you were"—he fished for tact—"close friends."

"That's not what you heard." She gave him an accusing look.

"No, I guess not. I heard he had a lady he was seeing somewhere in the neighborhood, and I was told you knew each other, and I guess I put two and two together."

She studied him for a long moment. "It wasn't any big thing.

Wasn't much to it at all. My husband passed ten years ago. Sam stayed with me a couple times, but mostly we were just friends." She smiled at Whelan, slightly embarrassed. "I don't know how that sounds to a young man like yourself, but it's true. He lost his wife years ago; you probably know about that."

"Yes."

"Well, we were working at the same place. I was working in a cafeteria in an office building and Sam was working with the janitor. He just came in and did some handyman things, you know. We got to talking, and pretty soon he was stopping by to see me, have a cup of coffee." She cast a sly look at Whelan. "Must sound pretty boring to a young man. Couple old people acting like fools."

"It doesn't sound boring at all. It sounds pretty normal." He laughed. "It sounds like a lot more than I've got right now."

"That's too bad. Nice-looking man like yourself, good manners, well-spoken. You ought to get out more, maybe."

"Maybe. It's something I'm not very good at anymore."

Mattie shook her head. "Sam was a good man, but we didn't have much in common. That's why we didn't stay together long." She saw Whelan's puzzled look and added, "Sam was a drinker. In the old days we said somebody was a drinkin' man, but it was more than that. He drank too much, he was sick from it a lot. I was through that once before, when my husband and I were first married. Wasn't about to go through it again. So…Sam and I, we were just friends." She thought for a moment. "Nice company when he wasn't full of drink. He was nice company."

"Did he ever talk to you about anyone he thought was following him? Anyone he was afraid of?"

She sipped her coffee and pursed her lips. "No. Lord, I don't think Sam was afraid of anything."

"Did he ever talk about his son?"

"Once or twice. I don't think they spoke. Not much, anyway. But he didn't say much about the boy. Said somebody else raised him. He was proud of him, though. Once in a while he bragged on that boy, told me how the boy went away to college. He was proud of himself, too, that he was the daddy of a college man."

She smiled at the memory. "He was a good man, and he was smart, he was a real smart man in his way."

Whelan nodded and took a sip of his coffee. He didn't want to tell her that Sam Burwell's relationship with his son had been unpleasant and that the boast about Perry being "a college man" was nothing more than a father's tall story.

"I really need to talk to anybody that knew him just before he died, ma'am. I heard that he had a…a friend…"

She wrinkled her face and then smiled. "Don't be beating around the bush, young man. You heard he had a lady friend. Besides me."

"Yes. Did you know her?"

"No. No, I didn't."

"I'd like to talk to her."

"I never even knew her name. I really don't know anything about her."

"Maybe if I knew where they met."

Mattie gave him a blank look. "Where they met? I wouldn't know anything about that, sir. I know she was a waitress. He told me she was a waitress." Mattie sipped her coffee. "Poor man," she said after a moment.

Whelan knew she genuinely felt pity for Sam Burwell. As he left, he thought about offering her money for her information and then realized she'd probably be offended.

"Thank you for the coffee, Mr. Whelan," she said, and when he pushed his way out through the heavy glass door she was still staring out at the street.

He stood outside his office and measured the heavy grayness that was taking over the sky and decided he needed a walk, a long walk through the neighborhood, a walk to think, to put names to the notions that now tugged at him.

As he walked a chill came into the air, but he kept walking, head down, trying to make sense of the chaos he'd walked into.

A man he'd been looking for was dead; another man, a man he'd spoken to, was dead. Two violent deaths with an undeniable connection. Other men were involved, and one of them—*at least* one of them—meant him harm. He thought about his own vulnerability, saw the many times in a day when he was alone and a killer could get the thing done. He saw himself walking alone down an unlit street, past vacant lots and overflowing dumpsters, then had a sudden image of himself peering into the empty space under the hood of his car. If this killer wanted him, why hadn't it happened then?

Why didn't he try to kill me then? Lost his nerve, Whelan told himself, then immediately shook his head. This one doesn't lose his nerve. This one doesn't even have a pulse. For the first time it occurred to him that the killer might be a woman.

Is that really who I've been looking for from the beginning? he wondered.

In his mind's eye he saw again Nate's dark swollen face and wondered if his questioning had led to the old man's death. Then he thought of Buddy Lenz.

"Shit," he said, and turned back in the direction of his office.

Time to see a lawyer who was not fond of the truth.

Pilar looked up from a magazine and gave him a half smile. "Hello, Mr. Whelan."

"Ms. Sandoval. I've got a question for you. Can you at least describe one of his clients for me? An older woman. Fifties or sixties…"

She'd begun to shake her head before he was through the first part of his question, and behind her stoic adherence to duty he saw something else in her eyes, confusion perhaps.

"I can't say anything about Mr. Hill's clients. I can't even—"

"It's all right. It was a long shot. Is he in? Can I go back there?"

"Yes and no. He's in, but you can't just walk right into his office." She seemed to disapprove of him for the first time, and he liked her better for it. Too young for the likes of Paul Whelan, but a nice lady.

"Okay. Would you please buzz him and tell him Mr. Whelan

is here to see him, and that if he doesn't see me we'll need the police?"

She shook her head. "You can't threaten—"

"It's not a threat. Just say it that way."

She picked up the phone and hit a button, waited, then gave Hill the message, word for word. After a half-second pause, she looked at the phone as though it had bitten her.

The door to Hill's office swung open and banged against a chair. David Hill blocked the doorway and glared at Whelan.

"What the hell do you mean coming here and telling me I'm going to need the police? Just who do you think you are?"

"No. I listened, and she didn't tell you that. She said *'we'll* need the police.' *We,* Hill, not you. It wasn't a threat, it was a statement of fact, at least as far as I can figure the situation out."

Hill conjured up a look of puzzlement, then gave an irritated shake of his head. "I have no idea what you're talking about."

Whelan shrugged and said nothing. There was no more intriguing bait than silence. After a few seconds of theatrical gestures to show his fatigue-and/or-irritation, including puzzled looks at the floor, muttering, and finally removing his glasses to massage the bridge of his nose, Hill sighed and took a step back into his office.

"All right, Whelan. I'll play along. Come in and let's get this over with."

Whelan followed him in and leaned against the heavy guest chair while Hill sat. The lawyer nodded toward the chair.

"No, thanks. I'll stand: I'm not here to camp out."

"What exactly are you here for?" Hill leaned back and tried to look bored.

"This morning the police discovered the body of an old man who lived in a bus on Maxwell Street. This was approximately fifty yards—no, not even that, thirty yards—from where Sam Burwell set up on Sundays."

For just a split second, Hill wasn't bored anymore. He stiffened, sat up, frowned. Then he caught himself. "How does that involve me? Was this a friend of yours?"

"No. And I didn't say it involved you. Maybe it does; you'd

know that better than I would. But this man was killed after several conversations with me. I went to him for information."

"About…Sam Burwell's death. I follow."

"And just before his death he had called me, I assume to tell me something else."

"And you believe he was killed to prevent his giving you information."

"I sure do."

"Did he tell you something so important that someone would kill for it?" Hill sat back in his big chair and gave Whelan a patient look, and Whelan thought he saw why Hill was probably a good courtroom lawyer.

"No, but then his killer wouldn't have known *what* the old man told me."

"How would he have known about your contact with this man?"

"He watched me." Whelan smiled at Hill and allowed a moment for the remark to sink in. For a five-count he poked around in his vest for his cigarettes. "May I smoke?"

"Certainly." Hill slid an ashtray along the desk toward Whelan, then went through his own ritual with the wonderful case and the lovely lighter and joined Whelan in polluting the office air. Whelan allowed himself several puffs on the cigarette and watched.

The lawyer's eyes fixed onto the desk blotter. Whelan could almost see him trying on different attitudes and stratagems, till finally Hill settled on one with which he was comfortable. He put his cigarette into the groove of a leather-bound ashtray, sat back in his chair, blew a little gray cloud of smoke into the air, and smiled. It wasn't much of a smile, there was very little behind it, but he held it for a moment and then sighed.

"I think I see where we're heading here, Whelan. I took a chance at watching you on Maxwell Street—after your bizarre intimations about 'secret information for my client'—and now you think I was watching this old man in a—did you say in a bus?"

"Yes. An old blue bus."

Hill shrugged. "I didn't even notice any buses. I was watching you, Whelan. I'll admit that. I believe I said as much when we spoke. But it's you I was interested in, not your contacts or your derelict friends. Now." He picked up the cigarette again and flicked a little cone of ash into the tray. "Let's think what this visit might be about. Money, perhaps. Is that it? That would shock me, Mr. Whelan, because I never made you for a blackmailer. A ne'er-do-well, a charlatan detective, but never a blackmailer."

"No, Mr. Hill, it's not about money. You *wish* it was about money because people of your sort generally think they can solve all their problems by handing people fistfuls of money. This is about a warning. I don't play games and I'm not going to pretend I understand what your game is in all this, or that I know anything more about your client than I did before. But I'm in this case and there's nothing anyone can do to get me out of it. It's a quirk of my personality.

"Here's what I'm going to do. I'm going to find out who killed Sam Burwell. When I do, I'll hand that person to the cops on a dinner plate. In the meantime, I think it's obvious that somebody will go to great lengths to get rid of anyone who talks to me. I've been talking to another person, and now I can't locate him. I've got a bad feeling about that."

Hill shook his head. "What does that—"

"I wasn't finished speaking. I want *you* to know that if anything has happened to the person I'm talking about, if he even develops a cold sore, you'd best be looking into the city's fine vocational training programs because they'll take your license to practice law and shove it up your ass and you'll be just another guy with too many college credits."

Without allowing the lawyer to respond, Whelan turned and crossed the room. At the door he looked over his shoulder.

"But that other stuff, about the information that I came across, the stuff I think your client'd like? That was no joke, barrister. You'd be surprised at how much I know. Oh, and now I've got something else."

Hill glared at him.

He pointed a finger at the lawyer. "I've got somebody who can place a certain lawyer on Maxwell Street *before* Sam Burwell died. In fact, this lawyer was watching Mr. Burwell."

Hill blinked and kept his perfectly rigid pose, saying nothing.

Whelan nodded. "You have a nice day now, hear?"

He stood outside for a moment, both pleased and disappointed. Pleased because he'd thrown a genuine scare into Hill—he could see it in the man's eyes, in his body language—disappointed that he didn't know where to go with this next. He was pretty certain Mr. Hill would be doing some fast dancing.

You won't be dancing so fast when I'm through.

The phone was ringing when he returned to the office. He caught it in mid ring.

"Paul Whelan."

"You hafta change your schedule so you can take some of your calls, doll."

"Hello, Shel. Who was it this time?"

"A Mr. Franklin."

"Doesn't ring a bell."

"He said you told him to call. He runs a building on Polk."

"Still doesn't…oh, wait, I know who he is. I talked to him the other day."

"Right. He left a message. He says Covington lives at sixteen hundred West Madison. And he says you can send the money to three-two-four-one West Polk."

Whelan laughed. "The money, huh? I like the trusting ones, Shel. He thinks I'm going to send him money in the mail, so I guess I better."

"It's as easy as that? Like makin' a wish?"

"Not quite. This is for information. Anything else?"

"How much business do you want? Toodle-oo," she said, and cracked gum in his ear.

Whelan slipped ten bucks into an envelope and addressed it to Mr. Franklin. When he'd stamped it, he stared at the other address for a while. Sixteen hundred Madison made it the corner of Madison and Ashland, three blocks east of Chicago Stadium, and he couldn't picture a residence at that corner. Then it came to him. Mr. Covington now had a different type of landlord.

Maxwell Street was already wearing its close-of-business ensemble. A couple of the smaller shops had already pulled their security gates out, putting the hurry-up into the last few customers of the day. The north wind made tumbleweeds of the sandwich wrappers and newspapers littering the street but couldn't budge or erase or hide the onion-and-grease smell.

He parked just off the corner of Halsted and Fifteenth and made his way backward toward Maxwell itself. He worked fast, questioning the tire and hubcap dealers and the kids selling Bulls T-shirts and Bears hats and the fast-talkers who wanted to sell him watches and gold chains. He talked to the counter boys in Reno's and the old lady in the window of Matty's and the sweating line working the window in Jim's, and though half the people he spoke with knew Buddy Lenz, no one had seen anything of the ragpicker in the gray sweatshirt.

A tight cold knot began to grow in his stomach. He went back to his car and made himself go through the motions of cruising the back lots, then checked out the viaducts where Buddy might be sleeping. Nothing. He killed the rest of dusk in the faint hope that the coming dark would bring Buddy Lenz out, but the feeling in his chest told him he was wasting his time.

At the corner of Fourteenth and Peoria he questioned a couple of older men sitting on the curb. It cost him three dollars and a couple of smokes to learn that one of the men knew Buddy from Whelan's description but neither man had seen him. He got back into the car. He was heading north toward Roosevelt Road when he picked up the other car in his rearview mirror. He took a sudden left, went a block down the side street, then made another left. The car in the mirror kept coming. He couldn't make out the driver's face, but something in the rigid posture told him who it was.

He went west to Blue Island, hung a right and decided to

play along. He went west on Roosevelt, cruised north on Racine, took a quick right at Taylor Street and parked in front of an Italian lemonade stand that had drawn a crowd in spite of the cool night. While he was standing in line the other car passed him and he got a fast look at the driver: Mark Durkin.

Whelan bought an Italian lemonade and stood at the curb eating it and waiting. Five minutes later the car returned. Whelan watched Durkin cruise by. The cop stared rigidly ahead as though noticing nothing.

Nice tail, Durkin. Nobody saw you.

He'd killed the entire evening and used up his options. Someone had to have seen something. He thought about the big cabbie who'd picked him up last night. Time to turn over a new rock.

There were three cabs in the cabstand at Lincoln and Halsted but none of them was the right one. He parked a few yards away in the alley near the Biograph, the selfsame alley where Dillinger had learned not to trust women wearing red. Dillinger was long gone, as was the old telephone pole with what every kid on the North Side believed to be the original bullet holes from that storied night.

The first cab contained a slender little Pakistani man who got himself excited at the prospect of a fare but didn't know Whelan's cabdriver. The second cab in the row was driven by an African man who had just gotten his medallion and shiny new cab the previous week. He said he knew nothing and Whelan believed him.

The third cabdriver was homegrown, a chubby black man with an animated face and quick smile. "Yes, sir. Can I help you?"

"Yeah, but I don't need a ride."

"I figured that, sir, when you skipped the first two cabs in line. What do you need?" He spoke in a precise, clipped sort of speech that reminded Whelan of a judge he'd once known.

"Information. I'm looking for a driver who uses this stand a lot. He's a white guy, big, an older guy, wears a blue cap and talks a lot. A little crazy, maybe."

The black cabbie nodded and smiled. "From the first part, it could be anybody. When you added the last part, I knew your man. Don't know his name but he's here a lot."

"Have you seen him tonight?"

"No, but I saw a cab parked back on Fullerton. I think he likes to eat at Peter's, just around the corner."

"I know where it is. Here, buy yourself a cup of coffee." He gave the cabbie two dollars.

"Thank you, sir."

Whelan knew Peter's well from his days as a beat cop. He'd never been sure what the name really was, for the bright sign out front used a hundred bulbs to announce PETER'S BROASTED CHICKEN but gave no hint as to the name of the establishment. Frequented by nurses from Children's Memorial and bartenders and waitresses and the occasional street person, it served breakfast all day, made a mean Denver omelet and pancakes that would stop small-arms fire, and had half a dozen daily dinner specials.

Half the booths were full and most of the stools at the long white counter, and in the middle of them sat the cabdriver, working his way through a perch dinner. He had an empty stool on either side of him, as though his bulk and body language had warned off potential neighbors. Whelan decided to ignore the warnings. He slid onto the stool to the man's left, weathered the frown thus earned, and smiled.

"Hi. Remember me?"

The cabbie glared for a moment, then broke into a grin. "Yeah, sure. Need a ride someplace?"

"Not tonight. My car has a battery again." A tall thin waitress appeared, pad in hand. She looked from the cabbie to Whelan with mild surprise, as though taken aback that the cabbie would talk to anyone.

"Just coffee," Whelan said. "How's the perch?" he asked the driver.

"It's all right. Whaddya want for five bucks, right?"

"Absolutely. What's your name, by the way?"

"Frank."

"Frank, I'm Paul. Listen, I wanted to ask you something."

Frank cut a piece of fish with the edge of his fork but left it on the plate. "Go 'head," he said, but there was a wariness in the man's eyes that made Whelan hesitate for just a second. Then the cabbie brightened. "Wait, you mean like detective questions?"

"That's right."

He grinned. "Sure. What do you need?"

"You said you drive up Halsted on your way home a couple nights a week."

"Right. Sometimes more, sometimes three nights a week. Depends on this blow job I told you about from City Hall."

"Okay, first I need to know if you saw anybody or anything unusual last night before you picked me up."

"No…but I was only down there for the time it takes to drive through."

"I know. It's a long shot. I'm thinking of a light-skinned black man in glasses. Well-dressed guy, late-model Buick Park Avenue, blue?"

Frank shook his head. "No. I ain't seen any of *them* that I'd call well-dressed, you know what I mean?"

Whelan ignored the comment and sipped his coffee. He wanted to ask about Nate's bus but the bus wasn't really visible from the street. He thought of Buddy.

"What about street people?"

"The bums? They're everywhere. Yeah, I see bums down there. Who do you think goes down there?"

"There are all kinds of people there, friend. I'm talking about real street people, the kind that live in doorways."

The cabbie shrugged and put a piece of fish in his mouth. He chewed for a second and then spoke through the mouthful of food. "Yeah, sure, I seen them. Almost hit a couple of 'em the other night. Run right out in front of me."

"Ever see one in a gray sweatshirt? White man with black hair, sweatshirt with a hood?"

Frank grinned and pointed at Whelan with his fork. "Yeah, sure, *him* I almost fucking punched out. I'm stopped at that corner by the hot-dog place and I can't move 'cause I got a guy pushin' a grocery cart across the street, and this asshole in the sweatshirt comes up and tries to hit me up for a buck. A buck! Like I got money to give away. What am I workin' for anyway?"

His face was flushed and he was half turned on the stool facing Whelan. He was about to say something else when he seemed to rein himself back in.

He grinned. "I get all worked up when people that don't work try to put the arm on me for money. If they want money, let 'em work for it like me. That's all I'm sayin'."

Whelan nodded. "When was this?"

"I dunno. Last week sometime."

"Have you seen him since?"

"Him I see all the time. I think he goes behind that beef place there, right across from the tire place. They go through the garbage and get food, those guys. I seen him there."

"See him last night?"

"No. Last night I didn't see nobody but you." Frank sipped at his own coffee, then called for the waitress. "You wanna warm this up, hon?" He waited till the waitress poured fresh coffee and took another sip. Then he turned to Whelan. "Wanna go have a beer?"

"Not tonight. Maybe some other time."

"Okay."

Whelan walked Frank back to his cab, and when the cabbie got in Whelan leaned through the passenger's side window. Frank's license picture made him look like a cartoon character.

"Nice picture."

Frank snorted. "You shoulda seen my last one. Anything else I can do for you, Paul?"

"That about does it. But if you're back down that way, keep your eyes open for the guy in the sweatshirt. And try not to run him over. I need to talk to him."

"You want me to bring him to you?" He grinned.

"No, kidnapping is still a federal offense," Whelan said, handing him a card.

• • •

Whelan thought about taking in a movie but didn't want to mingle with all the happy couples in the world. Eventually, he settled for a burger and a couple of dark BBK's in the wondrous chattery company of Joe Danno at the Bucket o' Suds.

He drove home feeling more tired than he should have, and wondering what he had to do to get a woman in his life. In his darkened living room he had a bottle of Berghoff's dark and a final cigarette and forced himself to admit what he'd been denying all day.

Buddy Lenz is dead.

Later, in bed, he lay in the dark listening to a jazz station on his radio and to the insistent voice in the back of his consciousness that told him his problem was not that he hadn't found the right people but that he'd missed something.

FIFTEEN

DAY 9, SATURDAY

Saturday morning broke warm and sunny, an Indian summer day. Whelan put on one of his beloved *guayabera* shirts, promised himself Mexican food for lunch, and made himself breakfast. Over coffee and toast and a pear he listened with one ear to the radio while he retraced a week's steps. The little voice once again told him he'd missed something, something simple, something early on.

An hour later he parked in front of the video shop on Broadway. The first wave was already assembled at the corner for the Salvation Army's lunch, and he scanned the crowd for a moment. There were a few familiar faces, even one or two he'd talked to in different investigations, and he moved closer to see if there was anyone who might be able to tell him something. A shapeless row of black and white faces, mostly men, a few women, a handful of small children, stared back at him till he was forced to turn away.

He was almost at the door to Sam Burwell's building when he spotted a familiar figure. Violet Haley waddled across the middle of Broadway clutching her purse and a small bag of groceries to her chest. In spite of the warmth of the day she wore a coat and had wrapped a woolen scarf around her head. She looked ready for the Yukon. Her slow progress across the street earned her a long blast on the horn from a truck driver, and Whelan heard someone in the line at the corner hoot as she tried to move out of the way of a station wagon doing forty up the street.

Mrs. Haley cast nervous glances at the various groups of men up and down her block, her gaze resting for a moment on the men outside the used tire place. She was almost at her door before she noticed Whelan. She came to a stop and opened her mouth. Whelan saw her eyes flit about as if she were looking for an escape hatch.

"Mrs. Haley? I want to talk to you."

Her eyes narrowed and she finally summoned up enough anger to look less frightened. "I got all kindsa work to do. I got no time to—"

"You said if I needed more information, I could come by again. It's worth money to me."

The promise of cash caught her in mid-protest. She moved closer to him, still clutching her purse. A Flash cab and a guy in a beater were engaged in a horn duel on Broadway. The noise seemed to frighten her, and she shot a worried glance at the two motorists. Then she looked at Whelan.

"I guess I got a couple minutes. I don't know what else I could tell you…" She stole a worried look toward the street.

"Can you tell me whether the apartment has been rented? The one you let me look at?"

She peered at him a moment through her glasses, then nodded. "I had that place rented, then the guy found someplace else. The owner's mad about it. Like it's my fault."

Shaking her head, she walked toward her building. She inclined her head toward the door.

"C'mon. You can look at it now. You wanted to see it now, right?"

"If it's no trouble, yeah. Thanks."

"Didn't say it was no trouble," she grumbled.

Once inside, Mrs. Haley made him wait a moment while she put her groceries away and took off her coat and scarf. He could hear her banging around in the kitchen and muttering to herself, obviously irritated. When she appeared, she was in the ratty smoke-smelling housecoat she'd worn the first time. Her hair hung down over her forehead and a cigarette had sprouted from the center of her mouth.

"C'mon," she said, and marched down the hall, leaving smoke.

The apartment at the end of the hall looked exactly as it had during Whelan's first visit. With Mrs. Haley standing in the doorway and squinting at him through her smoke, he made a quick inspection of each of the place's little rooms, looking in the cabinets and the refrigerator.

In the bathroom he paused for a moment and studied his own face in the mirror. The face was frowning. He was surprised to see that the face looked fatigued, a little sunburnt, a face in need of a change. He looked away for a moment, gazing at the empty shelves above the toilet. Then he saw the kit.

On the floor beside the little shower lay a man's toilet kit, a leather case with a zippered top. This one had cost money once but was getting on in years, with the dark brown finish of the leather worn through at corners and edges. It was closed, zippered tightly.

He bent down and opened it. Inside he found the usual jumble of old razors and Band-Aids and cough drops. There was a tightly rolled tube of antiseptic and a couple of the kind of toothpaste tube that comes in the mail as a sample. That was it. No stunning clues, no notes, no names scrawled on matchbooks, nothing—except for the fact that the kit hadn't been in the room on his first visit. He went out to see Mrs. Haley.

"How many times would you say you've been in here since you showed me the place?"

"I had to clean up. He left food in the fridge. I left all his stuff here, though. I ain't touched none of his stuff. I ain't no thief."

He shook his head. "I didn't think you were. Nothing's missing, as far as I can see."

She frowned. "What's wrong then?"

He thought for a moment. "Nothing, actually." Nothing you'd be able to understand, he thought. "Let me ask you a couple of things."

"Okay," she said but looked unhappy.

"Has anyone but you been in the room since I was

here last?"

"The tenant. I mean, the guy that was almost gonna take it."

"What did he look like?"

"He was a Filipino. Name was Santos. They got Filipinos up here now. Got everything, like the United Nations."

"You're right. But what did he look like?"

She gave him a puzzled look. "Like a Filipino. He was short and kinda chubby and he had black hair and he talked funny. They talk funny."

"I guess so. He's the only one who's been in here?"

"That's it."

"Last time I was here, we were talking about visitors the dead man might have had."

"I remember. We talked about that one that came to see him." Violet Haley's lip curled at the memory, her delicate sensibilities offended once more.

"What about men?"

"Who, me?"

"No, no. I'm sure you—" Dance faster, Whelan. "Your life is your business. I was asking if the dead man, Mr. Burwell, had any male visitors that you could recollect. Maybe you've remembered something since we talked. Did a man come to see him, a young man, maybe? A young black man?"

She gave him a blank look and shook her head.

"The police officers who were here to ask you questions—what did they look like?"

She held up two fingers. "Big one with blond hair, kinda young, and a little one, skinny, dark hair, kinda red face. I could smell liquor on that one. The big one, he asked all the questions."

"What did the other one do?"

"He just looked around, like he was bored."

"All right, Mrs. Haley. Here." He handed her ten bucks.

The cigarette came out of her mouth and she smiled as she palmed the bill. "I tol' ya last time to call me Vi."

"You did. I forgot. Well, thanks, Vi. I really appreciate it. And if you hear anything else, call me at this number." He handed her a card.

He walked down the stairs. Halfway down he turned to look at her. She held up his card and grinned at him.

The line outside the Sal Army office now stretched around the corner onto Sunnyside. Whelan walked to his car, got in, and sat there for a moment. Like his first visit, this one had served only to confuse him. He still couldn't put a name to the black woman who had visited Sam Burwell, and now it was obvious that someone had slipped into Burwell's apartment to drop off his kit. Why? With nothing in it to give even the identity of the owner, the kit itself was harmless.

He started his car, listened to his engine groan for a moment and thought about the bored Mark Durkin.

Sure you were bored, Durkin. You had the case made already.

Whelan thought about that for a moment. The real question was *why* Durkin thought he had the case made already.

He parked on Ashland in front of a burned-out liquor store, took a long look at the bunch of kids watching him from an alley and crossed the street. Half a mile away he could see the Stadium, and there was almost nothing to obscure the view but four blocks of vacant lots and liquor stores. There was a chapel on one end of the block, and a liquor store across Madison in the other direction, and set back a little from the street was the building Whelan was looking for. Covington's new landlord was the City of Chicago, and the median age of his new neighbors was probably close to seventy, for this was Senior Citizen Housing.

A security man on the ground floor halted Whelan's progress and a woman at the gray desk made a call to see if Mr. Covington was accepting visitors. She gave a short nod, put down the phone, and told Whelan he could go up.

"Ninth floor, apartment nine-oh-five," she said, and when he looked back at her from the elevator she was still watching him.

On Covington's floor the hall was hot, the air thick with the odors of frying lard and cigarettes and the acrid smell from the incinerator. At the door to 905 he knocked, and a deep hoarse voice said "All right," and Whelan then waited for almost a minute for the door to open. From within the apartment he could hear shuffling sounds and a scraping noise he couldn't quite place, and then the door opened and Whelan saw that he had reached another dead end.

George Covington was a big man in a blue flannel shirt and glasses. He was in his sixties, going bald on top. The man's face was deeply lined and his eyes were red-rimmed, made huge by the dense lenses of his glasses, and Whelan now understood the scraping sound, for Covington leaned his great bulk on a metal walker. He struggled to get out of the way of the door and nodded at Whelan.

"Mr. Covington? My name is Paul Whelan. I'm a detective working on…a case, and I wonder if I could ask you a few questions."

"Detective." Covington wrestled with this for a moment and seemed to weigh it against the opportunity for a little company. No contest. "All right," he said, backing slowly out of the way and motioning with a jerk of his big head for Whelan to come in. "You can sit over there in that chair," he said, looking at a lumpy armchair near the window, and Whelan crossed the room and planted himself in it.

Covington moved slowly back to his own chair, across a little side table from Whelan, put the walker to one side and dropped his large frame into the chair with a grunt. He peered into a cup, took a sip, and looked at Whelan. "You want some coffee? I can make you some coffee."

"No, sir, I've been drinking it all day."

"I like coffee. I can drink coffee all day. Used to be able to drink something else all day," he said, and chuckled. His voice suited him perfectly, deep and dry and beginning to show cracks.

"We all have to slow down eventually," Whelan said.

"Well, I'm gonna make me some more." He watched as the old man hauled his big frame out of the chair, could actually hear the cracking of the man's joints. Covington stood, wavered a bit before steadying himself on the arm of his chair, then grabbed his walker and crossed the small room to his kitchenette. Whelan could see the rest of the room now: on the floor just barely showing from behind the old man's chair was what appeared to be a small portable oxygen tank.

Whelan sighed. He could hear the old man's raspy breathing from across the room. "Talked me into it," he said.

"What's that?"

"I'll have some coffee too."

"Good," Covington said, smiling.

It was instant, mixed weak to make the jar go further. Whelan nursed his and shared a smoke with Covington and asked a few perfunctory questions about Sam Burwell. For his trouble he learned that Covington hadn't heard that Burwell was dead, hadn't seen him in ten years, if not twenty. Whelan knew he'd wasted his time coming here and something else as well. Without realizing it, he'd been counting on tying things together when he found Covington. He sipped at the bad coffee and allowed the old man to ramble for a few minutes about the old days. Covington allowed as he had made a few mistakes in his youth. When Whelan finished his coffee, he left the rest of his smokes, tossed in ten bucks for the old man's trouble and left.

He pulled up in front of the church at a little before seven, parked, and then sat in his car listening to the radio. The disk jockey had dug up an old Ramsey Lewis number called "Le Fleur." Dozens of people were entering the church hall, pausing to have animated conversations before they went in, calling to one another from across the street, holding up the food they'd brought. Whelan told himself he was watching the crowd, but he knew he was sitting there because he was an outsider and didn't want to go in till the last possible moment.

When he saw several of the people casting puzzled looks in his direction, he decided to get it over with. He crossed the street and went inside. At the door a young man blinked in mild surprise. Whelan said "hello," and the young man nodded and then said, "The donation is five dollars, sir. All you can eat."

"I feel like I'm stealing."

St. Anna's had a new school and hall to go with its museum-piece rectory, and at the moment the hall was flooded with light and music and people. At the far end, a long paper sign proclaimed the event to be A TASTE OF THE WEST SIDE, and just below it, a young man in a luminous lavender suit was playing deejay, and a couple of young schoolgirls were already dancing with each other. A few feet away, a couple of boys approximately the same age as the girls went through an impressive array of dance moves for an audience largely made up of other boys. Whelan wondered at what point the boys would deign to notice the girls.

He was intensely conscious, not of his color but of his intrusive presence in a private celebration. Not that he hadn't dressed for the occasion: he wore a new pair of tan slacks and a dark red long-sleeved sport shirt, and he'd made the gesture of polishing his old oxblood shoes.

Whelan walked the length of the hall, noting the many faces that turned his way, polite faces and some of them outright friendly, taking him perhaps for a friend of Father's, but all of them curious at the presence of this unknown white man. He realized he'd been hoping to see someone else there who was not a parishioner—a white cop maybe, or a firefighter, or the guy that ran the local Chinese restaurant. And he felt foolish for the thought.

If there was an overriding feature of that hall it was its smell: it was dominated by the aroma of food and by women's smells, a wondrous mix of perfume and cologne and powder, of clothing taken from cedar chests and, in the cases of a few of the older women, mothballs. He looked around for Father Brennan but didn't see him. He didn't see Perry Willis either. It was just as well: too early to spoil the evening. He scanned the crowd carefully for a moment and then his nose went to work: he sniffed at the air and began walking toward what would be the kitchen of the hall. He took a few more paces and then stopped.

At first glance it appeared to be a solid wall of food. When he was able to calm himself, he saw that he was standing before a row of tables laden near to breaking. Behind these tables were more like them, and behind these and at a slightly higher level were the windows of the hall kitchen, themselves stacked with Saran-wrapped pots and steaming bowls. His nostrils were overmatched. He'd expected a couple of nice tables of soul food and a few All-American standards, ribs and greens and maybe a ham and the usual church-supper array of potato salads and macaroni salads and cole slaw. He was thus unprepared for the splendors now encountered.

Hams there were, and several different recipes for greens, but there were dozens of other items as well, including catfish and three kinds of sausage and four different versions of Swedish meatballs. There was a smoked turkey the size of a German shepherd, and a sliced pork tenderloin, slabs of ribs cut into three-rib pieces for individual portions, and rib tips and short ribs of beef and the nasty little peppered sausages known as hot links. A few feet away to the left he found the dessert table, the sin of gluttony taking earthly form in the guise of sweet potato pies, pecan pies, angel food cakes, chocolate layer cakes, peach tarts, and apple cobbler.

He knew he was staring but was powerless to show his hard-earned manners.

"I died. I died and went to heaven," he said, and heard someone laugh. He turned and saw a young woman with a Tupperware bowl shaking her head at him. She set the bowl down on the table and looked at an older woman behind the table.

"Sound like this is one hungry man here."

"Better feed him before he dies on us."

They snickered and Whelan grinned at them. "My mother told me never to be the first one at a party to eat, but I notice nobody else is ready."

"Oh, they ready, honey," the older woman said. "They just waiting for Mrs. Simmons. Mrs. Simmons says eat, they'll eat."

"I can't wait."

He felt a hand on his shoulder and turned to see Father Brennan grinning at him. "Well, you took us up on our invitation and now you're meeting all the women."

"You throw a mean party, Father."

He cast a proprietal look around the hall and nodded slowly. "We sure do."

"I'm impressed."

The priest looked at him. "With what?"

"Your parishioners. They know how to enjoy themselves."

Father Brennan studied him for a moment. "They're poor, Mr. Whelan, they're not dead." He waved to a woman at the far end of the hall, exchanged wisecracks with the people beginning to belly up to the tables, then looked at Whelan. "Perry's here. He just came in. You want me to bring him over?"

"Did you already ask him to talk to me?"

"Yeah, but only because I don't think he's done anything wrong."

"If it makes you feel better, I don't either. But I think he might know something, and I'm running out of places to look."

"You could give it up," the priest said in friendly malice.

"I don't do that. Once I'm in, I stay in till it's over."

The priest smiled. "I'll bring Perry over."

"No. Enjoy your party. I'll find him myself in a few minutes."

"Well, good luck."

"I could use some." Whelan watched the priest join a group of his parishioners.

He had no trouble locating Perry Willis. Dark and intense, Perry stood along a wall by himself and sipped at a cup of coffee. They picked each other up at almost the same moment, and Whelan felt almost drawn over by Perry's close-set eyes.

"Mr. Willis." Whelan nodded.

Perry nodded, drank his coffee, and looked out at the room over the rim of the cup. He gave a short wave to someone at the door, then let his gaze return to Whelan. "You wanted to talk to me?"

"Yeah. Without the attitude and the sucker punch this time."

Perry looked down into his cup and made a halfhearted shrug, but Whelan could tell he was embarrassed. He waited for Perry to speak.

The young man looked around the room and shook his

head. "Father Mike, he said you think I'm some kinda crazy gang-banger."

"Not really. You seem to be wired a little tight, but under the circumstances—"

"I apologize. Sorry about that shit, man. I ain't popped nobody since I was in school. I felt bad about my poppa, I felt real bad, and I needed to hit somebody. And I didn't know nothing about you. You were just some white dude come around looking for him, and next thing he's dead."

"I was trying to find him. I never actually laid eyes on him. I think he was already dead when I started looking for him."

Perry nodded, looked down into the cup as though for answers, then squinted at Whelan. "What were you looking for him for? He owe somebody some bread?"

"No. I was hired to find him by a lawyer. He said a relative of your father's was trying to get in touch with him."

"That's what you said that time. On the phone." His voice seemed to lose a little steam at the admission about the phone call.

"And that just made you more suspicious. Because there *was* no other relative."

Perry gave him a frank look. "Right. Wasn't nobody else left, so I knew there was some weird shit going down, and my father was in the middle. Wasn't nothing new about that, but didn't mean I had to like it. So who's this lawyer?"

Whelan hesitated and Perry made an exasperated little hissing sound. "You gonna whip that lawyer-privacy thing on me?"

"No. I guess not. I'm not working for him now, I'm working for O.C. Brown. The lawyer's nothing to me. His name's Hill and he's got an office on the North Side. I can give you his phone number if you want it. But he still maintains that he's working for a family member that wanted to get in touch with your father."

The young man was shaking his head before Whelan could finish. "Wasn't nobody else. Just him and me. He had a brother in Georgia that passed when I was a little boy, and his sister, my aunt, she passed about five years back. That's all he had, man, except for me." He stared down at his shoes for several moments, and when he looked up his eyes were starting to moisten at the corners. "So what you want to know? O.C. and me, we had a talk. He says you're all right, and you know O.C. and my father were tight. So what you want to know?"

"Let's get the hard stuff out of the way first. Did you and your father have trouble?"

"Yeah, we did. Hard to be patient with a drinker, man. And he was a drinker. He come to me for money a lot of times and I give it to him, but I'm telling you he like to wore me out with it. My wife and I, we're trying to put the bread together for a house. So my father and me, we had some words. He give me some shit a couple times when he had drink in him, and I had to walk, man, 'cause I was afraid I'd smack him upside his head."

He stopped and looked at Whelan.

"Why you want to know how we got along? You think I hurt him?"

Whelan looked at him for a moment and knew the answer. He shook his head. "No, I don't figure you for a killer. But there's somebody out there who is, and he's still out there."

"What about those little-shit gang-bangers?"

"That's all they are. I think this was something different."

"What do you mean?"

"I'm not sure. I've learned that someone was looking for your father about a year ago, and he saw somebody following him in a car."

Perry nodded. "He told me that. Told me about all of it. But the dude in the car wasn't the one askin' about him. The one in the car was a brother, the other one was a white man."

"They could have been working together. How much did you know about his life? I mean his private life."

Perry shrugged. "He had him a crib on the North Side. He was makin' a little bread doing drywall and stuff like that for a dude out south beginning of the summer, but that was finished. Lately, he was just sellin' his stuff down there at Jewtown." Then he surprised Whelan with a smile. It was a broad boyish smile that made Perry seem little more than a teenager. "Had him a lady up north, too."

Whelan smiled. "God bless 'em both. What do you know about the woman?"

"I know she was white. He was kinda funny about telling me, behind that. Thought I wouldn't like him stayin' with a white woman, but I was glad for him. I don't get into that shit." He shot Whelan an embarrassed look. "Probably don't seem like that to you, but it's true. I don't have no problem with anybody."

"Do you know her name?"

"Tess. Called her Tess."

Whelan stared at him for a moment. "I heard her name was Mary."

"No, I never heard him say anything about any Mary."

"Ever hear him talk about another woman in his life, a woman named Mattie?"

"Sure, man, he used to see Mattie, but that wasn't no big thing. Mattie kind of religious."

"How about somebody from the old days. A woman named Mamie?"

"Never heard him talk about her, either. Seem to me, you know a lot about my poppa."

"For the past week I've done nothing but ask people about him. You get to enough people, you can learn things about somebody his family doesn't even know."

"You're pretty good at it, huh?"

"I know people who are better. But nobody as stubborn."

"You got that right," Perry said with a half smile.

"The people who were following him—did he ever put a name to them? Ever give you an idea who they were?"

"No. I don't think he knew."

"The last time you talked to him—can I ask about that?"

"It's cool. We didn't have any trouble the last time."

"How did he seem?"

"He was straight. And he was feelin' good."

"He didn't seem to have anything on his mind?"

"No. Everything was cool. It was a Friday. He come up for

dinner, and my wife made pork chops for him. I had a couple beers in the house for him, too. When he left, I give him forty bucks. It was payday."

Perry had to look away, and Whelan decided he'd asked all his questions.

When the young man met his eyes again, he seemed composed. "Not much help, was I?"

Whelan thought for a moment. "You gave me the woman's name."

"You said you had another name for her."

"Yeah, but I already knew it wasn't the real one. I just wish I knew why."

"You think you're gonna find out who did this?"

"Yeah, I do. It may take awhile, but…yeah, I'll find out. Thanks, Perry."

"Wasn't anything, man," Perry said, and they shook hands. "And I'm sorry about—that other thing."

"It's all right."

Whelan waited till the other man was several feet away and about to speak to some friends.

"Hey, Perry? Something I wanted to say the other night and I didn't get a chance. I'm sorry about your father."

Perry nodded and smiled.

"All right, y'all. Time to dine!"

The speaker was a heavyset woman of average height with a voice like the horn on a freighter and the bearing of a field marshal. Whelan figured this had to be Mrs. Simmons.

"Come on, get in line, let's eat." She took a slender boy by his shoulders and forced him into line. "Come on, baby, don't let these men keep you away from the food. You need to be putting some meat on those little bones." She spied a woman joining the line at the other end. "You finished already, honey? 'Cause that's the *part* of the line you're at."

A chorus of laughter forced the other woman to move to the other end of what was becoming a long line. Mrs. Simmons stood her ground, directing traffic and keeping order where chaos wished to take hold. Whelan watched her: men ruled the world only because women like this let them think they were in charge.

"How'd it go?"

He turned to see Father Brennan. "Not bad."

"Did it help any?"

Whelan thought for a moment. "Yeah, but I'm still not sure how. He gave me one piece I didn't have before: I just don't know where it fits."

"He's a good guy."

"Just doesn't want anybody to know it. But you're right."

"What are you going to do next?"

"I was thinking about eating."

The priest put a hand on his shoulder. "Better get in line, brother, and don't do anything to get Mrs. Simmons mad at you."

"And risk public humiliation? I'm not that stupid."

The priest walked away and Whelan stood near the food tables waiting for the line to wear itself out. Hundreds of people moved by and didn't seem to be making a dent in the incredible spread.

He filled his plate and found a seat at the far end of an empty table. Three elderly ladies took over the other end. They sat down, acknowledged him with polite nods, then noticed the steaming pile of food threatening to overrun the boundaries of his groaning plate. He squirmed. "I know," he said, "but the guy ahead of me had even more on his plate."

The oldest of the women peered at him from over half-glasses. "Young man, can you really eat all that?"

"If I can't, I'll die trying."

When he was finished with his little mountain of food and had made two runs at the dessert table, he had a smoke and a cup of coffee. Then he stopped by to thank Father Brennan again and left. The air had a bite to it, and he drove with the window down. He punched radio buttons and came up with Jimmy Smith, and cranked it up. At a stoplight on Roosevelt Road, a dignified black couple in a big Buick did a slow double-take at him, a white man and his moribund car in the middle of a black neighborhood.

It was still early, so he drove up Roosevelt to Halsted and made one slow circuit of Maxwell Street. The shops were all hiding behind their folding steel gates and the back lots were empty, but clusters of men stood on corners huddled over trash-can fires and a few slumming carousers lined up at Jim's for a late-night snack between taverns. He drove the back lots looking for Buddy and keeping his eye on the rearview mirror.

On his way home he thought about what little he'd learned: about the woman named Tess. Something told him that was her real name, that Sam Burwell had used her real name with his son. What Whelan had to figure out was why Burwell had needed to lie about her name to begin with. There was at least the chance that there had never been any "Mary," no white woman in Uptown who waited tables, that Sam Burwell was one of those lonely men who invent women for themselves.

He swung by the cab stand at Lincoln and Halsted, but Frank the cabdriver was long gone. Eventually Whelan admitted he had no real excuse to stay out. He went home and had a beer and watched half of an old Errol Flynn movie. In this one, Flynn, Tasmanian accent and all, was ridding San Antonio of riffraff. He got off good lines, romanced Alexis Smith, shot a hired gun, and brought justice to the city of the Alamo. Where was Errol when you needed him?

SIXTEEN

DAY 10, SUNDAY

On Sunday morning Whelan was already awake when the alarm went off at seven-thirty, and by eight he had showered and made a cup of coffee. He was blowing on the coffee to cool it off and half listening to the radio when he heard the news: another body had been found Saturday afternoon down on what the young woman newscaster called "the city's old Maxwell Street Market." The victim was described as a white male in his late forties or fifties, identified as Buddy Lenz, a homeless person known to frequent the area. The newscaster mentioned that this was the third body found in the area in a week.

Indian summer had gone south as quickly as it had shown up. Whelan could see his breath in the early morning air, and the Jet coughed and hacked and died when he tried to start it. Eventually it came to life, and though the heater was long since dead, it was slightly warmer inside the car.

He parked in the dusty lot behind the Maxwell Street Station and trudged east. It was nine-thirty and the side streets and back lots were jammed with vendors and bargain hunters and gawkers and kibitzers. Across the lots on Fourteenth the Mexican food vendors were already setting up shop, and the smell of corn tortillas mingled with the wood smoke and the ever-present odors of grilling onions.

He picked and shouldered his way through the crowd, stopping to watch a young man in jeans haggling with an old vendor over a china bowl. The young man turned the bowl repeatedly in his hands, quoting prices and not looking at the old man, and Whelan made him for a picker, the kind that sell to the big dealers. Eventually the old man said something and the young one finally looked at him and nodded. Money changed hands, the old one grinned and tucked it away in his pants, and the young one moved on toward Halsted with the bowl, peering at every table he passed.

Finally Whelan saw it. Over where the crowd thinned out near the viaducts, a group of small boys and several men were standing around a small square of weed-strewn vacant lot. He could make out the yellow tape of the police line.

They'd long since moved the body, and the early morning wind was making short work of the yellow tape. It was down on one side and beginning to work loose from a tree around which it had been wrapped. The loose end made a sharp flicking sound in the wind. Whelan could see no blood.

A few yards away, a squad car was parked at the entrance to the viaduct. Two uniformed cops stood outside, one leaning against the driver's side door. He didn't think either of them had been at the scene when Nate's body had been found. He stood there for a moment and lit up a cigarette, then walked over to the squad car. "Did you find the body?"

The cop leaning against the door gave him a long look and said nothing. He was gray-haired, with shrewd blue eyes and rosy cheeks.

The other cop took a step forward. "A citizen found the body, sir. Why?" He was younger, looked young enough to be in the Academy. He kept one hand on his belt as he spoke, reminding Whelan of Jack Palance's gunfighter character in *Shane:* a young cop striving mightily to cultivate a bad attitude and a hard-guy walk.

"I knew him."

"How'd you know him, guy?" the older cop asked.

Whelan shrugged. "I been coming down here for years. I buy produce over here." He nodded in the direction of the Mexican vendors on Fourteenth Street. "And this is where I buy, you know, all my light bulbs and batteries and stuff like that. I know a lot of these guys."

The older cop nodded and watched him.

"How was he killed?"

"Like the others," the older cop said, and tilted his head to watch Whelan's reaction to the lie. Doing a little fishing of his own.

Whelan squinted and shook his head. "There were others?"

The older cop pulled himself off the car door and reached in through the car window for his smokes. He shook one out and lit it up. "Yeah, there were others. But they weren't killed the same way. You don't know about them?"

"I'm only down here on Sundays."

"An old picker was shot couple weeks ago by a bunch of kids. And a guy that lived in a bus over there on Halsted, somebody strangled him. Friday, this was. This guy, somebody stabbed."

"Three guys in a couple weeks. Seems like a lot to me. I always felt pretty safe down here." The cop said nothing. Whelan looked again at the little plot of ground. "They cleaned it up, huh?"

"Wasn't much to clean up."

"I thought people bleed a lot when they get stabbed."

The older cop squinted at him and shook his head. "Not always."

Right, Whelan thought. They don't bleed where the body is dumped, just where it happens.

"Thanks," Whelan said, and walked away. He was careful not to look back.

He couldn't say it had come as a surprise, but now that he had seen the spot where they'd found Buddy Lenz, he felt worse. At the corner of Fourteenth Place and Morgan he stopped to light a cigarette. A traffic jam had formed between Morgan and Peoria, as cars attempted to move through the crush of people. A green station wagon bumped a pair of young Latino men and one of them pounded his fist on the hood. He and his companion glared at the driver, an elderly black man who just stared straight ahead.

Whelan puffed at his cigarette and totaled it all up for himself. Three men were dead and the killer was still out there, and the killer knew *him*. And who he talked to.

He tailed me, he took my car out, he watches me. I've talked to him, Whelan thought. I've talked to him. Time to finish this.

He took a final puff from the smoke and tossed the butt in a muddy puddle along the worn curb, then walked over to Thirteenth.

The dog with the holes in his coat was still there, as was the bear. The dog looked the same but the bear was showing the rigors of his work: stuffing was about to burst out of his stomach, and the dog had gnawed and worried at the ears till they were just ragged stumps. The old man was there too, ignoring the dog and watching for customers. He smiled and nodded when he saw Whelan.

"Hello, Jesse. How's business?"

"Pretty fair, pretty fair. Did me some good early. Sold a set of dishes, six-piece setting. Got a good price for it."

"I'm glad you're doing okay. It's getting to be a dangerous place to make a living."

Jesse squinted up at him. "You know about old Sam, then?"

"Yeah. And the others."

The old man nodded and looked down at his makeshift table. "That fella, that Buddy? I bought a few things from him. Wasn't bad, as a picker. Just a little—" and he tapped one finger at his temple.

Whelan nodded.

"Didn't know the old man in the bus, though. We didn't speak. He didn't speak to nobody I know of, 'cept maybe to the men there in that tire place." He rearranged a few items on his table and shook his head. "This always been a good place. All kinds of people come here and mix, and there's no trouble. Never been any trouble like this."

"It's gonna be over soon."

The old man gave him a sharp look. "How you know that, son?"

"A hunch. Just a hunch. See you around."

"Go easy, young man."

The pot-bellied knife vendor's spot was empty but the

blond sisters were there.

Whelan stood a few feet away from the sisters and watched them. They were in the middle of a sale and it was an education. A man was interested in a pocket watch, and as he dickered with the women over the price, they took turns commenting on his offers or on the qualities of the watch. They stood at opposite ends of the long table and forced the man to turn his head from side to side in order to address them. It soon became apparent that they were wearing him out. Then the negotiations ended and the man stared at the watch for a long time. Finally he said something and the woman closer to him, the younger one, shrugged. In the background, the older one nodded and the sisters let their eyes meet for a second. The man handed money to the younger one and she jammed it into a pocket of her windbreaker.

Whelan waited till the man had left with his watch before he approached. "Morning."

The older one nodded and smiled, but he could tell the younger one remembered him immediately. She said nothing.

"I was here last week and we spoke about a fellow who used to set up a few feet from here. Sam Burwell." The woman nodded slowly, still refusing to say anything. Whelan looked over at the older one and saw that she was as nervous as she'd been last week.

"I found out later that he died. Killed during a robbery, they told me." The two women both folded their arms and looked down, unaware that they'd adopted identical poses. "Now, you didn't know him, as I recall."

The younger one met his eyes briefly. "Right. We didn't know him."

Whelan nodded and looked around at the activity of the street. Then he caught the woman's eye and smiled. "Then can you tell me why you went to his funeral?"

The older one took a step back and the young one's eyes widened.

"We don't want no trouble, mister. We don't cause no trouble for nobody," the older one said. Whelan caught just the faintest hint of an accent: German, maybe Yiddish.

"But you did know him."

"Yeah, we knew him. So what?" The younger one had regained her footing and her moxie, and she wasn't about to be pushed into a corner.

"So you didn't tell me the truth when I was looking for this man, and now he's dead. And I'm real suspicious about everybody who lied to me because I think one of the people who lied to me killed him."

The woman's eyes grew enormous, and he heard a sharp intake of breath from her sister. "They said some kids did it. A robbery, like you said."

"I don't think so. I don't think it had anything to do with kids or robbery or anything else that the cops say. I think somebody down here killed him, and those other two men as well."

"You can't think we had anything to do with it."

"Yeah, I can. Women can kill."

The older one came forward. "We wouldn't have done nothing to him. He was a real nice man."

"So you did know him. And you went to his funeral."

The young one shrugged. "Like Minna said. He was real nice."

"If he was so nice, how come you can't help me find out what happened to him? Doesn't it matter to you?"

"Mister, we're scared to death now." Minna, the older sister, took a couple of steps forward.

"I need to know if you saw him talking with anybody unusual or if you saw anything at all that struck you as odd."

The younger one sighed. "We saw him talking to that white fella they found."

"Buddy."

"Yeah. That man came to see him a lot. Sometimes he had stuff to sell, but I think mostly he came by to borrow money."

"Anybody else?"

She shook her head.

"How about anybody that seemed to be hanging around here, maybe watching him?"

The woman gave him a wary look. "A man in a car."

"What kind of car?"

"I don't know. Dark, black or brown."

"A well-dressed young black man, maybe?"

She frowned. "No. I don't think so. I couldn't see him good but I don't think it was a colored man."

Whelan waited and, when it was clear that nothing else was coming, said, "He had a woman. A lady friend. If I could find her, I think I might be able to get somewhere. Did you ever see him with a woman?"

The younger one looked down and pursed her lips, but the older one let her eyes go big with suppressed excitement. She was watching her sister, and Whelan would have sworn there was mirth in her eyes.

"What do you want to tell me, Minna?"

She couldn't take her eyes from her sister. She nodded. "Helena went out with him a couple times."

Helena wheeled quickly. "That was nothin'. I wasn't his girlfriend. It was just some drinks." She swung her head back toward Whelan. "It was nothing."

"You went with him for a couple of drinks."

"That's all it was." She glared at Minna and Whelan saw her clench and unclench her fists. "All it was. A couple of drinks. He was a nice man and that was all there was to it."

"Well, thank you for your time, ladies. You've been very helpful." The sisters were still glaring at each other when he looked back. He took a long look at the woman called Helena.

He parked in front of the Blue Note and ignored the sullen glances of a trio of teenagers on the corner. When he pushed open the door, a rush of old tavern odors assaulted him. He could smell the cleaning compound and the fresh soap in the glassware sinks, but it would take days to cut the tobacco smoke from a busy Saturday night. It took a moment for his eyes to adjust to the darkness, but he was aware of the faces along the bar that turned to stare at him.

O.C. was behind the bar. "Hey, Whelan. You come down to visit with the folk in the hood?"

"Yeah. I need company. Isn't it a little early to be open on a Sunday? Or is there a new law that says you can start pouring as soon as the sun comes up?"

O.C. laughed. "Just coffee and orange juice till noon. Don't want to break no laws." He looked at his customers and indicated Whelan with a nod of his head. "Whelan here used to be the police. Now he's reformed." There was a chuckle from one of the old men at the bar, and Whelan took a stool near the front.

O.C. came down the bar. "Coffee?"

"Sure."

"You might not like it this time, Whelan. I just made it."

"Well, it's certainly not what I'm used to here."

O.C. poured him a mug of coffee and leaned against the bar, watching him drink it. "What brings you out today? I know you come to talk. Got that look in your eye."

"Buddy Lenz is dead."

O.C. nodded slowly. "Poor old Buddy. What happened to him?"

"Somebody killed him. They found his body yesterday."

O.C. watched him.

"And I think he was killed—"

"Because he knew something," O.C. finished.

"No. Because somebody thought he might know something. Maybe because somebody knew he talked to me."

"Not your fault, Whelan."

"Maybe not, but it doesn't feel good, all the same."

The older man watched him for a while. "You got anything?"

"Not sure. I feel like I'm close, real close. Close enough to be in a little trouble but..." He let the rest of it go.

One of the men down the bar called O.C., and the tavern keeper sidled back up his bar to pull a beer from the cooler. He smiled over at Whelan.

"Twelve o'clock yet, Whelan?"

Whelan consulted the bar clock. It said eleven-fifteen. "Twelve o'clock exactly." He watched as O.C. opened the beer, set it on a coaster, and slid a couple of quarters from the man's pile of change. O.C. tossed the change into the open register.

The tavern keeper came back down the bar and watched Whelan for a moment. "What kinda trouble?"

Whelan shrugged. "I'm close, and that brings you close to trouble."

O.C. nodded and then made a visible effort to cheer him up with a change of subject. "We got us an argument goin' here. Talkin' about old-time musicians. Horn players. My man Curtis here, he think this boy he used to run with was better than a fella used to play for Basie, and I'm tryin' to educate him. We had plenty of trombone players around here better than your boy, Curtis."

"Naw." The man frowned at his change.

O.C. walked over and put his face a few inches from his customer's. "I know about horn players. Curtis here, he always want to argue with me about horn players. Curtis, my man, we had half a dozen trombone men around *here* just as good as that boy Henry Green."

"Name one."

"Floyd Garnet. Red Willis. Pete McCoy. Frank Rickert, maybe. Had that quartet played on South State. Remember him?"

Whelan was smiling and watching the debate, and then suddenly he wasn't hearing a word of it. His heart began to pound and he wondered if he looked as stunned as he felt. To calm himself he took another sip of his coffee, then looked at O.C. He'd heard these names before, but now they meant something.

"What was the name of that last trombone man, O.C.?"

"Frank Rickert. White fella. Little crazy like most of them back then, but he was good."

Whelan forced himself to take another drink of his coffee. "You mentioned those men once before, when you were talking about Buddy Lenz."

"Right. All those boys from the old days."

"This man Rickert—was he the one involved with that young girl, the one Sam had been seeing?"

O.C. nodded and was about to say something when he

noticed Whelan's face. He waited a moment and then said, "Yeah, that was Frank Rickert. Why?"

Whelan cursed himself for not noticing the name when he'd run across it again. I should have caught it, he told himself. I should have picked up on it.

Now, standing in a little bar on the West Side, he was seeing the name clearly in his mind's eye, a name beside a ridiculous photograph that made its subject look cartoonish, the name on a cab license.

O.C. moved closer. "Something wrong, Whelan?"

"Depends on your point of view." Whelan was silent for a moment. "He was the one with the girl. The young white girl that had been seeing Sam."

O.C. nodded and watched Whelan.

Images and possibilities washed over him, and one seemed to fit better than all the others. It was a long shot but it pushed its way in and the others cleared out. He held this one and examined it from every angle, and now he understood about the name. They would have recognized her name, all of them.

"And when you heard that the girl died—who told you? Rickert?"

"Naw, that girl's family made things pretty hot for him. He left town." O.C. pulled at his lip and shook his head. "I'm pretty sure Sam told me."

Whelan nodded. O.C. studied him for a moment and then asked, "You think this is all about—that?"

"Yeah, I do."

O.C. looked around his bar and then at his customers and shook his head. "All these years. All these years, and I can't even remember that girl's name. Irish girl, Mc-something. McCann, maybe, but I can't even think of her first name."

Whelan looked at him. "How about Tess?"

"That's it! It was Teresa but she wanted folk to call her Tess. Goddam, Whelan. After all these years. What else you know?"

He finished his coffee. "I know she's not dead."

• • •

He killed time till the sky began to lose its color. The man he needed to see would just be coming out.

Like a vampire, he thought. It occurred to Whelan that there were only two potential victims left.

Well, let's make it easy for him.

Whelan tried the cabstand and the restaurant and struck out. No one had seen Frank Rickert since Friday. He got back into his car and cruised, and then he knew where he ought to be: where the big cabbie would expect him to turn up eventually. He headed for Maxwell Street.

The steel gates were up across the storefronts, and the lots where four or five hundred people had been trying to make a buck all day were now empty. The only evidence that they'd been there was the trash that the City of Chicago refused to pick up. A wind had come up and snaked its way through the back lots, sending newspapers and sandwich wrappers swirling into the air and down the streets. As he watched, a sudden gust of wind took a sheet of newspaper and slapped it against a chain-link fence.

He circled the area, slowing down to take a long look at the blue bus where Nate had spent his last days, pausing briefly to gaze at the spot where Sam Burwell had scraped together a few dollars on his Sundays, and finally stopping to study the barren weed-covered spot where they'd found Buddy Lenz. He parked and turned off his lights and had a cigarette, and when he was halfway through the smoke he saw the cab in his rearview mirror.

Just when I thought my luck had run out, Whelan told himself.

He watched the cab approach till it seemed huge in the mirror and wondered how long Rickert had been following him around town. Rickert's big body seemed to be craning forward, as though he couldn't quite see what was up ahead. Then the cabbie moved his car up till he was blocking Whelan's car from behind and killed his lights.

Whelan stepped out of his car and faced the cab. Rickert leaned out the window and grinned.

"Hey, buddy. Whatcha doin' back *here,* you lost?"

"You first, Frank."

The big cabbie shrugged. "I'm just lookin' to pick up one more fare."

"Where? Under the viaduct? You get a lot of fares under the viaduct, Frank?"

"No, I was just turning to get back onto Halsted. Hey, you got car trouble or something?"

Whelan smiled. "You mean like when you lifted my battery, Frank?"

The cabbie's eyes widened. "Me? What the hell do I need with a battery?" He forced a laugh.

"I had that all wrong, Frank. I thought somebody pulled my battery so I'd be stuck down here, so I'd be an easy mark. I thought somebody was trying to kill me, and that wasn't it at all—at least, not then. The idea was to get me stranded so you could pick me up and see who I was, maybe find out what I was doing down here."

"What would I care about that? I was just headin' home, and you flagged me down 'cause you needed a cab."

Whelan nodded. "Yeah, that's what I thought. Now I think something entirely different. I think you noticed me nosing around down here and got nervous. Then after you found out who I was, I think you followed me around, and I think you killed Nate over in that old blue bus after you saw me go in there. And then you killed Buddy Lenz."

"I don't even know these fuckin' people."

"Yeah, you do. You knew Buddy in the old days. You played the slide trombone. I know a lot about you, Frank."

"Oh, yeah?" Frank smiled and Whelan saw his hand move slowly down inside the car door. The cabbie would be coming out any second. Whelan took a step back and took out another cigarette.

"Sure. I was just talking with some of your old fans. Seems you were pretty good. Unlucky in love though, huh?"

Something new came into the small close-set eyes. Frank Rickert's mouth opened slightly. "Unlucky? That supposed to be a joke? You think you're pretty funny, huh? Unlucky. Tell you who was unlucky. *Him.* That fucking black—"

"Sam Burwell? Yeah, he was unlucky enough to take your girl."

"Yeah, he was unlucky all right. He fucked with the wrong guy and now he's shit outta luck." Rickert's face was flushed and his eyes were beginning to bulge. "He knocked her up, that sonofabitch—a white woman—and then they took off. But I found him, and now he's dead. And she's here. I know, 'cause I seen her with 'im."

"I know she's here. I've met her. And she still thinks you're an asshole, Frank."

Whelan took a quick step back as the big cabbie came barreling out at him. Rickert's quickness surprised him but Whelan was already moving, and he made it under the viaduct before Rickert could reach him.

The viaduct light was long gone, and as Whelan's eyes adjusted to the darkness, the street outside began to seem brightly lit. Frank Rickert was standing at the entrance, peering into the dark and listening. He looked like a bear tasting game on the wind.

Whelan moved slowly to the center of the viaduct and, when Rickert didn't move, realized the cabbie couldn't see him yet. He crossed the narrow street, crouched low, and watched the man on the other side. Rickert took a few steps into the viaduct, then stood motionless for several moments, and Whelan realized Rickert was letting his eyes adjust.

The cabbie took a couple of slow steps in and Whelan moved along the viaduct wall in the opposite direction, till he was directly across from Rickert. He realized he was now twice as far from his car as he'd been before.

Great strategy, Whelan.

He crouched again and groped around on the broken pavement for a weapon. His fingers stopped at a jagged piece of concrete. He pried at it but it resisted. He put both hands into it, and this time it came loose. Then he waited.

Rickert scanned the viaduct ahead of him and moved a couple of steps farther in. He shook his head, and then he began to turn. Whelan watched the big head scan the viaduct, and when it stopped he felt his heart stop with it. Rickert was looking directly at him.

Whelan remained in his crouch as though rooted in the old concrete. His chest was pounding and he could hear his breath come in gasps, and he would have sworn that Rickert was smiling as he came across the street.

The big cabbie covered ground quickly and changed his course as soon as Whelan began to move, cutting off his retreat. Whelan moved a few feet to his right and saw the other man move that way, like a fighter cutting off the ring, and he wondered if Frank Rickert had ever boxed.

When Rickert was just a few feet away, Whelan saw the knife. He ran at the cabbie, faked a punch at his head and, when Rickert raised his arm to protect himself, dodged by the cabbie's left. As he moved past, Whelan took a broad swipe with the concrete and felt a surge of satisfaction when it struck home.

Rickert cursed and the curse turned to a snarl. He took a blind backhand swipe with his free hand and got lucky, catching Whelan over the eye. Whelan spun around, moved to Rickert's left again to avoid the knife, and swung the concrete again. It caught the cabbie in a turn, just at the hairline. Rickert put both hands to his head and moaned. He started to crumple and then broke his fall with one big hand. Whelan moved back toward him and the cabbie almost caught him with a murderous sweep of the knife. Rickert started to get to his feet, wobbled, and then sank to one knee. He dropped the knife, put both hands to his bloody head and dropped back into a sitting position.

Whelan watched him for a moment, then walked back to his car. As he passed Rickert's cab he brought the concrete down on the windshield, and a starburst of cracks appeared like blue frost.

He jumped in and started his car. It took him four moves to get out from the neat blockade Rickert had set up with his cab but after the longest thirty seconds of his life, he was free. In his rearview mirror he could see Frank Rickert staggering out of the viaduct. His hair was matted at the point of the wound, and the left side of his face was nearly unrecognizable. In the unnatural light of the empty street, the blood looked black.

As he pulled away, Whelan took a quick look at the cab and for the first time noticed the sticker just to the left of the license plate. It said, HOW AM I DRIVING?

Not real well, Frank. And your personality could do with an adjustment.

He made the call from a pay phone on Halsted, giving as many of the particulars as he could to the sergeant who took the call.

"You want to leave your name, sir?"

"Paul Whelan."

"Phone number?"

"Durkin has it. This'll be his, right?"

"I wouldn't know that, sir. But if your information is right, yeah, Detective Durkin and Detective Krause."

"Good. Just give Durkin a message for me. Tell him I said, 'Congratulations on a great piece of detective work.' "

The sirens were already piercing the night as he hung up, and he watched as blue-and-whites from three different directions converged on the viaduct where he'd left Frank Rickert.

SEVENTEEN

DAY 10, SUNDAY

He drove back north through empty streets, past darkened bars and restaurants all shut down for Sunday night, and listened to some jazz. The disk jockey played an old Wes Montgomery tune, and Whelan decided there was no lonelier, more melancholy sound than a guitar in the night. He wondered what kind of music the woman listened to, what she did with herself on nights like this.

It wasn't Sunday night in Uptown. There was no calendar here, no clock. The homeless roamed the streets and stood in doorways, and those with places to live leaned out their windows or sat on their stairs and stared at traffic. He parked on the west side of Broadway across the street from the Salvation Army office. A few feet away, an elderly white woman dug through the contents of a trash basket, looking for something to eat or sell.

This time the smell of rotting plaster on the staircase was overlaid with the thick odor of disinfectant. Somewhere in the building someone was frying something, and the place was overrun with smokers, so that the air in the hallway was bluish gray.

He paused outside the door and listened for a moment. Inside, there was music from a radio, and a woman's voice, surprisingly youthful, joined the song and worked out a little two-part harmony. Whelan remembered she'd been a singer once. He knocked.

The song vanished, both singer and radio went cold. There was silence from within the apartment for a moment, and then he heard her shuffling footsteps just as before. She was less than a foot away now, and Whelan could imagine her craning forward to listen for him.

"Who's there?" came the hoarse voice.

"It's Paul Whelan."

She was silent and he could sense her panic, and the answer when it came was no surprise.

"I'm sick. I can't talk to nobody now." There was a groaning quality to her voice and for a moment he felt pity for her, till he remembered her other talent.

"Mrs. Haley, I've got to talk to you and it's got to be now. I have some things you'll want to hear."

She was breathing audibly now. "I don't want to see nobody. Maybe tomorrow—"

"No, tonight, *tonight*. Now—Tess." He spoke her name slowly and clearly and then waited.

He heard the sound of the chain being removed and a deadbolt being drawn back, and then the door swung open. The woman gazed at him with a crushed look behind the tinted glasses and said nothing. Her shoulders sagged, her skin had gone pale: a portrait of defeat.

"I haven't come to cause you any trouble. I came here to tell you that you're safe now. It's over. But you have to talk to me, you have to give me some answers: real ones this time."

She stared at him and ran a hand through her hair and shook her head slowly from side to side, and for just a second Whelan thought she'd refuse to let him in. She was wearing the tattered peach robe but it seemed to have been washed. Then, abruptly, she stepped aside. She sighed.

"Come in. You can sit anywhere you like." Whelan noted the sudden disappearance of the Bridgeport accent. He stepped past her and lowered himself into an old blue armchair.

The woman stood at the door for a moment as if debating whether to run out, then closed it with a shrug. "Excuse me for a second. I want to comb my hair."

While she was in the next room Whelan studied her tidy little apartment. He'd seen many such places, in many parts of the city, and he read them all the same way: a little oasis of order in the midst of poverty or filth or violence or chaos. At the far end of this miniature living room was a nook just large enough for a kitchen-size table. Just above this table, almost exactly at eye-level, were three photographs. From where he sat, they looked to be pictures of mountains. It took no effort of the imagination to see the woman sitting there, sipping at a cup of tea and staring at those pictures.

The accent was gone and, when the woman emerged from her bedroom, Whelan saw that Violet Haley was gone as well. In her place stood an intelligent-looking woman in her fifties. She had changed into a dark blue dress with a bright print pattern that suggested Japanese paper houses. Her hair was pulled back and tied with a little elastic band, and from the ruddy glow of her skin, he suspected she'd thrown a little soap and water on her face. The greatest change, however, was in the eyes. Violet Haley's heavy-lidded gaze was gone, the tinted glasses were gone, and the woman who faced him was clear-eyed, unafraid. And something else: they were large bright eyes, pretty eyes and she'd needed the tinted glasses to hide that.

"Can I get you a cup of coffee? I think I'm going to have some. It's just instant."

Caffeine at 10:30 P.M., he thought. I'll be up till Tuesday.

But he knew the way people need to busy themselves at such times, so he said, "Sure, I'd like some."

She came in with the coffee and the forced smile of someone making an effort to observe good manners.

"Now you fit in with the room." He sipped at his coffee.

The remark seemed to catch her off guard. She paused with her cup at her lips and blinked. "What do you mean?"

"Little things are falling into place for me. Each time I came here, you took a few moments before letting me in. I think you were using the time to become Violet Haley: putting on an old dress, messing up your hair, making sure it hung in your face. Putting on the tinted glasses to make yourself look a little older. The last time, you even had your dress buttoned wrong."

She looked down with an embarrassed smile and sipped

her coffee.

"But when I came here the first time, I caught a glimpse of your living room. It was—well, like this. It's neat and tidy and, in every possible way, it's a place Violet Haley wouldn't have. I didn't spend a lot of time thinking about it, but I remember noticing and wondering."

"Well, now I don't have to be her anymore." She looked down at her hands. "How did you find out? I know Sam didn't tell anyone about us."

"No, he was throwing up his own smokescreen. I've spent most of the past week and a half juggling a lot of conflicting stories, but gradually it struck me that of all the people who knew Sam Burwell, you were the only one to describe this tall well-dressed black woman who visited him. Other people told me about a white woman named Mary. This flamboyant black woman you made up for my benefit. It was all pretty convincing. When I finally put it together I still had trouble reconciling the two images I had of you. Then I remembered you had been an actress."

The woman called Tess shrugged and looked away suddenly. In profile, her face showed her sadness.

"I was no actress, Mr. Whelan. I was just a very stupid girl who eventually became a very stupid woman. I only thought I was an actress."

Whelan couldn't think of any response. He sipped at the coffee and decided to change the direction of things.

"By now, the police have Frank Rickert in a hole somewhere."

She faced him. "He'll get out."

"No. He told me he killed Sam Burwell."

She nodded. "I knew it."

"I think they'll be able to get him for two other murders, and I'll press charges: he tried to kill me too."

She stared at him in horror. "Two other murders. Oh, my God. Three people dead because of…because of me."

"No. Because of him. He killed them, without any help from anyone else and over things that happened almost thirty years ago."

"You know?"

"Not exactly. I think I've got the bare outlines; you have to give me the rest. I know you had a love affair with Sam Burwell back in the fifties. You were just a kid."

She shrugged. "I was twenty-two. It wasn't like I was in high school."

"And you had some kind of relationship with Frank Rickert; before or after Sam, I'm not really sure."

"I knew Frank from another club where I waited tables. We went out a few times but there was nothing special to it, at least I didn't think so, and we just let it go. Then I started seeing Sam. People didn't like it."

"Because he was the wrong color."

She nodded once. "I don't know who started spreading it around, although later I wondered if it might have been Frank. Anyhow, it got back to my family, so we had to cool it. But we never stopped seeing each other. We just took it—" She paused, looking for the word. "We took it underground. It was easy enough. Sam was a bit of a lady-killer anyway, always had girlfriends, and I had guys asking me out, so…" She made a little wave of her hand.

"And one of them was Frank Rickert."

"Yes. That's when I started to see it was more than just a good time to him. I was seeing several people but Frank was around more than anybody else. And getting demanding about it."

"And then you found out you were pregnant."

She blinked. "How do you know that?"

"I was starting to put it together—you went away, and a little later Sam did—but Frank Rickert told me. Your family made his life unpleasant for a while."

"Yes. My father and my brother went looking for him, and then my father sent some men who worked for him. Frank left town. And a little later, so did I. I went out to California. I wanted to—" She gave Whelan a self-deprecating look. "Guess what I wanted to do. Like every other empty-headed young girl in the country, I wanted to get into movies." She shrugged.

"Whose idea was it to put out the story that you were dead?"

"Mine. Just for the people that I knew there, the ones who didn't like the idea of me and Sam together. And for Frank, although I didn't think he'd be back for a while.

"Anyhow, Sam put out the story about my being dead; then he came out west two months after I did."

"And a little while after that, you had a baby."

"Yes." She nodded slowly. "I had a baby. And now that he was here, I realized I wasn't going to be in the movies. And I couldn't accept it. I had a baby and a husband—"

"You were married?"

She chanced a little smile. "Yes. I was Sam's wife. So there we were, living in a little frame house in Los Angeles near a Mexican neighborhood. Sam couldn't get started out there. He always worked, but he never really found anything he liked or made any money. He couldn't make what he called 'a connection.' So he wasn't happy. A lot of time, he was just doing odd jobs. And I was miserable. I wasn't ready for a baby and marriage, I wasn't any kind of a wife to him. And we were both drinking, real heavy." She paused, sipped her coffee. "And then I just left. I left my husband and my baby and tried to force my way into the movies. What a joke! A twenty-three-year-old alcoholic trying to get people to take her seriously as an actress."

"Did you get any roles?"

"Oh, sure, I got to be an extra. They used a lot more extras then," she said with a smile. "You had to have somebody for the Romans to kill, or the giant crabs, or the flying saucers. And I got walk-on parts in some of those B-movies. The best thing about it was that it only took about a year for me to know I was finished. Some folks hung on out there in that candy factory for five, ten years.

"So I left Hollywood and went to work waiting tables and working in department stores, and I drank my way from LA to Portland."

Where was Sam by then?"

"He was in Texas, although I didn't know it at the time. He went south and gave the baby to his sister because he knew he couldn't raise him. Then he went out west again. He lived in Texas and Mexico for a while, and then eventually he came back here and started a decent life for himself."

"Why didn't he take the child back?"

She shrugged. "His sister moved to California about a year after he gave her the baby. She had no idea where Sam was, and by the time they got in touch with each other, he was in Chicago with a new wife and a baby of his own and she was all settled on the Coast. His sister convinced him it was better to leave the boy where he was. His wife was happy to go along with that; she had a baby of her own. He never meant to let the baby go, Mr. Whelan. He always thought he'd get him back but it didn't work out that way. But he didn't abandon the baby. Not like me. I think about that little boy all the time. I wonder how he turned out."

"So Sam's sister raised your baby as her own."

"That's right." She lit a cigarette from a pack on a side table.

"When did you come back?"

"About two years ago. I got tired of life out there." She waved her hand toward the west. "I was married for a while." She gave him a little smile. "Nice man but a drunk, like me. We were both practicing drunks."

"And when you came back, you found Sam."

She nodded slowly. "Not right away, but yeah, I found Sam. And Frank. He always knew I was still alive. The other ones, they just accepted the story. Frank checked it out, he found out through my family or somebody, I don't know. Then he came out west looking for me."

"Did he find you?"

"No. I saw him once, though, on the street. This was maybe three years later. He was sitting in a cafeteria. I think he went all over the Coast looking for me."

"And back here?"

"I saw him driving a cab. A couple months later, he spotted me. I was walking down Clark Street from a restaurant I worked at. I felt these eyes on me and I looked up and he was across the street in his cab, waiting for a light to change. I ducked into a tavern and left by the back door. Then I saw him again here on Broadway, but he didn't see me."

"That's why you looked so frightened the other day, when I approached you on the street. A couple of motorists started leaning on their horns and you looked scared. I thought you were just jumpy, but one of those cars was a cab. It was the presence of a cab that made you jumpy."

"Yes."

"How did you find Sam?"

"In a little restaurant the other side of Lawrence. I was getting a cup of coffee and he was at the counter. We talked for a minute, stiff as two boards, and then I sat down next to him, and we started over. We started all over again."

"He moved in with you."

"No, we didn't want to do that. He took the flat at the end of the hall, but yes, he stayed here."

"I could tell he didn't live in the apartment."

"How?"

"It didn't look like a place that was lived in. There was a little of everything but not what you'd get if a person lived there. Not enough food, not enough mess. Not enough cigarette butts in the ashtrays. The bed looked like someone took a nap there, not like someone slept there every night. And there were none of the little things a man keeps around in the bathroom."

She gave him a rueful smile. "His kit was always in here."

"Until you snuck in and planted it there. It was there the second time I checked out the place but not the first."

She shrugged. "He only used the apartment to stretch out for a nap after work. Or when he drank. We had an agreement: if he was drinking, he couldn't come in here. So a few times he took a bottle back there to his own place. I was trying to get him to quit." She looked away. "If he had lived, he'd have been sober."

"Did Frank see you together?"

"I don't know. He must have. Sam saw him in the cab around here a couple times, and he said he saw Rickert down on Maxwell Street. I think Frank heard Sam was down there from a man they both used to know, a drummer."

"Buddy Lenz."

"Yes."

"I'm pretty sure Frank Rickert was looking all over the West Side for Sam."

She nodded. "He said he heard a white man was looking for him, and it never made any sense to him till I told him how Frank had been looking for me."

For a moment she appeared to be deep in her own memories. When she looked up, she was smiling at him.

"I know how I look to you, and how it must seem, a couple of down-on-their-luck people our age, but I swear to you, Mr. Whelan, to us it felt like we were a couple of kids again. Like we had a second chance. It sounds stupid, doesn't it?"

"Not to me. I'm envious."

She smiled again and offered him more coffee.

"Sure, I can use another cup. It's been a long day."

When she had poured him another cup of bad instant, they drank in silence for a moment, and then she frowned.

"There was one thing I never figured out. Sam thought he was being followed a couple of times. He thought it was Frank, but one time he was followed on the street by a man in a car. He said he thought the man was black."

"That," Whelan said, "is another story."

EIGHTEEN

DAY 11, MONDAY

Pilar's eyes widened and Whelan made a placating gesture.

"Sir, he told me not to let you—"

"It's all right. There won't be any trouble. I even brought him some coffee." He held up a white paper bag.

The young woman sighed and it was clear this was the last complication she needed on a Monday morning. She was still shaking her head when the door to the inner office opened and David Hill emerged, studying a contract.

"Pilar?" he began, still looking at the paper. His shirtsleeves were rolled up and his collar button was open, and Whelan thought he looked like the workingman's lawyer. "I need you to run something off for me." He held out the paper and then saw Whelan. He let his arm drop to his side and stared for a five-count.

"Do you have five minutes?"

"I don't have *any* time for you, Whelan."

"We have to talk. Just hear me out. It won't cost you a thing. I even brought you coffee." He held up the bag.

"I don't need coffee."

"Come on, Hill. Give me five minutes and then I'll get out. You can have Pilar toss me into the street."

"I can't think of a single reason why I should—"

"Because you owe me the courtesy."

"I don't owe you a—"

"You sent me out looking for someone you had already found. If I did that to you, I'd at least give you the courtesy of a hearing."

Hill began to shake his head, seemed to think better of it, and stopped. He frowned and looked from Whelan to Pilar, who was studiously pretending to proofread copy. "All right, Mr. Whelan," he said, backing into his office. "Come in. Pilar, hold my calls for five minutes."

"Yes, Mr. Hill." She gave Whelan a little smile as he went in.

Hill shut the door behind Whelan, then crossed the room and sank tiredly into his chair.

"Cream or sugar?" Whelan asked.

"Black," Hill said.

"Me too." Whelan made a show of sipping his coffee and shifting his body in the client chair while Hill fidgeted with a pen on his desk. With his stern facial expression and dark-rimmed glasses and prominent jaw, he still reminded Whelan of a young Malcolm X, all fire and force, not to be screwed around with. Except this was not Malcolm X. This man had lied to him, had come pretty close to setting him up. Time to clear the air.

"Let's deal with the basic issue first. You misrepresented the facts from the very beginning. You held back significant portions of the truth."

"Excuse me?" Hill leaned forward.

"You're insulted, right. You're getting ready to challenge me to a sword fight. Come on, Hill, you lied to me. You had me out there chasing my tail when you had already found Sam Burwell."

The glasses came off. Hill's forehead shone with perspiration. He massaged his eyes, then put both hands against the desk, as though to shove off from it.

"Mr. Hill, we don't have time for you to go through your repertoire of lawyerly gestures. Save them for an unsuspecting jury. I want to know why you hired me to find someone you had already located."

"I have already explained to you that I was representing a client who—"

"There was no client," Whelan said quietly. He took a sip of coffee and put the cup down on the desk. "There never was a client. The client was you. You found this man, and then you hired me to cover the same ground you'd already covered. I had a feeling from the beginning that there was more to this than you were letting me know. In our first meeting you let something slip that puzzled me. I was never able to forget it completely and now I understand it."

"What?"

"You had nothing but old pictures of Burwell, and your client had supposedly not seen him in many years, but you told me he was going bald on top. That's something only a person who'd seen him recently would know. Other things didn't add up. You did that bit about being the New York lawyer coming here to hicksville, and I found out that you were indeed a lawyer in New York—but only for the last three years. On the other hand, that part you let slip about your client being a woman, that was a nice touch. It confused me, because I wound up spending so much of my time looking for a woman."

Hill studied Whelan for a moment. "What is it that you want from me?"

"Nothing. Actually, I came here to tell you what I've learned and to see if you'd let this facade come down just for a few minutes."

"And what have you learned?"

"I know who killed Sam Burwell and I know why. I know you found Burwell and I think you had been looking for him for some time. He was followed once by a black man in a car and I think that was you, in a rented white Ford. You followed me in the same car." Whelan allowed himself a smile. "I assume it was rented: Fords aren't your style.

"And I think a black man seen running from a blue bus down there one night was one scared New York lawyer. But I know you didn't kill anybody."

Hill kept his poker face, but his eyes were moving as though he were making a decision. Whelan decided to give it a push.

"And I think Sam Burwell was your father."

The lawyer blinked and the color seemed to drain from his face. Hill bought a little time by lighting a cigarette and taking a long drag on it. He blew out smoke and for just a second allowed his face to take on an incredulous expression. Then his body seemed to sag a little, and he nodded.

"Yes. He was my father. But we never knew each other. I don't remember him at all because I wasn't even two when he left. I never really knew about him, because my aunt—you know that she raised me?"

"Yes."

Hill blinked. "You're better than I thought, Mr. Whelan. Anyway, my aunt raised me to believe that she and her husband, who'd died many years earlier, were my parents. She let a few things slip over the course of many years, and she finally told me when I entered college who my parents really were, that my mother had run out and that my father had left me with her. She told me she didn't know what had become of him.

"I became obsessed with my parents, finding out about them. She told me a little about my father but nothing about my mother. She wouldn't tell me a thing about her, wouldn't speak her name. I didn't get very far in my search. My aunt didn't really want me to succeed. She had lost touch with my father in later years and believed that he was dead. And she made it pretty clear that my mother wasn't worth finding out about."

"So how did you?"

"When she died I went through her papers and I found a lot of old letters, some of them from my father. And there were a number of later ones from other people, including a couple from Chicago, apparently in response to her trying to locate him. I took all of it with me when I went east. I went to New York to prove to myself that I wasn't going to waste any more time on the past. But I spent so much time going through it, over and over again, that I decided to come here and take care of business."

"The letters are where you came up with the addresses you gave me."

"Yes. And I found him, Mr. Whelan. I came here and set up a practice and in my spare time I looked for him. I hit some of the places you did and probably got the same responses you did. I never did find out where he lived. But I found him down on Maxwell Street. Your informant was right: I went down there and watched him. I stood across the street from him and stared at him like a moonstruck little boy."

"But you never got the chance to speak to him."

"No. What do you say to a parent who left you? I'd spent the past ten years rehearsing what I'd say but when the time came none of my little speeches fit the occasion. I was looking at a man who seemed to be from a different world. He was a shabby-looking man selling junk and other people's castoffs down in a funky place, and none of that bothered me—but I was afraid he wouldn't accept me, what I was. After all, the man hadn't seen any reason to stay around and raise me." A little of the anger came back into Hill's face.

"He left you with someone he trusted with your well-being. He didn't think he could raise a child by himself, and from what little I know, I think he took some time getting over your mother's leaving. And a lot of it was his trouble with liquor. Your aunt convinced him to let her raise you."

"How would you know that?"

Whelan waved him off. "I also know"—Whelan hesitated, fumbling for a way to tell what he knew without being patronizing—"he was proud that his son was in college."

Hill shook his head. "He didn't even know I went."

"Yeah, he did. He told someone how proud he was to have a son in college. So he knew. Your aunt must have told him before they lost touch for good. He knew about you. He knew he'd left you in good hands and that you'd turned out to be someone he was proud of."

David Hill swallowed and looked away, and for a moment Whelan wished he were somewhere else. Then he went on. He told David Hill how his father had died and at whose hands, taking care to give only the sketchiest outline of the story and leaving the most vital part to the end.

"And I have other information you should know, but I don't know if this is the time—"

The lawyer blinked. "You playin' God now, Whelan? You settin' yourself up as my guardian angel?"

The transformation caught Whelan off guard. David Hill had gone from New York lawyer to streetwise homeboy, and he looked as though he were ready to come over the top of the desk.

"You think you can come in here and stick your white face in my life and then decide how much you gon' tell me and how much you gon' hold for later? You gonna sell it to me, Whelan?"

"You've spent enough time playing God with me, Hill. How does it feel?"

"I hired you because he disappeared. He disappeared, and I was afraid something had happened to him. I made some inquiries but no one seemed to have seen him. I thought a trained investigator might be able to find him."

"Why didn't you tell me the truth?"

"I was embarrassed about my…my situation. But that wasn't all. I was afraid you wouldn't take it seriously, looking for a down-at-the-heels black man on the West Side."

"Unless you made it a little more grandiose, by creating a mysterious client who had means."

Hill nodded. "That's right. Would you have taken it seriously otherwise?"

"Yes. You don't know me, so you wouldn't know if that's true, but each case is about a person, not about money. I've taken cases where clients couldn't pay me much, and I've taken on a few where I knew I wasn't going to be paid at all. You should have given me the benefit of the doubt." He saw Hill's sardonic smile and nodded. "I know, you couldn't do that because I was white."

"You blame me?"

"I guess not. So why didn't you hire a black detective?"

"If somebody had recommended one, I would have. I asked around for somebody good, especially at finding people. I got you."

"So now you know you can trust at least one white private investigator."

Hill gave him a slight smile. "I don't have as much of a problem with white people as you think, Mr. Whelan. I didn't mention this earlier but…my mother was white. I've known that for years." The smile grew wider and Hill took a last puff from his dying cigarette.

"Yes, I found that out too. And that brings me to the last piece of information I have, which will complicate your life more than anything else you've learned in the last year."

And Whelan looked down at the floor and told David Hill that his mother's name was Tess and that she was alive and well and living in a small apartment on North Broadway. And when he had finished, he left David Hill to his own thoughts.

Nineteen

O.C. Brown listened carefully, watching Whelan and saying nothing. When Whelan was finished, O.C. poured him a fresh cup of coffee and came out from behind the bar. He walked over to the jukebox and used a key to open it, pressed some buttons, and closed the front up again. He hit some numbers and came back behind the bar. Whelan heard the scratch of needle on plastic, and a moment later the dark empty little tavern was under the spell of Billie Holiday.

O.C. ran a rag across the shiny surface of his bar and then set out a pair of coasters and a pair of highball glasses.

"Have a drink with me there, Whelan?"

"Sure."

"Not too early in the day for you, my man?" There was a faint glimmer of amusement in O.C.'s eyes.

"Special occasion."

"That's my boy." O.C. held up a bottle of Crown Royal for approval. Whelan nodded and the old man poured them each a healthy shot. "I don't use shot glasses." O.C. studied the whiskey, swirling it around in the glass. "I can't drink this stuff no more but just this one time." He held his glass up to Whelan. "To my boy Sam," he said.

Whelan touched his glass to O.C.'s, nodded, and drank.

A pair of customers came in, younger men, and both gave Whelan a long second look. O.C. greeted them, nodded his head in Whelan's direction and said, "Friend of mine, *good* friend. This here is Paul Whelan."

One of the men said, "How you feel?" and the other nodded. O.C. left to serve them. When he came back, he picked up the coffeepot again.

"No, no more for me, O.C. I've got to run."

"You sure?"

"Yeah. I know me and taverns. I've spent days in taverns. Spent eight hours in a saloon once just because it started raining."

O.C. chuckled and nodded. "We got to talk about money before you leave."

Whelan held up two fingers. "Two hundred."

O.C. shook his head. "I asked around. Some folk in your line of work make that in a day."

"Not me. Two hundred. And a lifetime tab at the Blue Note."

O.C. laughed. "How you gonna make a living like that?"

"I own the house I live in, and rich lawyers keep sending work my way."

O.C. reached into the register and came out with a white envelope. Out of it came a sheaf of bills which he counted and handed over to Whelan. "Two-fifty. Take it, my man."

"Cash, huh? All right!"

O.C. Brown held out his hand. "You're a good man, Whelan. And a smart man."

"A lot of it's luck. You keep at it and ask enough questions and think about what you've learned, and sometimes you come up with answers."

O.C. was shaking his head before Whelan was finished. "Naw, man, couldn't nobody else do it. Only you. Only you, Whelan."

"I'll see you around, O.C."

"Gimme a holler sometime. Come in and use that tab."

"I will. Maybe we'll go see the Sox."

"All right. Those are my boys. They gonna take it next year."

"Yeah. In this town everybody's gonna take it next year."

Whelan waved and left.

On Tuesday morning he sat in his office and read the paper. The unseasonably warm weather had brought on dozens of shootings, assaults, and armed robberies. Less than a block from his home, an off-duty police officer had been assaulted and robbed. The unidentified cop had been treated for facial injuries at a local hospital.

Another caption caught his eye: RESTAURATEURS SUE CITY. Somehow he knew what this one would say, but he read it anyway, to make his day. According to the story, the owners of the House of Zeus restaurant, citing what they called "harassment, anti-Iranian behavior, and blackmail," had brought suit against the authorities. It was, Whelan reflected, what one might call the shotgun approach to litigation: the suit named a Sylvester Janus, said to be a health inspector, as well as the Board of Health, the City of Chicago, the Mayor, and the Governor of Illinois. The attorney for the House of Zeus was apparently a Mr. Reza, who promised that "this suit will bring the whole corrupt system to its feet." Whelan remembered Mr. Reza, who before law school had worked in the A and W kitchen for his cousins Rashid and Gus. He laughed and rubbed his eyes.

"Nice going, guys," he said. "You sent a little business to your cousin."

He was paging through the ruminations of local sportswriters who seemed to think the Bears were on the verge of something big, when the phone rang.

"Hey, sweetie!"

"Hello, Shel. What's up?"

"Seems your clients think you never sleep. You got a call at eight A.M."

"Must be a stranger. Nobody who knows me would think I'd be at work that early. What's the point of being self-employed?"

"This was a Mr. Hill. Said he'd come by and visit. I told him you struggled in around nine-thirty."

"Nicely done, Shel. How's the milkman?"

"He thinks his ship came in. Later, baby."

At precisely nine-thirty, David Hill came into the outer office.

"Come on in, counselor. I got your call."

Hill held up a white bag. "Brought you coffee."

"I can always use a cup of coffee. Sit down." Whelan busied himself with the coffee and waited for Hill to announce his business.

"You laid a lot of news on me yesterday, Mr. Whelan, and I don't think I was in the frame of mind to thank you properly."

"You thanked me."

"Yeah, but, man, I'm not sure there's even a way to do it the way it should be done."

"Did you see her?"

David Hill nodded. "Yes. I called her, and then I dropped by in the afternoon."

"How did it go?"

Hill shrugged. "It was very uncomfortable for both of us, and painful, and…I stayed for three hours." He smiled.

"I thought you'd work it out."

"I have no idea what will happen—"

"Who does?" Whelan sipped his coffee. "You're lucky, both of you."

"Now I'm going to call Sam's son, my…" Hill made a nervous gesture with one hand.

"Your brother," Whelan finished.

"Yeah. I have no idea what I'll say to him."

"You're a lawyer, you'll think of something."

Hill shook his head, looking embarrassed, then glanced around the office.

"You'll be staying in Chicago?"

Hill gave him an incredulous look. "Hell, yes, Whelan. Every other lawyer I've met, white, black, or brown, is talking about running for office. Everybody in this town seems to talk about running for office."

"It's either that or play softball. So you're going to run for office?"

"No. If all the other lawyers are going to run for office, I'm going to be an attorney. Sounds like I'll make a whole lot of money. Speaking of which." He drew an envelope from the inside pocket of his coat and slid it across the desktop.

"What's that? We settled already."

"Retainer," Hill said, straight-faced. "I'll need an investigator sometime, and I don't want to stand in line behind

G. Kenneth Laflin."

Whelan pulled the envelope over and nodded. "Deal."

He decided to take a walk and was just leaving when the phone rang.

"Hey, Snoopy."

"Bauman. You still on furlough?"

"No, I'm back at work. I made it." He spoke with the air of a man who has survived something bleak and harsh. "Listen, you been reading the papers? That's some neighborhood you live in."

"About the cop? Yeah, I saw it."

"Hell of a thing. I—uh, I know the cop."

"Oh, yeah?" Suddenly he had a feeling about what was coming next.

"Yeah. So do you. Mark Durkin."

"Durkin? Around here? What was he doing around here?"

"Beats the hell outta me, Whelan. What do you think?"

"Looking for girls, maybe."

"Right. That's what I was thinkin'. They busted his jaw, did you know that?"

"No. No, I didn't know that." Whelan thought for a moment, and dark notions danced through his imagination. "How would you know?"

"You know me, Whelan. I know everybody."

Whelan thought for a moment. "I bet you know how much they took from him."

Bauman snickered into the phone. "Seventy-seven dollars. And his wallet. Got his badge, too. I got a feeling old Mark won't be prowling around up north no more."

"I think you're a danger to us all, Albert. I feel like finding the guy who did it and saying thank you."

"I'll let him know, Snoops. You can buy him a cocktail sometime."

• • •

The rest of the day was slow. No other visitors came in to see him, he received no other calls. He finished the paper and wondered what he'd do that night, and he thought of Pat, who had said she'd call him when she had it all sorted out with her ex-husband. No call yet, and he was beginning to feel that the call, when it came, would not bring good news.

He found himself thinking about Ms. Sandra McAuliffe, of the Illinois Department of Public Aid, and wondered if she'd take a dinner invitation seriously. Why the hell not?

He called her and asked her out for that night.

There was a pause. "Paul…I think you should know, I'm… in a relationship."

Figures, he thought, and he was about to let the conversation end when he found himself pushing on. "Well, so am I. Is yours any better than mine?"

No, he thought, it's dog shit or you wouldn't be talking about it like a psychologist.

Her laughter took him by surprise. He hadn't heard her laugh before, and this was a good one, deep and practiced.

"It's that obvious, huh?"

"You could have said 'I'm spoken for,' or 'I have someone,' or 'I'm involved with someone,' or 'I live with a guy,' or even the old standby, 'I've got a boyfriend.' I've got a relationship too, and it's…moribund."

"Moribund. A good word." She was silent for a moment. "So where are we going?"

MORE FROM MICHAEL RALEIGH

DEATH IN UPTOWN

A killer terrorizes Chicago's diverse Uptown neighborhood. Private investigator Paul Whelan's specialty is tracking down missing persons, but when his good friend is found slain in an alley, Whelan is steered down a path of violence as he searches for answers.

His investigation is interrupted by the arrival of an attractive young woman, Jean Agee, who is on her own search for her missing brother. But as clues lead Whelan to believe the two cases may be connected, the body count rises quickly, and he finds himself racing to catch a killer before he strikes again.

A BODY IN BELMONT HARBOR

The body of a small-time drug dealer washes up in Belmont Harbor among the yachts of Chicago's wealthy. Convinced that this murder connects to her husband's suicide two years prior, wealthy widow Janice Fairs hires private eye Paul Whelan to investigate.

Whelan's investigation takes him into the rarefied air of the wealthy, where he begins to discover unlikely connections between the two men in the harbor. But Whelan isn't the only one snooping, and he discovers himself an unwitting player in a game of cat-and-mouse, with deadly consequences.

KILLER ON ARGYLE STREET

Chicago Private Investigator Paul Whelan takes the case when an elderly woman asks him to look into the disappearance of Tony Blanchard, a young man she'd taken in after his parents died. Instead,

Whelan discovers a string of murders, all tied to a car-theft ring.

All the evidence suggests that Tony is dead as well, but Whelan keeps digging until he finds himself surrounded by a dangerous maze of silent witnesses, crooked cops, and people willing to kill to keep the truth from surfacing. When a friend from Whelan's past emerges—a friend Whelan thought long dead—his investigation takes a dangerous turn; one that brings him no closer to Tony, and a lot closer to his own demise.

THE RIVERVIEW MURDERS

Margaret O'Mara's brother disappeared thirty years earlier, so when his last known associate is found murdered, O'Mara hires Chicago PI Paul Whelan to investigate.

Whelan makes the rounds through seedy bar and dilapidated apartment buildings where he discovers connections to a long-gone Chicago amusement park where another murder took place forty years prior.

Soon, Whelan finds himself navigating his way through dark pasts, deep secrets, and a mystery that may cost him his life.